Without Proof

REDEMPTION'S EDGE
BOOK THREE

JANET SKETCHLEY
janetsketchley.ca

Without Proof, A Redemption's Edge Novel

© 2015 by Janet Sketchley

ISBN (print) 978-0-9938743-4-5
ISBN (electronic) 978-0-9938743-5-2

Edited by Angela Breidenbach. Additional editorial input by Matthew Sketchley.

Cover by Amanda Walker.
Photography by Amanda Walker Photography (forest) and Can Stock Photo (model).
Series cover design by Christina Fuselli, Fuselli Art & Design.

Published in Canada by Janet Sketchley.
Printed in the United States of America.

DEDICATED TO YOU, THE READER. ENJOY!

Books in the Redemption's Edge Series:

Heaven's Prey
Secrets and Lies
Without Proof

Books in the Green Dory Inn Mystery Series:

Unknown Enemy
Hidden Secrets
Bitter Truth
Deadly Burden

Daily Devotions:

A Year of Tenacity
365 Daily Devotions to Warm Your Spirit and Encourage Your Heart

Tenacity at Christmas
31 Daily Devotions for December

Readers' Journals (print only):

Reads to Remember:
A book-lover's journal to track your next 100 reads

NOTE TO MY AMERICAN READERS:

This novel uses Canadian spelling, which is sort of a hybrid of US and UK English. You'll see words like colour, neighbour, practice, and licence, and they're not typos. That said, and despite the many eyes that have checked the manuscript, I can't guarantee perfection. But I've done my best!

Also, you'll encounter some French-Canadian and other words and names. Here's some basic pronunciation help:

ami: say "ah-MEE" (friend)

Ayon: say "Ay-ON" where the "ay" rhymes with "hay" and without saying the "n" in "on"

chérie: say "sha-ree" (a term of endearment, like dear)

Dafiq: say "dah-FEEK"

finis: say "fin-NEE" (the end)

Gilles: the "g" makes a zh sound as in "treasure," and the name rhymes with "hill," so say "zhil" (If you have to, call him Jill. Please don't call him Giles, or he may haunt you.)

Luc: say "Luke"

Honore: say "on-ORE"

Renaud: say "re-NO" (like the car)

Safia: say "sa-FEE-ya"

toujours aimée: remember the "zh" sound from "treasure" and say "too-zhoorz ay-may" (always loved, and a play on Amy's name)

ACKNOWLEDGEMENTS

I'm indebted to Darrel and Lee Carver and Jan Warren for their input into possible sabotage details for Amy and Gilles' plane. (Google helped too.) Any mistakes in writing are mine. Readers familiar with Nova Scotia may be aware that there's no longer a flight club in the Halifax area since the Shearwater Flying Club closed. I've invented a fictional one in that approximate location for the purposes of the story.

Sharon Horgan helped me understand how Michael might react to the events of chapter 30. I thank her and Donna Morris for answering my painting-related questions.

I think my whole family joined in on discovering the fireworks incident, which turned out to not have much page time but which solidified Michael's and Gilles' friendship. The character of Nathin owes his existence to my son Matthew, and is duly grateful.

Thank you to my editor, Angela Breidenbach, editorial assistant, Matthew Sketchley, and cover artist, Amanda Walker, for their diligence and skill in shaping the finished novel.

A huge shout-out to my sharp-eyed early readers, Ruth Ann Adams, Heidi Newell, Russell Sketchley, and Beverlee Wamboldt.

Much gratitude to Sonya Benjamin and Tammy Wamboldt for their amazing support for this series. I hope book 3 lives up to your expectations!

From the deepest part of my heart, I thank God for giving me the gift of writing... along with the occasional "kick of love" to keep me moving.

Without Proof

REDEMPTION'S EDGE
BOOK THREE

JANET SKETCHLEY

A father to the fatherless, a defender of widows,
is God in his holy dwelling.
God sets the lonely in families,
he leads out the prisoners with singing;
but the rebellious live in a sun-scorched land.

Psalm 68: 5-6, NIV

Chapter 1

The doorbell echoed from the main floor. Amy dropped the square of sandpaper onto the frame she'd been finishing and flexed her aching fingers.

Overhead, light footsteps headed for the door. Michael's aunt could sign for the delivery, but Amy wanted to check the boxes. She rolled her shoulders to work out a kink, then slid from the stool and brushed a layer of dust from her clothing.

Aunt Bay's voice met her at the top of the basement stairs. "She may not want to talk to you."

Not the printer order after all. *She, as in me?* Amy took a few silent steps but stopped out of sight.

"Please, I'm on a deadline." A male voice, light and with a hint of a quiver.

Amy grinned. Aunt Bay had that effect when she wanted. It might be fun to let her soften this guy up a bit more, but Amy stepped into the hallway. "Is there a problem?"

Aunt Bay huffed at the man. "Come in, then. But if she says no, you'll be leaving."

The visitor took three quick steps inside before Michael's aunt could change her mind. "Amy Silver?"

"Yes?"

He wasn't much bigger than Aunt Bay, but closer to Amy's age. A bit older, maybe in his late 20s. Black, with tight-curled hair and black-framed glasses. Despite the

1

passive voice, his gaze spoke determination. "I'm Troy Hicks, a friend of Michael's. I'm a journalist."

"Okay." Amy nodded, waiting. Did he want to write about the art studio? But why would Aunt Bay object?

Troy adjusted the laptop bag strap on his shoulder. "I know this is a sensitive topic for you, but I'd like to ask about your accident."

Amy glanced at Michael's aunt. Felt the quiet of this rambling house that had become her sanctuary. Looked back at Troy. "Why? It's been almost two years."

Dark eyes studied her. "There was a similar crash in the States recently. The local paper is interested in a follow-up on your recovery. Just a short human interest piece."

Pain radiated in Amy's hip and she shifted her weight to her good leg. "I live with the after-effects every day." She wasn't crazy about being in the paper, but after all Michael and his aunt — great-aunt, really — had done... A positive mention of the painter and his studio could bring him a new customer or two. She smiled at Troy. "Okay."

Aunt Bay's face relaxed. "Good for you. I knew you were healing."

Amy turned to Troy. "If Michael gets back soon enough, he can join us." She led the way into the living room and sank into the nearest chair. Pain lanced her hip, then began to ebb. She pulled a steadying breath.

Troy settled opposite her, and opened his laptop on the low table in front of him. He pulled out his smart phone and tapped the screen. "All right if I record this? I'll take notes, but I like a verbatim backup."

"That's fine, I guess."

Aunt Bay entered the room carrying a tray with three glasses of ice water. Amy reached for a glass. "Thank you. My hip started to go. I needed to sit."

"I saw it in your face, child."

"You're too good to me." Aunt Bay and Michael, both.

They'd taken in a virtual stranger because she had no family of her own. Amy had met Michael, what? Four times before the crash? Five?

Troy moved his laptop onto his knees. He held Amy's gaze for a few seconds, and flashed a reassuring smile. "I appreciate this. I'll ask a few questions, we'll chat, then I'll distill it into an article once I leave."

Aunt Bay set the tray on the coffee table beside Troy's phone, and carried her glass to a chair that let her observe them both. "You'll let Amy see what you've written first?"

One side of Troy's mouth curved down. "That's actually discouraged. Second-guessing dilutes the original tone and causes missed deadlines." He glanced at Amy. "Are you concerned I'll misrepresent you?"

Amy shook her head.

"Okay." Troy checked his laptop screen. "Two years ago this November, a private plane carrying you and your fiancé, Gilles Renaud, crashed on a rural highway." He looked up. "I'm sorry, Amy. There are no words for your loss."

Amy's throat tightened. "I'll always miss him. We talk about him a lot, and sometimes that makes it easier."

Aunt Bay sniffed. "Far better than stuffing away the grief and pretending he never existed."

Troy nodded. "Gilles was an experienced pilot, and weather conditions were fair. I'm told it took a great deal of skill to bring the plane down in one piece." He glanced back at his laptop. "According to my notes, Gilles died from internal injuries, and you spent weeks in hospital. Everything changed that day, but you've found strength to carry on. And you've stayed in Nova Scotia instead of moving back to... Ottawa?"

"I brought everything with me when I came here to marry Gilles." She'd had nothing — and no one — to return to. "Michael and Gilles were best friends. In his own grief, Michael gave me a place to stay when the hospital discharged me. His great-aunt moved in to help me."

"And to keep folks from talking." Aunt Bay levelled a stare. "I should have introduced myself. Beatrice." She pronounced it *BAY-a-triss*, then spelled it for him. "If you can get your tongue around that, feel free to call me by name. Otherwise, it's Miss Rockland."

A grin split Troy's face. "BAY-a-triss it is. Thank you."

Amy looked at the older woman. "It was Gilles who nicknamed you Aunt Bay. Michael told me."

"Yes. That first summer Gilles stayed here. An irrepressible teenager ready to take on the world." Beatrice turned to Troy. "This was my home then. When I bought a condo in the city, Michael took over the house for his studio. The light off St. Margaret's Bay is perfect in his work room, and he gets tourist traffic in the summer."

Troy typed a rapid burst and paused, hands over the keyboard. "Amy, you mentioned your hip. Is this related to the crash?"

"My leg was trapped when the plane crumpled, and I ended up with a dislocated hip. The surgeon repaired it, but if I stand too long, or over-exert it, the pain comes back." Amy grimaced. "When I'm out with Aunt Bay, I'm the one with the cane. At twenty-five."

She waited until Troy stopped tapping keys. "I wanted a way to give back to Michael and Aunt Bay, so I started helping with the paperwork and accounts between physiotherapy appointments. I'm good with numbers. Michael, your typical artist, isn't. Then I learned how to do framing and other support work, to give Michael more time to paint."

Amy sipped her water and rested the glass on the arm of her chair. "I could get back up to speed with the banking world and apply for work in my field, but I like it here. Less money, but less pressure, and right now I don't want any stress." Her fingers twisted the end of her ponytail. "So am I still healing? Or am I hiding?"

Troy grinned. "I'm a journalist, not a doctor. Sounds to me like you've got a good thing going, win-win all around. Have you kept in touch with Gilles' family?"

Speaking of stress... "Please don't mention them in your article. They wouldn't appreciate it."

"Okay. Now, there's one other angle I wanted to look at in passing. Are you satisfied with the investigation into the crash?"

Amy pressed her back into the chair. "Why?"

"Coverage of the American crash suggests there are a few ways to sabotage a small plane that are virtually untraceable. Did Gilles do a pre-flight inspection?"

"I followed him around the plane. It was fascinating."

Troy nodded. "Forgive me — did he take it seriously, or was it a formality?"

Amy stiffened. "Gilles may have had a reckless streak, but he was obsessive about mechanical safety."

Aunt Bay snorted. "Daredevils can't risk equipment failure. Not that he'd try anything crazy with Amy in the plane. He treated her like spun glass."

"Here's the thing." Troy positioned the laptop more squarely on his legs. "Gilles' pre-flight should have caught any ordinary mechanical issues. After your crash, I asked his flight club about the possibility of sabotage — just to cover every option. They shut me down faster than you can say 'No comment.' Fine. I thought it wasn't likely anyhow. But now I know it's possible. I asked again this morning, and they hit me with a guilt trip. Said to respect you, not to dig up past pain."

"Yet you're asking me about it."

"Because I do respect you." Troy sat forward, one elbow on the edge of his laptop. His features hardened. "If someone did this to you and Gilles, you have a right to know. To see justice done."

Amy stared. "But who? Why?"

"That's the other reason I'm asking. You and Michael knew Gilles best. Did he have enemies? Personal or business conflicts? I won't put anything you say now in my article, but I'd like to keep recording for myself."

This conversation was unreal. Amy rubbed her hip. "Gilles didn't seem worried about anything. He was, when we met. Said he was running away from God — don't repeat that. We fell in love, he settled whatever was bothering him, and we came here to get married."

"Gilles had a reputation with the ladies, but this would be a pretty extreme response from a spurned lover. I don't suppose you have any enemies yourself, Amy?"

Amy's scalp prickled. Enemies? She forced a laugh. "Not the murdering kind." Gilles' mother. Her own unseen father. "Besides, I'm an easy target and I'm still here."

Aunt Bay reached over and squeezed Amy's arm. "Thank God for that."

Troy checked his phone. "Michael hasn't replied to my text yet. When he does, I'll ask if he remembers anything. Thank you both for your time." He shut the laptop and slid it into his bag.

Amy sat forward in her chair, preparing her hip joint to stand. "It's been nice to meet you. Thanks for checking on me, and good luck with your article. I really don't think there's anything to the sabotage idea, though. Just because it could have happened doesn't mean it did. Everyone loved Gilles."

Aunt Bay stood without any effort. "I agree with Amy. But I hope Michael invites you back socially. He works too much."

Troy looked at the older woman. "Are you a praying person like Michael, Beatrice?"

At her nod, he took her hand. "Then pray for the truth to come out."

~~~

Troy's visit left Amy on edge. She popped a couple of painkillers and forced herself to finish sanding the frame she'd abandoned, but instead of applying the final layer of clear-coat, she cleaned up and roamed into the kitchen.

Aunt Bay looked up from sliding a meatloaf into the oven. "You have an hour, if you'd like to lie down." She added foil-wrapped potatoes and closed the door.

"Thanks, but I think I'll make some tea and sit down with the heating pad. Maybe read a bit, unless you'd like to chat." Amy filled the kettle and opened the tea cupboard. "Would you like a cup?"

"If you're making herbal." Sharp blue eyes studied Amy. "Don't fret over what that young man said. If there was the slightest hint of sabotage, Gilles' parents would have never let it rest."

Amy reached for the chamomile tea box, then chose spearmint instead. She tossed two bags into the teapot. "Honore wouldn't. And heaven help the culprit if she found him. But Luc's been different since the crash. I'm not sure he'd notice." Amy couldn't blame the man for retreating into his grief, but in the hospital, injured and alone, her encounters with Honore had shredded what was left of her emotions. When Honore cut her off completely, it was a relief.

The kettle clicked off. Amy hadn't heard the water bubbling. Thoughts of Gilles' mother would do that. Amy's hand trembled as she poured water into the teapot.

The doorbell rang. "This time it'd better be our delivery." Amy set the kettle down and started for the door. She should have grabbed her cane from the closet.

Beatrice slipped past her. "Let me. I'll have him bring the boxes out to the table."

Amy changed direction and grabbed the nearest chair. At seventy-plus, Aunt Bay could likely still heft those boxes herself, one at a time.

The courier drivers never let her try. One stamped into the kitchen now, box in his arms. "Afternoon, Miss. Here on the table good?"

"Yes, please. Thank you."

"No problem." He left and returned with a second box. "The other lady already signed for them. Have a good one."

"You, too."

The front door banged shut. Aunt Bay stepped back into the kitchen, Amy's cane under one arm. "In case you need it." She propped it against the wall by Amy's chair and handed Amy a knife. "You open the boxes. I'll pour our tea."

Amy had forgotten the tea. She slit the packing tape and folded back the box tops.

Aunt Bay set two steaming mugs on the table at a safe distance from the boxes. Both women reached into the nearer box at the same time, bumping hands. Beatrice laughed and drew back. "This was your idea. You go first."

Amy pulled out a memo pad, faintly printed with water lilies from one of Michael's original paintings. She held it to the light. "I like it. Not too washed out, but light enough to write on. And his name and website at the bottom are clear."

Beside her, Aunt Bay studied another pad. "The hand-written letter may be nearly extinct, but people always need note pads."

They'd chosen elements from a few of Michael's paintings: the white lilies, an antique bucket overflowing with water, ducks on a lake, a waterfall. As well as the muted pads, the boxes held full-colour note cards, desk calendars and fridge magnets. Michael sold the original of each painting, but he kept digital copies to use in smaller reproduction prints. Why not expand the idea and use snippets from a larger work for gift items?

8

They had the second box half empty when the front door opened. "I'm back!"

Aunt Bay called, "We're in here, Michael."

Troy's words about sabotage flooded Amy's mind. Her hand froze around a bundle of magnets. What would Michael think? She listened as he went into the office and fiddled around.

Then he came into the kitchen, hair still tossed from the breeze. His smile sweetened something deep in Amy's heart.

She'd loved Gilles, always would in a way. But this unassuming painter had no idea how she felt now. Would he ever stop grieving enough to see her as a woman instead of a co-worker — or his dead friend's fiancée?

Michael stepped toward her, smile sliding away. "Of all the times to leave my phone in the car. I just saw Troy's messages. He had no business bringing up the accident."

Amy flipped her ponytail behind her back. "I don't mind him writing something short for the paper. He seems nice. But did he tell you his sabotage idea? Can you think of anyone who'd want to hurt Gilles?" She swallowed hard. "Or me?"

Michael's eyes darkened to almost brown, drowning the gold flecks Amy loved. "Nobody. Troy's a great guy, but he tends to see conspiracies everywhere. Gilles wouldn't want him planting ideas like that."

Aunt Bay pushed her chair away from the table. "Sit here, Michael, and tell us what you think of the new products. I need to get the vegetables cooking."

Chapter 2

The two men worked their way around the small gallery, pausing at each painting, occasionally sharing a word or two.

Watching them, Amy stepped closer to Michael. "Business customers are so different from tourists."

He shuffled his feet into a wider stance, but he still looked like a soldier standing inspection. "They make decisions faster."

What did these two see, besides the art? Did they notice the wide, aqua-stained floorboards? The pebbled glass ice-water decanter? The subtle splash of the tabletop fountain?

Michael had designed his home gallery to complement the theme of his paintings. More than one tourist, after a glance at the paintings, had approached Amy with a whispered "Which way is the washroom?"

The trickling water likely didn't penetrate the Middle Eastern men's focus. Reza Zarin bought paintings each year for his string of hotels. Today was the first time Amy had met his son, Ross. The younger man's dress was less formal than his father's suit and tie, but both wore an air of understated elegance. Business must be going well.

The office phone rang.

"I'll get it." Amy walked into the adjoining room. Yes, that cut off Michael's escape, but he needed to practice his sales skills. She picked up the handset from the desk.

"Stratton Gallery, Amy Silver speaking. How may I help you?"

"Amy, this is Luc Renaud."

As if she knew other Lucs. As if she'd forget Gilles' father. "Could I phone you back? We have clients in the gallery, and Michael will want me to do up the paperwork."

"If you answered your own phone earlier, I wouldn't be using the business one." He sounded weary.

Amy sighed. The man had never recovered from his son's death. She should have kept in better touch. Except his wife hated her. "I'm sorry, Luc. I promise to call you as soon as these gentlemen leave."

"You should never have done that interview."

"What — oh, is it in today's paper? He didn't mention you or your family, did he? I asked him not to."

"Honore is beside herself. Sabotage indeed! That reporter's words are hurtful."

Amy stepped around the desk and sank into the chair. "Luc, I need to—"

"Hurtful and untrue. It was an accident. Let it rest. Why bring back all our pain?"

Her forehead dropped into her free palm. "I'll read what he wrote, and talk to you later. Of course it was an accident. They checked out the wreckage, and they know what to look for. Now, I do have to go." Amy disconnected the call before he could start another round.

Troy's visit had seemed so innocent, if his suspicions a bit far-fetched. Now she'd added to the grief of a kind man and given his wife another log for her fire. At least Amy didn't see Honore anymore.

Amy pushed up from the chair and grabbed her cane on the way back to the gallery. She tried not to use it in front of the tourists, who were prone to pity and questions. The Zarins wouldn't gush over her. If they even noticed.

They stood in the middle of the room now, turning to

11

face each painting in turn. Some customers liked to see the effect from a distance as well as up close. A few more quiet words, then they stepped toward Michael. He met them half way.

As Amy approached, Zarin Sr. pointed out a peaceful duck scene and a heron, stick-legs in shallow water, head poised to strike its prey. "I wish the ducks in a more rustic frame, like the one beside them."

Michael studied the two frames, then nodded. "I don't have another frame that size, but I can have it for you by next week. Monday's Labour Day, but we'll be open."

Zarin nodded. "My son will collect both paintings on Monday, then. He will settle the paperwork now."

Ross Zarin matched his pace to Amy's as she headed for the office. "You were in the crash with Gilles Renaud?"

Luc's words welled up in Amy's thoughts and she held back a sigh. "You read the interview too?"

Ross glanced at his father and Michael, still in conversation. "My father showed me the article today in the paper. That's how I knew you. Gilles and I had mutual friends. I'm sorry for your loss. And your injury." He passed Amy a business card. "If you ever need to talk about it with someone outside of the grieving process, please call me. Even just to have a change of scenery or a coffee. I understand grief."

"Thank you." What else could she say? No amount of sympathy could change the past.

Ross lowered his voice. "I was surprised by the sabotage angle."

"Me too. It doesn't make sense."

"Sabotage implies enemies. Gilles had rivals, and — forgive me — ex-girlfriends, but I only heard good things about him. I wouldn't worry about enemies."

~~~

12

Amy brought up the *Halifax Herald* website on the office computer. She didn't do this often enough to know her way around the site, and Troy's story would hardly be a main headline. Eventually she found it. "Plane Crash Survivor's Second Chance at Life." *Gag.* Complete with photo.

She skimmed the article. No mention of the Renaud family. Good. And Troy had included the name of Michael's studio as part of her new life. If this gave Michael's business a bit of free advertising, she could live with the sabotage foolishness. Where was that part, anyway?

Troy had included it as an almost throwaway line near the end. "Experts investigating the recent crash of a light aircraft in Maryland confirmed that certain methods of sabotage are virtually untraceable. Given Gilles Renaud's skill as a pilot and the clear flying conditions at the time of the crash that claimed his life and maimed his fiancée, one can't help but wonder if this was truly a random accident."

Maimed. Amy bristled at the word. Troy knew better than that. He must be playing the sympathy angle. She rubbed her hip. The surgeon and therapists had done a good job, and as long as she kept up with her exercises, it only hurt if she over-taxed herself.

Michael poked his head in the door. "Is Aunt Bay back yet?"

"Nope."

"Great. I'll see if she can pick up more wood stain for that frame. I forgot we were almost out of that shade."

Amy glanced at the time. "Catch her fast. She'll want to get out of the city before rush hour."

Michael nodded. He pulled his phone from his pocket and headed back the way he'd come.

Phone. Amy should call Luc back. Try to calm him. She pushed back her chair and reached for her cane. Better listen to his messages first, and see if anyone else had called.

Before leaving the gallery, she checked the parking lot.

No customers arriving. If someone came while she was upstairs, she'd hear the gallery door chime.

Amy climbed the stairs and went into her bedroom. Her phone lay charging on the bureau. She picked it up. Two voice messages from Luc, an hour apart. He was upset, but demanding an apology would only reinforce the suspicion of sabotage. Would a man used to getting his own way understand that sometimes the best solution was to do nothing?

No other phone messages. Just a text from three days ago. Honestly, she had to remember to check this thing nightly. Except it had been weeks since the last message. This was from Gilles' sister Emilie. *Weekend plans? Call me?*

Amy set her phone back on the bureau and headed downstairs. She'd call from the office instead of using her pay-as-you-go cell.

Back in the office, she brought up Emilie's number on the land-line and hit *talk*.

"Hello?"

"Hi, Emilie, it's Amy. I just got your text."

"Don't you ever check your phone?"

Amy closed the newspaper web page and checked the studio email. Two new things to delete, and one to read after her call. "I kept putting it down around the studio and losing it, so I leave it in my room. It's not like I'm in high demand."

"Amy, it's been long enough. You need to start living again. Find a new guy. You know Gilles wouldn't want you to turn into a hermit."

"Not everyone's a social butterfly like you two. I'm more of a wallflower."

Emilie's snort sounded a lot like her brother. "You're not even in the garden. You're hiding on a shelf somewhere."

"I'm not hiding! I have a job, friends... I'm happy." When was the last time Amy'd gone out anywhere that wasn't related to studio business?

"A job. With Michael. Friends. Michael and his aunt. It's like he's keeping you hostage or something."

Amy twisted her ponytail around the fingers of her free hand. "He's just protective."

Emilie's suggestion was even crazier than Troy's sabotage theory. Which Amy was not going to think about. Gilles had no enemies, so it couldn't be true.

Could it?

Chapter 3

"Thank you!" The two middle-aged ladies left the gallery, each carrying a small bag of Michael's new greeting cards.

When the door closed behind them, Amy arched an eyebrow at Emilie. The girl's short hair was dark today, with bright green tips. "Did you really think you could up-sell them to that painting by acting like you wanted to buy it yourself?"

Emilie flashed a very Gilles-like grin. "Never hurts to try."

Amy shrugged. "Let's go relax for a bit."

"You go. Michael and I can tend to customers."

Michael crossed the floor toward them. "If someone else comes, we'll see them." He glanced at Amy, then back to Emilie. "We were hustling around before you got here, packing for the trip."

"Trip?"

"Didn't Amy tell you? I have an exhibit in Toronto next weekend. Same spot as a couple of years ago." He left the room, Emilie at his heels.

Her words floated back to Amy. "...the year Gilles died."

Amy limped after them. Michael wasn't tired, just sensitive enough to know that she was. And not wanting to point out her weakness to Gilles' energetic sister. *The year Gilles died.* Was that why Michael invited Amy on this trip? They'd be home before the actual anniversary of the crash, but did he think repeating his part of the events might trigger Amy's grief if she stayed behind?

What about Emilie? The girl had fought her parents to attend university here in Halifax instead of at home in Montreal. She'd hero-worshipped Gilles. Now she pulled at Michael's arm. "I didn't know anyone here. You ran away, and Gilles died."

Michael turned, as if waiting for Amy to reach them. "I didn't run away."

Emilie tipped her face to his. "You left us — left your best friend — just for your art." She broke away from him and fled toward the living room.

Colour washed Michael's face, and his eyes squeezed shut.

Amy touched his wrist, more gently than Emilie's tug of war. "It hurt them that you didn't say goodbye. Gilles understood. He said it was the right choice. You know Emilie, though."

Michael's eyes popped open. He stared at Amy. "He knew." He nodded slowly. "Of course he knew." The whisper sounded strained.

Amy's heart went out to him. "I'm sorry it didn't work out to relocate. But you're doing well here. And this house is a fantastic setting."

One corner of his mouth quirked. "Just a bit far from the major markets."

"You didn't leave because of someone here, did you?"

His face froze. "What do you mean?"

How could she say this that wouldn't sound ridiculous? "You and Gilles were close. If someone made you leave town, he might also have sabotaged the plane."

Michael groaned. "I chose to leave. Gilles chose to fly. No sabotage. Period."

Emilie breezed back into the hallway. "Fancy Audi just pulled into the parking circle. Maybe this time I can sell a painting."

With his back to the girl, Michael rolled his eyes.

They started for the gallery as the outside entrance chimed. Emilie opened the connecting door, flashing Amy an impish smile. "Young, rich and gorgeous. Go work your magic."

Michael's mouth firmed. Instead of speaking, he hurried past them to greet the customer.

Amy followed. "Emilie, you're a nut. I don't have any magic."

"Gilles thought you did. When you smiled."

"Gilles made me smile. Nobody else does." Except Michael, on whom the "magic" didn't work. Amy peeked into the gallery. "Ross Zarin. He came with his dad on Friday. Up-sell him if you can, but they seem kind of restrained to me."

Ross beamed over Michael's shoulder as Amy and Emilie stepped into the room. "Two assistants, today."

Michael swept a hand toward them. "Ross Zarin, this is Emilie Renaud. "

Ross bobbed his head and shoulders in an abbreviated bow. "It's a pleasure to see you both. I hope you're enjoying the long weekend."

Emilie mimed mopping her brow. "Michael works us hard."

Michael snorted. "Everything's ready to go, Ross. Would you join me in the office? I left the packing open on the piece we re-framed to be sure it's what your father wanted. While you're signing, I'll close the wrap."

A shadow crossed Emilie's face. "Could Amy do that? Your aunt was looking for you."

Ross reached for Amy's elbow. "Lead on."

Before Amy knew it, she'd been escorted to the office chair and Ross was inspecting the unwrapped painting propped against the filing cabinet.

"Perfect." He dropped into the visitor's seat across from

her and picked up the invoice. He gave it a cursory scan and placed it back on the desk.

Amy handed him a pen and showed him where to sign. "Are these for your local hotel?"

Ross scrawled something bold and illegible. "I think Winnipeg. Or perhaps Edmonton. My father has a theory that if guests see scenes of another part of the country, they might decide to travel there as well. Staying, of course, in one of his establishments."

"You never know."

Leaning back in his chair, Ross gave a lazy grin. "My father breathes strategy. He came to Canada as a young man with nothing, and now he's training me to manage his empire."

"He must be proud of what he's accomplished." Amy slid the signed invoice into the file folder in front of her. "Do you have the same entrepreneur's spirit, or would you rather be doing something different?"

Ross stretched his legs out in front of him. "I never asked that question. A good Muslim son obeys his father, and I find the old ways... satisfying."

Because you're a man. Had that shown on her face? Amy softened her features. "We have Muslim neighbours, but not from one of the stricter sects. The wife is allowed out on her own, and she covers her hair but wears North American clothes. She's been very kind to me since the accident."

"I'm not surprised."

Footsteps sounded in the gallery. Amy looked up as Michael reached the office door.

He walked over to the paintings. "Everything's fine, I trust?"

Ross stood. "Perfect."

Michael plucked a roll of tape from the desk and closed the packaging. "I'll carry these to your car when you're ready."

"I'll get them." Ross scooped the paper-wrapped paintings up in a fluid motion and turned to face Amy and Michael. "Thank you both. Enjoy the rest of your day."

They escorted Ross to the door. When he'd gone, Amy turned to Michael. "What did Aunt Bay want?"

He shrugged. "She put Emilie to work making a salad to go with dinner."

~~~

The salad's vibrant greens and glossy cherry tomatoes complemented Michael's homemade lasagna when it was finally time to eat. The scent had been teasing Amy for the past hour.

Aunt Bay glanced around the heavy oak table and fixed her eyes on Emilie, whose hand reached for the garlic bread. "Let's pray. Father, thank You for this fragrant meal and the hands that prepared it. Bless it to our use, and us to Yours. Amen."

Emilie snagged a thick slice of bread. "Sorry. I forgot." She turned to Michael. "So when are you leaving?"

"M-m." He made an exaggerated chewing motion. Or maybe not so exaggerated, given the huge bite mark in his slice of bread.

As Aunt Bay dug into the lasagna pan, Amy passed the salad to Emilie. "Michael wants to start tomorrow. We're going to take an extra day, because it hurts if I sit too long."

Emilie clanked the serving spoon against the salad bowl. "You're going with him?"

Michael held up a finger. "We're camping. Separate tents. And two rooms in Toronto."

A smirk touched Emilie's lips, but her brow smoothed. "You're so old-fashioned. It's cute."

"Whatever." He lifted a square of lasagna onto her plate, then one for Amy, before serving his own. "See, I'm chivalrous, too. And I can cook."

Aunt Bay snorted. "Doesn't matter how great a catch you are, if you won't swim near the bait."

He reached for the salad. "Two wonderful ladies in my life already."

Amy's cheeks warmed. She stared at her plate. In his life but not *in* his life.

"Two single ladies you're keeping out of circulation." Emilie rapped twice on the tabletop. "Especially Amy. Michael, don't bury her with my brother."

Heat washed Amy's face and down her neck. Her fingers felt like ice.

Michael touched her arm and she flinched. He pulled his hand back. "Emilie, that's enough. Amy will move on when she's ready. Here, in my house? Under my protection? Let her grieve."

Amy made eye contact with Emilie and shook her head.

Emilie held her gaze. Her lips moved in a silent *I told you so.*

Chapter 4

Amy had assisted with Michael's exhibits before, but never more than a few hours' drive from his studio. With frequent stops to stretch, her discomfort wasn't as bad as she'd feared. Nonetheless, she opted to use her cane throughout the show at Toronto's Linden House Gallery. As art appreciators, these patrons would be less concerned with sympathy than informal tourists.

Returning from the washroom, she paused at the exhibit room entrance. A gentle hum of conversation drifted from the visitors as they circulated among the paintings in pairs and clusters.

How many of the arts reporters invited to last night's opening soiree had written reviews? How many of the press releases she'd sent out had been noticed? She'd created a Facebook event, too, for Michael's local followers, and sent a newsletter update to his email subscribers. Linden House staff had done the same with their contacts.

Amy's job was to raise Michael's business profile, as well as rescuing him from the paperwork he dreaded. He didn't like these functions either, although the moral support of her presence seemed to help. At least he accepted shows as a necessary evil. The most beautiful art in the world wouldn't do much good if nobody saw it.

Look at him now, standing with an elderly couple, head tipped, listening. Smiling gently. Being authentic. He didn't need to sell — just to be himself.

Amy stepped into the room and wove her way through the visitors, pausing to greet anyone who made eye contact. Snippets of conversations lapped at her ears.

"Such natural colours... it's so clear, like looking through a window... I can almost feel the spray from that wave... see how the raindrops glisten."

A mother and daughter chatted in front of a painting of two chickadees splashing in a birdbath with two more of the little birds flying to join in. The girl, maybe nine or ten, spotted Amy's name badge. "Miss, how did he get the birds to pose like that?"

Amy smiled. "Michael works from photographs. He'd never get the birds to hold still, and water's always changing too. He spends a lot of time observing, with his camera ready. Sometimes he'll even combine two or three shots to match the image in his mind." She pointed. "This is the birdbath outside his studio. You should have heard the racket these little guys were making. We think they'd just left the nest, from the way they carried on. Just like human brothers and sisters."

The little girl grinned back. "Me and my brothers are louder."

Her mother lifted an eyebrow. "You can count on that."

Chuckling, Amy moved on. She caught sight of Michael talking with a couple closer to his own age. The woman was pregnant. Another patron stepped nearer, and the woman placed a protective hand over her stomach. Michael beckoned Amy to join them.

Up close, the couple were older than she'd thought. Mid-thirties?

The woman smiled and put out her hand. "Amy? I'm Carol. Your cousin? From a thousand years ago. Almost twenty, anyway."

Amy shook hands instinctively, trying to match the face

to her memory. She'd been so young when her cousin Carol, who'd lived with them, had gotten pregnant and married — in that order. To a shiftless guy a few years her senior, reinforcing Amy's mother's repeated message of abstinence. Could this be the same guy? Maybe Mom had been wrong.

Carol gestured to the man beside her. "There's been a lot of water under the bridge since then. This is my husband, Joey."

Another handshake, warm and somehow caring. Amy glanced between the two of them. "How did you find me?" Why did they bother?

Carol stepped closer to Joey. "We tried last year, to invite you to our wedding."

Joey nodded. "I Googled you again a few weeks ago, on a whim, and found you on Michael's website. Carol was actually here at his exhibit two years ago, and this gave us a great reason to come back."

"We'd love to offer you both a meal while you're here," said Carol, "or dessert after the exhibit closes tonight."

"What do you think, Amy?" Michael's expression said his question really meant *how's your hip?*

She could pop an extra painkiller for the chance to reconnect with an actual family member — one who wanted to spend time with her. "Could we?"

Michael checked his watch. "We'll be here until eight. Is that too late?"

"Not at all."

"Perfect." Michael glanced around. "I need to mingle. Would you give Amy your address for the GPS? And thank you."

Amy watched him sidle past a knot of well-dressed women and approach a solitary visitor admiring a painting. "It'll be good to sit and chat. We don't need to put you out for a meal, though."

Joey linked hands with Carol. "She likes to feed people. I

married her for her cookies."

"You did not!" Carol slapped her other hand against his stomach. She grinned at Amy. "I married him for his music collection. I'm glad you can come tonight. I'd love you to meet my son, Paul, if we can track him down."

Their banter stirred the empty spot in Amy's heart where Gilles had been. The spot that Michael's friendship somehow made emptier. She pulled a notepad and pen from her pocket. "How do we find you?"

After she'd taken down the address, Amy excused herself to circulate. She left Carol and Joey lingering in front of a dew-drenched clump of pansies in a blue earthenware pot.

They stayed at least another half hour, and intercepted Amy to say goodbye when they left.

By closing, a handful of Michael's paintings bore a "sold" sign. The atmosphere had been positive all day, with smiles and hushed conversations. Amy leaned on her cane. Satisfaction didn't ward off fatigue. Or pain.

The GPS did most of the talking on the drive to Carol's place. Amy leaned against the headrest, glad not to be peering at a city map.

Michael hummed quietly under his breath. Relieved to escape the crowd? He navigated the van through a network of residential streets and pulled up in front of a two-storey home.

Amy stirred. "They said it's a basement flat, and to use the back entrance. I really appreciate this, Michael. You have no idea what it's like to have no family."

"Maybe Carol remembers some of your childhood escapades. I might learn something."

Carol — and her dog — met them at the door. "Settle down, Chance. Let them in!"

A warm, spicy scent set Amy's taste buds tingling. Amy put out her palm for a doggy nuzzle, then wiped it against her leg while Chance inspected Michael's shoes.

"Just hang your coats on the pegs, and come have a seat. I wasn't sure how quickly you'd get away, so our chicken needs a bit longer in the oven." Carol led them into a cozy living room with a Monet print over a brown cloth sofa. A matching armchair and faded green recliner clustered to the side, facing an ottoman with a tray of four tall glasses.

Amy nudged Michael. "Does the Water Garden make you feel at home?"

"Or like I need to go back to school."

Joey stepped into the room from a short hallway, buttoning a sweater over his shirt. "I should have warned you, Michael, Carol's into Impressionists. Have a seat." He dropped into a corner of the couch. "Whoever's the most tired gets the recliner. It's comfier than it looks."

Michael made a sweeping motion with his arm. "Amy? Even the best chair won't help my tired brain."

Her hip twinged as she lowered her body into the seat. "I may be here for the night."

Carol offered Amy a glass. "Water?"

"Yes, please. I'm parched. There's only so much I dare drink at a 'Waters' exhibit." Amy balanced the glass on the armrest and kept a light hold on it. Chance had lain down between the couch and other chair, but a single bound and one swipe from his tail would be all it took to soak her.

Michael took a glass and sat in the other chair by the dog. He trailed one hand along the furry head. "Schmoozing is hard work."

Carol settled on the couch. "Especially being on your feet the whole time. I'm glad you could come tonight, though. There wouldn't be a lot of time tomorrow between church and the gallery opening, and we have an evening meeting."

"Church?" A hint of energy lifted Michael's tone.

"Would you like to join us?" Joey stretched his legs out in front of him. "It's pretty informal, good teaching, and it's not far from your exhibit."

The air thickened in Amy's lungs. Michael was smiling, agreeing. Saying there'd be time for a quick bite before the show. Amy took a mouthful of water.

Michael knew how she felt about church. He wouldn't expect her to go with him. Would Carol and Joey?

Carol caught Amy's eye and nodded, eyebrows barely lifted. "That was me two years ago. A little free advice — the sooner you choose God's way, the easier it is."

How could Amy change the circumstances of her birth?

"That's what my aunt and I keep telling her. Life's too complicated to navigate alone." Michael ignored the look Amy gave him. "Thank you again for finding us. I didn't know Amy had family here."

"I moved to Toronto a couple of years ago, but that's another story." Carol slid closer to Joey on the couch and tucked her feet up beside her. She smiled at Amy. "This guy kept me sane and held my hand through the worst bits — about the same time as your plane crash. Gilles had invited me to your wedding, but his mother sent a letter saying it was off. I assumed you'd broken up. Sad, but not tragic, and with everything going on here I just let it go."

"Gilles didn't tell me he found you. That's the way he was — he'd do anything for anyone. Especially for me." Amy pulled in a steadying breath. "I was in hospital for weeks. Mrs. Renaud's way of helping was to cut me out of the picture. I didn't see the body for closure. They held the funeral without me." But she remembered Gilles dying. Remembered his final words. *Toujours aimée* — always loved.

Amy gathered her hair in one hand and twisted it. "Michael and Gilles were best friends. Michael and his aunt took me in while I recovered, and then I talked myself into a job."

Michael's gaze felt like a hug. "Losing Gilles hit us all pretty hard."

Joey sat forward, palms on his knees. "There was a recent plane crash in the US that made me think to look for you again. Do they know for sure yours was an accident?"

Amy darted a glance at Michael. "They said it was. Then this month a local reporter suggested sabotage, because of the one you mentioned. It makes no sense, though. Even the best pilot can have an accident. Gilles had no enemies."

"Do you?" Joey's eyes held hers, clear and serious.

The hairs raised on Amy's arms. "No! I've been perfectly safe since the accident." Please, it had to be an accident. Somehow she could handle the randomness of her loss. If it was planned, if someone meant to kill Gilles—

Michael frowned. "There's no motive."

"I hope you're right." Joey blew out a sigh that ruffled his moustache. "Carol was a target because of her brother."

Carol froze, then turned to her husband. "It was the same time, but Harry didn't mention any other threats."

Amy grimaced at Michael. "Yes, that Harry Silver. He doesn't know I exist. Who'd target me for him? Or leave me alone when I lived? They had to be after Gilles."

Michael stared at her. "There is no they. It was an accident."

Amy's teeth caught the inside of her lower lip. What had she said? She didn't believe Troy's theory. Did she?

~~~

"Goodnight, Michael." Amy's electronic key buzzed to release the door to her hotel room. "I'm glad things went so well today. Thanks for giving me time with my cousin."

Michael squeezed her shoulder and stepped away. "You don't want to come with me to church, do you?"

She put one foot into her room and tried for a smile. "I can't."

"I'll text you when I'm on my way back. We should still

have time for a quick lunch." The gold flecks were dancing in his eyes. "It'll recharge me for the rest of the show."

"What did you do last time?"

"Went to one of the mega-churches. It was great, but I didn't know anyone."

Mega-church? Amy's mind flashed a picture of towering walls of reinforced steel, thick as a bank vault's door. Walking, like an old-fashioned movie robot. Crushing people beneath its feet. She shivered. "See you in the morning."

"Sweet dreams." A gentle smile drifted across Michael's face before he turned away.

Her hip needed a soak in the tub. The hot water loosened her thoughts as well as her muscles. An hour later, dry and in her pajamas, Amy booted up her laptop and signed onto the Wi-Fi network. It wouldn't hurt to look into that crash in Maryland. See for herself what people said.

Watching news footage of the crash set her hip aching all over again and tripped her heart rate into overdrive. Amy shut the laptop. She roamed the room, but the images lingered. Memory provided the sensations, the feelings of helplessness. Of fear. Gilles' desperate grip on her hand. His fierce whisper.

Amy filled a glass of water in the bathroom and gulped it down, avoiding her reflection in the mirror. She rapped the glass onto the counter and fled to the window. Cars, and a few pedestrians, moved outside. In the distance, a horn honked. She pressed her forehead against the cool glass and let her breath fog the pane.

A pizza delivery car turned the corner. Amy's stomach quivered. She stepped back and let the curtain fall into place.

She could phone Michael's room, wake him. He'd hold her, pull her out of this terrible place, but his brotherly support brought its own brand of agony.

Suddenly the desk lamp's glow wasn't enough. Amy

flipped on the overhead light and the one beside the bed. She reopened the laptop and navigated to her favourite site for mellow jazz, then flopped on the bed, eyes closed, and let the music lull her.

She must have drifted to sleep eventually. When she opened her eyes and turned her head, the clock said three fifteen. Her teeth felt fuzzy. Amy sat up, rubbing the worst of the stiffness from her neck. She turned off the music and lights and climbed under the covers.

Outside, a siren wailed and faded. Amy flopped over and fluffed her pillow. Why did hotels have so many strange sounds? And why hadn't she taken a painkiller while she was up? Groaning, she pushed up from the bed and dug her pills from her purse.

Music would mute the night sounds. Amy turned the laptop on again and plugged it in so the battery wouldn't die before morning. She propped pillows behind her and drew the covers over her legs, then settled the machine on her knees. Waiting for the medicine and music to take effect, she'd try that plane crash again. Text files only, this time.

A few news reports hinted the investigation might not be conclusive, but they didn't give details. Sighing, Amy pushed her hair back from her face. She typed *Maryland plane crash sabotage* into the search box. The first page of links were mostly blog entries, plus a flight club discussion forum.

She scanned the possibilities, then copy-pasted the believable options into a new file. Damaging the fuel line, or the tank selector. Or contaminating the fuel. Those made sense, although Amy couldn't believe anyone would want to hurt her or Gilles. One of the posts made her laugh. Lizard men used their electromagnetic weaponry because the pilot had proof of their machinations?

The drugs had taken the edge off the pain. Amy yawned and slid the laptop onto the bedside table. She'd leave the music streaming to help her sleep. Sunday would be brutal.

~~~

By the time the exhibit closed Sunday night, the dull throb behind Amy's eyes was beyond medication.

Michael closed the gallery door behind her. "Last night in the big city. Anywhere special you'd like to go?"

She looked up at him. "I'm exhausted."

The sparkle left his eyes. "I found a nice little jazz club online."

"I can't, Michael. Drop me at the hotel and you go — I hardly slept last night." Amy's brain caught up. Rooted in place, she stared at him, replaying his words, his tone. "That almost sounded like you were asking me out."

He shrugged. "Let's grab something quick to eat." His emotionless tone was a stone wall.

Her throat tight, Amy turned and limped toward the parking lot.

Michael caught up before she reached the van. "How about the burger joint across from the hotel?"

"Whatever you like. I'm sorry, I just—" Just what? *Need to sleep? Think I ruined something special? Love you?* Amy choked on a sob.

Michael reached for her, then let his hand fall away. He unlocked the van and opened Amy's door. "We'll get drive-thru. You can eat in your room and go right to sleep."

Amy dragged a sleeve through her tears and climbed into the passenger seat. The emotional see-saw from Gilles' death should be behind her now. Her jaw tightened. She had to leave the sabotage theories alone.

Chapter 5

When Amy's alarm sounded the next morning, she couldn't remember dreaming, but the aftermath weighted her emotions. Or maybe it was just the overload from yesterday.

It didn't take long to pack up at the gallery. More paintings had sold than she expected. They'd leave some smaller ones on consignment with gift shops on the way home, along with some of the new art products.

What could have been two solid days of driving became a week-long working holiday. Amy had contacted the gift shops ahead of time, so Michael knew which owners wanted to see him.

Mornings and evenings in the campgrounds were the best part of the trip. With the light at its best for pictures, Michael led Amy on a hunt for water scenes. They found tiny streams, raindrops on leaves, a raging waterfall. Michael snapped photos and sketched rough pencil details. Over the winter, he'd paint the best images.

Amy loved watching him work, seeing the before and imagining the after.

He chose areas with easy access and short walks. What kind of inspiration might he have found if he'd left her behind with the tents?

Late Friday afternoon, Michael pulled the van into the studio driveway. Emilie's bright blue Honda sat beside Aunt Bay's purple four-by-four.

Amy's chest tightened. Might as well stamp *The End* in all caps. "Michael, this has been so good. I know I slowed you down, but thank you." She clicked open her seatbelt and turned toward the door. "I wish we could have tried the jazz club."

The key scraped as he pulled it from the ignition. Amy opened her door, keeping her face averted.

Michael let out a slow breath. "You were a big help. I know it was hard. Thank you."

Emilie raced toward them from the house, as if Michael might change his mind and drive away. Aunt Bay followed more slowly.

Amy climbed out of the van, testing her hip, just in time to see Emilie launch herself at Michael with a squeal. Amy caught Aunt Bay's eye, and the older woman shook her head.

Michael disentangled himself and hauled open the side door of the van. Amy did the same on the passenger side. The sooner they had everything unloaded, the better.

Emilie grinned at her across the boxes. "Hey, Amy. Welcome back."

"Thanks."

The girl reached for one of the smaller boxes. "I came to help Michael unpack. You can't carry much."

Aunt Bay spoke in Amy's right ear. "We'll all help."

The bare gallery walls gave Amy a creepy feeling, but it didn't take long to unwrap the paintings and restore the room's atmosphere.

Michael stacked the extra boxes of notepads and other products in the office, and spread his hands to his helpers. "All set to re-open. Thank you. Did we miss any customers this week, Aunt Bay?"

"I returned a couple of messages and said you'd be back on Monday. Didn't notice anyone come to the door, but I've been on the go a lot."

33

The phone rang, and Aunt Bay picked it up. "I was expecting a call. You three go relax."

They settled in the living room. Emilie tucked her feet under her and fixed Michael with a bright stare. "So tell me all about your trip. I wish I could have cut classes for a week and gone, instead of poor Amy having to do it."

Michael's lips quirked. "She didn't have to do it. I could've gone alone again." The look he gave Amy soothed the prickle from Emilie's words. "Amy's a great assistant. She made the trip a lot easier."

"What are you going to do when she finds another bank position?"

"Sell her a painting for her office."

The girl tossed her head. "If you let her go. Honestly, Michael, sometimes I think you're keeping her prisoner, like some kind of weird memorial to my brother."

Amy lifted one foot, then the other. "No ball and chain. You're as bad as the conspiracy speculation about Gilles' and my accident."

Michael raised an eyebrow. "In Toronto, you sounded like you believed it."

"I got caught up in the puzzle. The what-if. But there's no motivation, not even money. Any life insurance Gilles had would have gone to his parents, or to the company if it was a work policy."

"He should have transferred it to you."

Amy blinked. Michael never criticized his best friend. They'd been inseparable — until whatever happened to separate them. Even then, each spoke well of the other. She shrugged. "I'd be surprised if he had life insurance. Gilles was too alive to think about death."

Emilie shrugged. "He had no one depending on him, until you came along."

"I didn't come along. He found me." The whirlwind romance and engagement. Leaving everything to start fresh here in Halifax with this captivating Québécois. He'd carried her away from a carefully-ordered life like some dashing — but good-hearted — pirate.

He'd said he was running away. Amy looked from Michael to Emilie. "Gilles left something here, something that upset him. He sorted it out and came back, but what was it? Could that be the clue?"

Michael's hands slapped his thighs. "Not again!"

Emilie shot him a glance. She faced Amy, eyes slitted as if to see the past. "He was furious with Papa. He shouted and stormed out. I didn't see him again until he came here with you. I'd been counting on him to help me move into my dorm." She grinned at Michael. "But Michael helped me instead. And bought me pizza."

Amy resisted rolling her eyes. "Do you know what upset him?"

"I couldn't catch the words. Papa had appointed him manager of the Halifax dealership, and Gilles had been here a few months. He flew home to Montreal for the weekend. We could tell he was upset about something, but he'd only speak with Papa, in private."

"Would you ask your father about it?"

Emilie's mouth turned down. "I don't know. He's different now. So sad."

Michael groaned. "Leave the man alone. Please say you don't suspect him of killing his son."

"Of course not!" Heat swept Amy's face. "But whatever upset Gilles might be important."

"You don't think Luc could see that for himself?"

"Maybe he's too broken to care."

Chapter 6

Late Saturday morning, Amy carried a cup of tea into the gallery and flipped the sign to *open*. Not that she expected customers on such a rainy day. She'd glimpsed a stack of mail on the desk last night when they were unpacking. Might as well tackle it now.

She logged into the office computer and sorted envelopes while the email loaded. Junk, junk, request for a donation for the firefighters' silent auction. Amy set that one aside. Michael might be interested. More junk. An envelope addressed to her. She slit it and pulled out a letter.

Dear Amy... A glance at the signature stopped her breath.

Aunt Bay tapped on the door jamb. "Don't you think you deserve a break after your road trip?"

Amy gasped. Her fingers refolded the paper and clasped on top of it with a thump. "I—"

Michael's aunt raised an eyebrow. "Am I intruding?"

"Of course not!" Her giggle sounded guilty. Or sick.

Aunt Bay advanced into the office and claimed the visitor's chair. Ignoring the telltale paper, her shrewd gaze held Amy's. "That's not a good colour on you."

Amy picked at her collar. What had she put on, again?

"Your face, child. What's wrong?"

"I don't know. Really." Amy smoothed the letter against the desk blotter. "I don't know if I want to read it. It's from—" She stared at her hands: ring-less, nails too short... twitchy.

"Not that reporter again. I'll straighten him out."

"No, Aunt Bay, it's—" Amy sat taller. Pulled back her shoulders until they hurt. Looked Michael's aunt in the eye. "My father and I are not on speaking terms."

After a minute, the older woman nodded. "His choice, or yours?"

"His." Complete with the threat of a restraining order if she communicated with him again. Heat swept Amy's body. Gilles had said the man wouldn't be at their wedding. Amy had known from her fiancé's expression that he was angry, but he hadn't shared the conversation. Definitely nothing about further contact being forbidden.

"Does he know about the accident?"

Amy nodded. Crushed by grief, unsure of her own injuries and cut off by Gilles' mother, asking the father she'd never met for help had seemed better than continuing to rely on the kindness of virtual strangers. "Without you and Michael, I don't know where I'd be."

Aunt Bay's lips formed a straight line as she studied Amy. "Have you tried to forgive him?"

"He doesn't want me."

"His loss. Forgiveness wouldn't change his mind, but it would help you heal."

"I am healing." Amy rotated the letter on the desk.

"I'm talking about the ache in your spirit. The one that makes you think less of yourself. And avoid God."

Amy pushed her chair back from the desk and stood. She snatched the letter, folded it smaller. Stuffed it in her pocket. "I can't have this conversation right now."

The phone rang when she was half-way to the door. Amy jerked back and picked up the handset. She recognized the soft, rapid tones of their neighbour, Safia.

"I'm sorry to impose when you've been away, but could I possibly come and get a package of Michael's new cards? I need to visit a friend in the hospital."

Amy met Aunt Bay's eyes and mouthed *Safia*. "Come whenever you like. I'm sorry about your friend."

"I'll be there shortly. Thank you."

Amy set the phone back in its cradle. "She needs some cards."

Aunt Bay nodded. She hadn't moved from her chair, likely hadn't stopped watching Amy.

The woman's patience was as powerful as direct speech. Amy sighed again. "Aunt Bay, I love you, but sometimes you push too hard."

"How many times did you say that to your physiotherapist? The pushing, not the loving."

Amy shook her head. "You're the only person I've ever met who's actually incorrigible. You know that, right?"

"In that case, perhaps I'll rescind my invitation."

"You haven't made an invitation."

Aunt Bay smirked. "Tea and homemade cookies, this afternoon? Just the two of us."

"What are you plotting?"

"Moi?" The older woman placed her palm on her chest, eyes artfully wide. Then her expression clouded. "Something's not right with Michael. I want to know what happened while you were away."

Amy perched on the edge of her chair and planted her elbows on the desk, supporting her chin in her hands. "It might be this sabotage thing. I can't get it out of my head, even though it's messing with my sleep. He's so protective, he hates anything that might upset me."

Aunt Bay's eyes narrowed. "I still want to hear the rest. Although that could be it."

"Safia will be here soon, and I should deal with our email, but you know how Troy suggested you pray about the sabotage idea? For the truth to come out? Have you?"

The gallery door chimed, and both women stood. As Amy stepped around the desk, Aunt Bay said, "If you're asking did the Archangel Gabriel appear with an answer, no. But I find it interesting that the idea keeps coming up. Perhaps there's a reason." The lines around her mouth deepened. "I hope there isn't."

A chill drifted across Amy's shoulders.

They stepped into the gallery as Safia closed the outer door. Rain spotted her headscarf and coat, and her little boy's raincoat.

The boy made a dash for Aunt Bay. Behind him, his mother called, "You're wet!"

Boots squeaking on the floor, he barrelled into Michael's aunt. She caught his shoulders. "Well, now, Dafiq. What are you up to today?"

"We hafta go to the hospital and visit Mommy's friend. I hafta be quiet."

Aunt Bay snorted. "That should be interesting."

Amy grinned, and stepped closer to Safia. "The cards are over here. Don't worry about dripping rain. I have a mop in the office. Would you like us to keep him while you're in the city?"

The neighbour's dark eyes lit up, but she shook her head. "You'll have too much to do after your trip."

"Look at the two of them." Aunt Bay had bent to the boy's eye level. Whatever he was saying, he had her full attention.

Safia's lips twitched. "She's remarkably patient."

"And effective. You go on your own. You'll have a better visit."

"Thank you." Safia chose a package of cards and followed Amy into the office to pay. "May I use the edge of the desk to write my note?"

When they went back into the gallery, Dafiq was galloping in tight circles around Michael's aunt, laughing. Aunt Bay had positioned herself in one of the few spots where the boy could move safely, and she called to Safia,

"Let him stay and play."

Amy grinned at her neighbour. "See?"

Once Dafiq said goodbye to his mother, Amy headed to the office for the mop. "I'll catch the puddles, and join you two in a few minutes. I think Michael is going through photos from the trip, so we don't have to worry about noise distracting his painting."

She took time to skim emails, and dashed off a quick reply to a gift shop's question. A message from Troy jolted her. *Gilles' flight club still won't talk to me. Would you try?* He included the club's phone number. Amy jotted it on a slip of paper and stuck it in her pocket with her father's letter. If she called, she'd better use her cell in private.

~~~

Flour and globs of cookie dough littered the kitchen counter. Amy tackled it with a wet dishcloth while Aunt Bay supervised Dafiq's hand-and-face washing in the bathroom. The warm, sweet aroma wafting from the oven had them all smiling.

The timer beeped, and Amy slid her hands into oven mitts to bring out the first tray. Dafiq bounded into the room with a whoop, and climbed into his favourite chair at the table.

As Aunt Bay poured the boy a glass of milk, Michael stepped through the back door, dripping rain. He inhaled deeply. "Perfect timing!"

Dafiq pointed at the water on the floor. "You hafta take your boots off right there, or they won't let you have any cookies."

Michael grinned. "And you have to visit more often, so I'll get more cookies." He set his boots by the door, and hung his hat and coat on the doorknob.

Amy reached for the carafe. "Coffee?"

"Did I mention you're my favourite assistant?" Michael ruffled the boy's loose curls, then settled on the chair beside him.

She slanted him a look. "I'm your only assistant. And this does not count as 'other duties as assigned.' Where were you?"

"Down by the water with my camera. I took some interesting shots."

Amy set his mug on the table and filled a plate with gooey chocolate chip cookies. Behind her, Dafiq said, "Sometimes my mommy sends me out to play in the rain, too."

"Careful with these. The chocolate is still hot." Amy plopped a stack of paper napkins on the table with the cookies. She pulled out a chair as Aunt Bay joined them with two cups of tea. Amy slid a cup toward herself. Sitting felt good. "Thanks."

Safia arrived just as they finished cleaning up. Aunt Bay had tasked the "men" with washing the cookie sheets. Dafiq ran to his mother with a metal tray in one hand and a tea towel in the other. "Look what they let me do!"

Amy smiled behind his back. "How's your friend?"

"She'll be fine. It was routine surgery, but she finds the time long."

Amy remembered the feeling. Aunt Bay and Michael had spent an incredible amount of time with her in the hospital, but the nights had crawled by.

When Safia and Dafiq left, Aunt Bay motioned to Amy. "I need a little lie-down before our chat."

Amy followed her up the stairs and went into her own room. She unrolled her exercise mat and worked through her physio stretches, then unplugged her phone from its charger. No messages. Surprise.

It couldn't hurt to phone the flight club. She pulled the papers from her pocket, dropped the letter on her bureau, and keyed in the number.

"Halifax Flight Club." The gruff voice didn't make it easier.

"Hi, um, this is Amy Silver. I was in that crash a few years ago with Gilles Renaud? Is there someone I could talk to?"

The man on the phone took his time responding. In the background, another male voice shouted, and something metal crashed. "Listen, miss. Even if you came in here with proof you're legit and not some tabloid writer, there's nothing to say. The investigators ruled it an accident. If you're really her, I'm sorry for your loss and for what you've been through. But spreading rumours won't bring him back." He hung up.

Amy hurled the phone onto the bed. It bounced hard and hit the floor. Growling, she spun on her heel and stalked out of the room.

~~~

Later, in the living room, Aunt Bay fixed Amy with a stare. "Now that it's quiet, give me the scoop on your trip."

Amy leaned one elbow on the armrest. Should she ask the older woman to tackle the surly guy from the flying club? What good would it do, other than revenge?

Beatrice and Michael had fought enough of Amy's battles since the accident. This one she'd handle on her own. Or better still, let it go. The man and his attitude weren't worth it. He probably didn't know anything useful, anyway, or he'd have told the investigators.

She imagined her resentment melting into liquid, beading through her pores, then lifting from her skin as a gas. Happy thoughts. Toronto. Memories of the gallery brought a smile. "I wish you could have heard the comments at the show. People love Michael's paintings. The images refresh something in us."

"Which is why I expected him to come home satisfied, even with the long drive." Aunt Bay walked to the door and listened before returning to her seat. "The music's still on in his studio. He seemed okay with your relatives?"

Amy stared at a corner of the ceiling. "Fine. Especially when he found out they were church people. I don't think he understood how much it meant to me to have actual family want to see me."

"He doesn't know about your father?"

"He'd be as protective as Gilles was, and as angry. Please don't tell him." Amy still had to read the man's letter. At least it was short. And not signed by a lawyer.

Raindrops scurried down the windowpane. Amy snuggled deeper into her chair. "On the way home, Michael found some good ideas for paintings, even though he kept to easy terrain for me. I told him to go without me—" The last night in Toronto. She'd said it then, too. And accused him of asking her out.

Aunt Bay tipped her head forward. "What is it, child?"

"He doesn't go anywhere that means leaving me unattended. You don't think Emilie's right, do you? That he's trying to keep me in some kind of bubble?" Only wishful thinking could interpret his friendly invitation as a date, but Emilie's ideas were just as far out.

"Emilie's perspective of life is somewhat unusual."

"But could he have... I don't know... an obsession?" The back of Amy's neck prickled. She lifted her hair away from the skin.

Michael's aunt's mouth snapped shut. Her lips twisted from one side to the other, as if she were trying a new taste she wasn't sure she liked but was too polite to spit out. Finally she shook her head. "Michael lived with me since his teens, until I moved into the city. He's as stable as they come. Except when he was with Gilles." A grin split her face.

"Ask him about fireworks sometime. He doesn't know I know."

"But you and I want him to be stable. What if he's not?"

"Then we'd notice. And we'd help him. But I need more than Emilie's drama-queen theories to convince me." Aunt Bay tapped her fingers on her leg. "Besides, if he successfully kept watch on you all week, why would he be morose? Unless you sneaked out to a strip club or something."

"Aunt Bay!" Amy's cheeks flamed.

The older woman glanced at her watch, and stood. "I'll just remind him he's cooking tonight." At the doorway, she turned back. "Don't worry, Amy. And I won't either, now. It must be the airplane issue stirring up his grief. Which does not mean to drop it, if the Lord keeps putting it in your path."

Amy listened to Aunt Bay's footsteps on the stairs, and pushed up from her chair. Her hip twinged at the change in angle. God wouldn't "put anything in her path." Amy did her best to stay out of His way so He wouldn't have to notice her and be offended.

Thinking of offence... better to read her father's letter now instead of before bed.

Michael met her on the stairs. "Homemade macaroni and cheese. With bacon, if we have any. I hope you can wait an hour. I got caught up in what I was doing."

"Awesome."

Amy closed the door to her bedroom and took a deep breath before picking up her father's letter. She carried it to the chair by the window. Outside, at the edge of the property, rain pelted St. Margaret's Bay. A lone seagull huddled on a rock.

Sighing, she looked at the folded paper in her hands. Nothing her father could say could hurt her more than he already had.

Dear Amy,

I was wrong. There are no words to apologize for how I treated you after you wrote me — and you, injured and grieving at the time.

I have no excuse, but I'd like to explain: my wife's cancer had returned, and we knew it would be fatal. She didn't know about my affair with your mother. Your wedding invitation was the first time I knew about you. I was afraid if my wife found out, it would kill her. (Yes, I was also ashamed to tell her.)

Not knowing what your mother told you, I'll offer some background: I was a hockey player. When I was traded to the Senators, my wife didn't want to move, so I rented an apartment in Ottawa. It was a trial separation for us after years of drifting apart.

Your mother and I met at a party, and it was love at first sight. I started divorce proceedings, and she agreed to marry me as soon as I was free. Then came my wife's cancer diagnosis. She had no one to help her through the treatments, and my duty was clear. I took a leave of absence from my team and went home, promising to come back to your mother once the situation resolved.

My wife lived, and the ordeal rekindled our love for one another. I still had feelings for your mother, but it seemed right to honour the longer-standing, legal commitment. When I phoned to tell her, we both cried. She didn't tell me about you. She had a high-paying job, but I would have sent child support, tried to secretly be part of your life. Instead, we agreed to cut all contact. I didn't know she had died until you wrote. For that loss, too, I am sorry.

There's no other way to judge me than harshly, and I deserve it. But please know I wish the very best for you, and I would count it a privilege to help you in any way I can. It's a surprising joy to discover I have a daughter.

I hope you don't throw this in the trash. If I don't hear from you, I'll assume you did, and I'll write again. So please respond, even if it's just to curse me out.

I remain,

Most humbly sorry,

Your father, Neal Williamson

Amy stared at the typed words. The nerve of the man, waiting until his wife died, so he'd be safe, then deciding he wanted a daughter after all. Curse him out indeed — except her mother had loved him.

Not that Mom ever said his name, or gave any clues about his identity. Amy didn't learn that until she turned twenty-one and a registered letter arrived from the lawyer overseeing her mother's estate. Even then it wasn't much, just his name and last known address. With a request to only contact him if Amy required medical records or urgent help. By then she'd been on her own for four years, her childhood fantasies of finding her father long dead.

She re-folded the letter. Mr. Neal Williamson had turned down his daughter's desperate plea for help two years ago. She didn't need him now.

Nor did she need Michael or his aunt to know she was illegitimate.

The letter crackled in her fist. Nobody used that word anymore, but it's what she was to God.

Why did Michael and Aunt Bay have to be church people? Her background didn't matter to anyone else, but it put her outside the boundaries of their faith. How could God accept her when she should never have been born?

Chapter 7

Amy loved Sunday mornings. With Michael and his aunt at church, the entire house was hers. She could bake, read, soak in the tub... not that she couldn't do the same things with them home, but it felt different. Today, solitude let her process her father's letter without worrying what they'd see in her face.

She poured a second mug of coffee and looked out the kitchen window. The deck was still damp, but little waves on the bay glistened in the sunshine. Not much wind. With a sweater, and a cushion for one of the wicker chairs, she could take her thoughts outside.

Amy scooted up the stairs to her room and pulled a fleece-lined, brown hoodie from her closet. Music would help, too. She glanced at her bureau. Where was her phone?

Had it been in her purse since the trip? So much for using that for the music. The battery would be dead. No, the end of the charger wire lay across the cut-glass box on her bureau that held her hair elastics. She wouldn't have plugged that in and forgotten the phone.

The flight club call. Amy remembered the phone hitting the bed, bouncing onto the floor. She walked to that side of the bed and knelt to peer under the nightstand. Nothing. She twisted, grinding her knees against the laminate floor. The phone lay under her chair by the window.

Oops. She'd been mad, all right, to give it that much

momentum. At least it was still in one piece. When she picked it up, the message light was flashing. That could explain the giant singing bumblebee in her dream last night.

One new text. *Please let go of the plane crash. Asking questions could cost your life. A friend.*

Fingers locked around the phone, Amy stared at the words burning themselves into her mind.

A faint thud from downstairs caught her breath. Amy whirled, trying to look everywhere at once. She closed the text message and typed *9 - 1 -*

Thumb hovering over that final *1*, she grabbed her cane and tiptoed to her doorway. Silence. Only the tick of the wall clock from the living room and the background ringing from overstraining her ears.

She crept down the stairs, pausing on each one. Nothing stirred. The sound had come from beneath her, at the back of the house. At the bottom of the stairway she turned toward the kitchen, then hesitated. Sneaking up on an intruder had to be her worst idea ever. What was she going to do? Club him with her cane? The light-weight aluminum would bounce off his head and barely dent his hair.

There'd been no further sounds. No reason to call emergency services, nor flee to the neighbours. But just in case...

Amy cancelled her partially-entered call and brought up her contacts list. Why hadn't she added the neighbours? She hit Emilie's number.

At the sound of the girl's groggy voice, the pressure eased around Amy's lungs. "Sorry to wake you, but I'm home alone and I heard a strange noise. Stay on the line with me while I do a walk-through?"

"Amy, if you think someone broke in, get out!"

"It wasn't a crash or anything, just a sort of thump." Emilie the drama queen should understand overactive imaginations.

"Well, be careful. And keep talking. If there's anyone there, you might scare him away."

Unless it was the person who sent that text. Amy kept the phone to her mouth as she stepped into the kitchen. "Okay so far." Nothing out of place.

Could the sound have come from outside? She peered through the window. "There's something on the deck. Small and brown."

"It's not a brick, is it? Like they throw through windows with threatening notes?"

Amy shook her head. "Way to help me stay calm, Emilie."

"Sorry. Do you think that made the noise?"

"Dunno. It's just lying there—" As she spoke, the bundle fluttered. "Hey—" Amy backed up and studied the windowpane. "It's a bird, a starling or something. I can see the smudge where he hit the glass. Poor little thing."

The bird stirred again. A third try brought it to its feet. It took a couple of tottering steps and flew away from the house, weaving and keeping low to the ground.

Amy smiled. "He's okay."

"Well, now you've scared away the big, bad noisemaker, I'm going to hit the shower. Say hi to Michael for me, and Aunt Bay."

"Thanks for being my backup."

A bird. She'd panicked over a bird. Amy's fight-or-flight had settled down, but the phone in her hand reminded her of the anonymous text. A new shiver prickled her scalp.

Leaning against the kitchen counter, she opened the message. *Please let go of the plane crash. Asking questions could cost your life. A friend.* Was it a warning, or a threat?

The sender's number meant nothing, except to show an out-of-province area code. Where was 431, anyway?

Amy's phone was a basic pay-as-you-go with no browser option. She went back to her room for her laptop, and set it up at the kitchen table. It didn't feel safe to stay upstairs right now.

She retrieved her coffee mug from the counter and took a sip. Not quite cold enough to reheat, but not hot enough to dawdle over, either. Amy settled in front of the laptop and finished her drink while the machine booted up.

Reverse phone number lookup tagged Winnipeg for the area code, but couldn't match a name to the full number. Amy frowned at the screen. She didn't know anyone in Winnipeg, and how would someone that far away even hear she had doubts about the crash?

She tapped her fingernails against the side of her empty mug. The message's tone wasn't threatening... at least on the surface. Hardly worth going to the police. Her eyes narrowed. Especially since they'd tell her to let the accident go, too.

Showing it to Michael would be worse. He'd not only agree, but the phrase *cost your life* would stick him closer to her than a straightjacket. Not in a good way.

Aunt Bay wouldn't overreact, but she might feel obligated to tell Michael. Back to claustrophobia.

Troy. Amy nodded to herself. A reporter might even be able to dig up this person's identity.

Fingers tapping the keyboard, Amy tried the local newspaper's site first. No luck. Troy had said he was a freelancer, after all. Searching for him by name returned too many options, including a neurosurgeon and an Australian rugby player.

Amy logged into Facebook and brought up Michael's profile, then the list of his friends. Troy was there, and he'd helpfully set his email address as public. Likely a good idea for a journalist looking for tips.

She fired off a quick email with the subject header "Plane crash." That should get his attention.

Three minutes later, the house phone rang, showing a local cell number. Troy's voice asked, "Amy? What's up?"

Amy tapped a foot against the nearest chair leg. "Someone sent a text about the accident, warning me to drop it. I thought you might know what to do."

"Drop it."

"What?" Amy pulled the phone away from her ear and stared at it. "You're the one who planted the idea in my head. Don't you dare pretend it's nothing now."

"Whoa... I didn't say that." Troy paused. "Tell me exactly what the message said. And whatever you do, don't delete it."

"So you do still think there's something."

"More than ever. I got a text, too. Mine said to leave you alone or I'd be responsible for whatever happened to you."

The hairs on the back of Amy's neck stood slowly to attention. She recited the unknown phone number and the message she'd received.

Troy grunted. "My gut says this person's more concerned about your safety than about bringing the truth to light. Must be nice to have someone looking out for you."

Someone looking out for her. "Troy, this isn't Michael, is it? Tricking us to convince me to stop thinking about it?"

A hoot of laughter, then silence. Finally, Troy asked, "Would he think it'd work?"

"He shouldn't."

"Then, no. I'm not sure he'd know how to set up a fake number, and I'd certainly hope none of his friends would send messages like that on his behalf. They could be charged."

Amy wandered to the window. The bird hadn't returned. "So you think I should obey the warning."

"Yes."

"But you'll keep investigating."

"They've as much as told me there's something to investigate. I have a few ideas, and I'll be careful. In the meantime, you stay out of danger."

After the call ended, Amy stared out the window, idly tapping the edge of the phone against her chin. She wasn't brave, or resourceful like Troy. But it didn't feel right to let someone who hadn't even known Gilles put his safety on the line alone.

She'd been with Gilles every step of that day. Had she seen anything that seemed insignificant at the time?

Shoulders set, Amy turned from the window and left the kitchen. Time to make another call.

~~~

Amy waited until halfway through lunch to drop her bomb. "I want to visit the crash site."

Michael's jaw froze in mid-chew, but Aunt Bay kept eating as if Amy had suggested a trip to the mall. Michael's throat jerked convulsively. He gulped some water from his glass. "Are you sure?"

"I'm stronger than you think. It's time."

Michael squeezed his eyes shut in a long blink, then nodded. "Maybe it is. The closure could finish the doubts you've been having."

Or help Amy remember even a small clue. "I'm going with Ross Zarin. He's picking me up in about half an hour."

Aunt Bay set her spoon gently in her soup. "Is that wise?"

Heat rose in Amy's cheeks. She'd expected Michael's feisty aunt to take her side. "We were talking about the crash, and he offered to drive me."

Michael's face had taken on a mottled, reddish tint. His lips pressed together, twisted, slackened. Finally he pulled in an enormous breath that seemed to free his tongue. "Wouldn't it be easier to go with one of us?"

Amy stared at the half-eaten grilled cheese sandwich beside her soup bowl. She'd been ready to fight him, to push for her independence, but the hurt in his tone undid her. She fiddled with her spoon. "You two have done so much for me, and you know I'm grateful. But I need to start facing things on my own."

"This isn't on your own," Aunt Bay said. "It's trusting a stranger instead of those who love you. Michael or I, even Emilie, for all her foolish chatter. We'd have gladly gone with you, and paid our own respects. On the side of that road, when it all comes back at you, you'll break down in front of a stranger instead of in the arms of friends."

"If I went with you, we'd all be crying. Being with Ross should help me hold it together."

Aunt Bay snorted. "God gave us tear ducts for a reason. I've often wanted to visit the site myself and say a proper goodbye."

Amy reached across the table and took the older woman's hand. "You missed the funeral so I wouldn't be alone."

"And I don't regret it. I gave my condolences to the family at the funeral home, but it was so..."

Michael cleared his throat. "Proper. Stuffy."

Without having been there, Amy understood. "Not Gilles."

"Exactly." Aunt Bay rapped on the tabletop. "The portrait, the fancy coffin and floral arrangements, those said nothing about the free-spirited young man we loved." Her index finger wiped the corner of one eye. "I was going to suggest we go this year on the anniversary of the crash. I wish I'd spoken sooner. Steps this big should be taken in a group where you belong."

Amy sighed, ignoring the twist in her stomach that said Michael's aunt was right.

Chapter 8

Amy's engagement ring lay in a corner of her jewellery box, a thin chain nestled inside it. She'd worn it around her neck after losing Gilles. Putting it away on the first anniversary of his death had felt terribly final, but her life-loving fiancé would never have wanted Amy to tie herself to his memory. Now, she slipped the chain over her head and tucked the ring inside her shirt.

Downstairs, the doorbell rang. Amy zipped her brown hoodie, grabbed her purse from her bedroom chair, and headed for the door.

Michael and his aunt both stood in the entryway chatting with Ross. Amy reached the bottom of the stairs and collected the cane she'd left propped by the closet. "Thanks for coming, Ross. I'm sorry to keep you waiting."

Ross flashed a broad smile. "It's a beautiful day to get out of the city, even for such a solemn trip." He nodded to the others. "A pleasure to meet you, Miss Rockland. Michael."

Amy tried to fill her eyes with apology as she said goodbye, but Michael wouldn't meet her gaze. She crossed the paving stones with Ross to his pristine silver Audi.

Ross ushered her in and closed her door.

Amy pinned on a smile and tried to relax. A girl could get used to chivalry like this. When Ross slid behind the wheel, she said, "Lovely car. Did you get it from Gilles' father?"

Brown eyes flicked her way and then returned to task.

"Yes. My father has a fondness for luxury cars. I tell him he should buy a Renault from Mr. Renaud."

Amy settled her cane more securely between her seat and the door and said nothing.

As Ross put the engine in gear, he shot her another glance. "R-e-n-a-u-l-t. It's a type of car. Sorry, bad joke. But that's the first thing I thought when I heard the name." He turned onto the narrow pavement and headed back to the highway.

The Audi glided on the straight bits of road and hugged the curves so smoothly that a peek at the speedometer surprised Amy. She snuggled into her seat. What a difference from Michael's rattletrap van. Even from Aunt Bay's little four-by-four. This was like driving with Gilles again. Except Gilles had insisted on a high-end SUV for his sports equipment.

They cruised up behind another car and Ross slowed. "Peaceful place to live, but these drivers would stress me out."

A steady stream of vehicles travelling toward them gave no chance to overtake. After a few more turns Ross seized an opening, swung into the opposite lane and powered past the car that had held them back.

Amy barely heard a change in engine pitch. She assessed the man beside her. His shiny black hair was almost military-short, just long enough to reveal a hint of curl. His sweater looked like cashmere and probably cost a fortune. The dark green complemented the soft brown of his skin. A simple gold ring on his right hand held a dark, square stone.

Ross Zarin was made of money, and it had done a quality job. Amy smiled, remembering Gilles. He'd been raised in privilege, too. She'd been scandalized at how he'd taken it for granted. Wealth let him have what he wanted — toys, adventure, and from what she'd heard of his past, women. But Gilles never acted rich, neither the spoiled snob nor the cultured elite. Ross bespoke a type of affluence that emphasized his natural confidence. The difference intrigued her.

Amy's mother had been a successful executive, but she'd funnelled as much as she could into savings for Amy in case anything bad happened. Like the cancer that took her life in Amy's teens.

Ross glanced sideways. "You're very quiet. Having second thoughts?"

"Maybe. I couldn't attend the funeral, and I thought this would be the final bit of closure. What if I'm not ready?"

"Then we drive past the site and find a spot for coffee. You will have at least come one step closer." He flexed his fingers on the steering wheel. "Why did they hold the funeral without you?"

"The crash dislocated my hip. I was in the hospital."

"Was Gilles not cremated? They could have waited for your release."

Amy stared at the passing buildings. "Gilles' mother insisted."

"Grief does strange things."

So did petty nastiness.

Amy pictured the surge of bitterness receding from her like the tide. She would not give Honore Renaud the satisfaction of poisoning her life. Of course, Beatrice said that only Jesus could help Amy let it all go and start over.

Ross followed a ramp onto the highway. "My mother died when I was very young. Attending the ceremony would have been too much for me, but my grandparents took me to see her body. I've always appreciated that."

"Oh, Ross, I'm sorry. How old were you?"

"Four. My one memory of my mother is saying goodbye. And a terrible sadness." He switched lanes to pass a delivery truck. "My father took it very hard. I spent the rest of my childhood with my aunts and uncles in Iraq."

"So far away... Were you lonely?"

His lips twitched. "Hardly. Between two households, there were thirteen cousins. I was never alone. Of course I missed my father, but he visited when he could."

"I'm surprised he didn't remarry."

Ross spared a brief look from the road. "Please, never tell him I shared this. When he came to Canada, my father fell in love and married against my grandfather's wishes. My mother was a faithful Muslim, but my grandfather was a stern man with plans of his own. My mother's death in a car accident destroyed my father. He saw it as a punishment from Allah, and he remains single in penance."

The distance sped past as they chatted, and before long the GPS instructed Ross to leave the highway. They navigated secondary roads to reach the stretch of pavement where Gilles had made a desperate, glider-style landing. Amy's pulse quickened at the mental echo of the engine's last gasps in the sky. "Gilles took a chance, landing on the road, but it was the best option he saw with so much forest. We couldn't believe it was clear."

Ahead a white, wooden cross stood sentinel in the overgrown ditch. Ross pulled to a stop on the shoulder of the road and turned to face her. "This may be the only roadside memorial for a plane crash instead of a car." He squeezed Amy's arm and quickly let go. "Do you want to get out, or is this enough for today?"

Her mouth went dry. She stared at the white marker, eyes burning. What was she thinking, to try this? Could she set foot on the spot where her dreams had died? Face the pain again? Amy lowered the zipper of her hoodie and touched her breastbone, rubbing the faint bump of her engagement ring beneath her shirt.

She blinked away the tears and set her jaw. For Gilles, she could do this. One scrap of memory, one faint clue, could bring him justice. Her hand found the door handle. "I need to go alone."

"I understand. Call if you need me. I'll be right here."

Amy climbed out of the car. The ground beside the pavement was soft from yesterday's rain. Her cane tip sank in. She tugged it free.

Low undergrowth had filled in the spot where the plane came to rest. The damaged trees had been cut down, and new growth hid their stumps. Amy stood beside the car for a long moment, studying the scene. Remembering. Rescue vehicles with flashing lights. Two ambulances and a fire truck, plus a police car. No traffic. They told her other police cars had blocked the road in case of an explosion.

A tear tracked down Amy's cheek. She'd lost it then, crying that if there'd been fuel they'd still be in the air. But the emergency workers hadn't known what brought down the plane.

One slow step at a time, Amy picked her way down the bank and through the bracken. The marker's paint was already fading, and a few spots marred the brass plate. Using her cane for balance, Amy squatted and wiped the metal with a tissue. Her fingers slid across the text: Gilles Renaud 1988 - 2013.

A packet lay at the foot of the little cross, and the growth seemed to have been pulled away. Frowning, Amy bent nearer. Flowers. Dead and decomposing, but laid here as a bouquet. From whom? She straightened. If someone who loved Gilles wanted to turn this into a proper memorial like some of the other crosses, they'd have used an artificial funeral arrangement, maybe even cleared a bit of space and added a tiny white fence.

She could do that. With his grave in the family plot in Montreal, Amy had nothing here for a connection point. She brushed two fingers across the top of the cross and stepped farther away from the road.

The plane had come to rest... roughly here. She set her

feet, leaned on her cane, and stared at the trees.

It had been a perfect flying day, and Gilles practically glowed with the thrill of giving her a new experience. He'd walked her around the plane for the pre-flight inspection, pointing out every single thing on the checklist and explaining why it mattered. Inside the plane, he'd completed what he called an engine run-up before going back to the flight operations office for a minute.

When he returned, they'd taxied onto the runway, picked up a thrilling amount of speed, and lifted into the sky.

She'd been surprised at how hot the sun made the cockpit. Enchanted by the scenery... the coastline, farmer's fields. Lulled into timelessness. When the engine first sputtered, Gilles switched tanks. Switched back, when it didn't help, insisting they should have fuel for another hour.

Teeth gritted, swearing – or praying – in a rapid monotone, Gilles had finessed the wallowing plane down onto the pavement, telling Amy to watch for approaching cars. Nose up until the last possible moment, speed nearly gone, they hit hard. A sound like a shot came from beneath them and the craft skidded sideways off the pavement onto the soft shoulder. The plane lurched, spun. Tipped as the ground fell away beneath it.

Eyes closed now, Amy fell into a memory kaleidoscope of helplessness and screaming. The tortured sound of shearing metal. Gilles' voice, louder now, definitely praying. The tang of burnt wires. Bumping, jostling. Pain – such pain. And something wet on her skin.

Gilles' voice calling her name. She'd smiled, touched his face. Something in his eyes... "Medical tag. Around my neck." He sucked a breath through clenched teeth. "Phone 9-1-1." A shuddering sigh. "Find Michael." His gaze held hers, desperate to communicate, but what?

Crying, Amy scrabbled her phone from her pocket.

Before she could enter the numbers, Gilles grabbed her

free hand. His eyes were too bright, his skin pasty white. "Amy... Toujours aimée..." He slumped against his safety harness, eyes shut. His hand slipped from hers.

Amy caught his wrist. Her fingertips found his pulse, and the terror backed off. Adrenaline made her tremble enough that it took three tries to punch in the emergency call.

He'd never regained consciousness. Now, standing here with his final words echoing in her mind, Amy slumped heavier against the support of her cane. He'd wanted to say something. But what?

"Gilles, I don't want to fail you..." Amy's words ghosted into the trees, and she could almost see her breath. Surely it wasn't that cold. Cane propped against her leg, she rubbed her arms.

Behind her, a car door slammed. Ross called, "Amy? Are you all right?"

Amy nodded. She took time to wipe her eyes and pull together the shreds of her composure before turning back to the car.

Ross waited on the bank to help her climb up to the road. When he touched her hand, he frowned. "You're freezing!" He steadied Amy on the pavement and studied her face. "Do you think it helped?"

"I don't know. But I needed to come. Thank you."

He bustled her into the car and cranked up the heat. "Coffee now. Or tea. And talk as much or as little as you like." He pulled a u-turn and headed back the way they'd come.

So understanding... except he didn't understand the weight of defeat. Couldn't she have remembered one tiny clue?

Chapter 9

Amy closed her eyes and leaned into the headrest, letting the powerful engine carry her. "Ross, this was very kind of you, giving up a free afternoon to help a stranger find some closure." Couldn't she have found clues instead, in the resurfacing memories?

"Not quite a stranger. And I'm glad I could help." The turn indicator clicked, and Ross pulled into the gallery's driveway. "I didn't want to raise this in the café, but visiting the crash site was hard for you. Is it settled in your mind now, or did it raise more questions?"

He'd mentioned questions earlier, too. The words of the anonymous text cut through her thoughts. *Asking questions could cost your life.* Amy shivered. "The thing is, Gilles landed safely, against all odds. If one of the tires hadn't blown and sent us into the trees..."

"They said it was a fantastic piece of flying, to get down in one piece."

That was Gilles. Anything he did, he did well. Amy's heart twisted. "It just seems so — I don't know, futile. He pulls off this amazing landing, saves our lives, and then dies because of a faulty tire."

Nodding gently, Ross didn't break eye contact. "The pain of an accident is bad enough, without that reporter spreading rumours of sabotage."

Amy gathered her hair in both hands and let it fall behind

her back. "I don't think anyone's taking him seriously."

"You should ask for a public retraction."

"That would only remind people what he said. I'd rather let it go." And hope Troy knew how to investigate discreetly, for his safety and for hers.

Amy thanked Ross again and climbed out of the car. What a waste. No remembered clues, and nowhere to turn next. Going to the flight club would scream "questions" to whoever sent that text, and at this point, she had no questions to ask. If not for the warning, she'd have written off her recurring doubts as one more stage of grief. Could a person loop back into denial?

Ross waited until she opened the front door before driving away.

Amy stepped inside. "I'm back!" No way would she give in to the guilt that demanded she slink home in repentance. It was past time Michael and Aunt Bay stopped coddling her. If they had a little more faith in her, she could have shown them the text. They could have helped. Amy's lips twisted. In that case, the three of them would have visited the crash site together.

She pulled off her boots, and carried them through the house to the back deck. Clapping them together over the railing let the worst of the dirt fall into the grass. She scanned the scattered trees leading down to the water. Was the little bird still around? Not that she'd recognize him. A board creaked behind her, and Amy turned from the view.

Michael took another step and stopped, hands in his pockets. "How was it?"

She raised the boots, then set them down beside her. "Muddy." Leaning against the railing, Amy breathed in the fresh air. Someone, not too far away, had mowed a lawn today. "But better than I expected. I didn't know how steep the bank was. No wonder we hit so hard. Have you seen the spot?"

He nodded, slowly. "Once."

"Did you leave flowers?"

"I did."

Amy's lips twisted. "I'd like to clean it up and make a proper memorial."

"Is that... something you'd need to do alone?"

Amy closed the distance between then and laid a hand on his elbow. "Michael... today wasn't about shutting you out. It was time to see where he died, and I thought you'd find a reason to keep me away. I'm sorry I hurt you."

A muscle spasmed in his cheek. He stared over Amy's shoulder toward the water. "I would do anything to see you whole again."

Loyalty vibrated in his voice. Dedication and sympathy. But not what she wanted to hear. Amy tried to smile "You're a good friend." She squeezed Michael's elbow and stepped past him toward the house.

At the door, Amy stopped and spoke without turning. "You're a good protector, too. But sometimes healing involves stretching and taking risks."

She hurried inside. Behind her, the door opened. Michael carried her boots through the kitchen. Before he reached the front closet, the doorbell pealed.

"It's just me!" Emilie's voice.

At least the girl would take their minds off the tension between them. Amy straightened her shoulders. So she hadn't found a clue. She still knew something had happened beyond a simple accident. And she'd taken that step of closure to return to the scene. Not that she'd forget Gilles, but she could live in his absence. Would Michael have believed that, if she'd asked him to drive instead of Ross?

Emilie's hair was pink-tipped today, matching her bright pink sweater. She grinned at Amy. "Thanks for waking me up this morning. I got my laundry done in time to escape from my roommates." She kicked off her shoes and launched into a slide across the floor in fuzzy, pink-striped socks.

Michael caught Amy's eye and smiled.

Emilie spun to face them. "Where's Aunt Bay?"

"She went next door to stay with Dafiq. His parents had to go out." Michael checked his watch. "She should be back soon."

The girl's eyes widened, and she shook her head. "Is he that little terror who doesn't know how to walk? By which I mean he's always running around? I don't know how she puts up with him." She headed for the living room.

Amy followed. "Aunt Bay worked hard to love the little guy, but she really does. And he's more settled around her. He knows his limits." Safia and her husband had no family in the area. The young mom had needed plenty of support when Amy first arrived.

Behind them, Michael asked, "Anyone want a drink? I made lemonade to go with supper."

Amy declined, but Emilie rounded her eyes at him. "Yes, please. And do you have enough food for a starving university student? If not, that's okay. There's leftover pizza at my place. Unless my roommates finished it."

Michael laughed. "You two can help me get it ready once Aunt Bay's back. When Safia asked her to babysit, I said I'd cook."

Amy dropped into a chair and put her foot up to ease her hip, while Emilie trailed Michael to the kitchen, chattering all the way. Did Michael even know the girl had a crush on him? She wasn't subtle, but for all his sensitivity, Michael perpetually misread Amy's own emotional cues. A sigh pushed from the depths of her lungs. Maybe he knew how they both felt, and thought ignoring it was kinder than rejection.

He was kind. Why couldn't Amy be content with that?

The two of them came back into the room, each carrying a tall glass of lemonade. Michael set a third glass on the table beside Amy. "Just in case you change your mind when you see how good it looks."

Emilie drained half her glass and gave a satisfied sigh. "So, Amy, have you recovered from your scare this morning?"

Amy caught her breath. Had she mentioned the anonymous text? She tried to warn Emilie with her eyes to say nothing.

Michael leaned nearer. "What happened?"

"It was nothing. I was in my room, and I heard a thump while you and Aunt Bay were at church." She shrugged. "I overreacted, and phoned Emilie so I'd have someone on the line while I checked it out. A bird flew into the window. He was okay, though." Please, she couldn't have said anything about that text.

An impish light gleamed in Emilie's eye. "You'd better take her to church with you, so she won't be home alone."

Michael's lips twitched. "Fine idea. Why don't you join us?"

Emilie's hands flew up as if to push back his words. "I'm a student. I need my sleep."

"Go to bed before midnight on Saturday. You'll be fine."

"I'm Catholic."

His grin deepened. "They won't excommunicate you for entering a Protestant church. Or would you like us all to go with you to Mass?"

Pink darkened her cheeks to match her hair. "No thanks. I was just trying to help."

"So was I." Michael glanced from Emilie to Amy. "You're both more than welcome any time, no strings attached."

The back door banged. Michael stood. "Sounds like our intrepid babysitter is home. I'll go see if she needs a lie-down before we start supper."

A minute later, he popped his head back into the living room. "All right, sous-chefs, we're on. She'll have a quick rest while we cook."

Emilie lifted an eyebrow at Amy. "Sous-chefs, no less. Sounds fancy. You stay here and rest. I'll help."

Michael's voice floated from the hallway. "Both of you. Now. Come and learn the ways of the burger master."

Laughing, they went to the kitchen. Michael was tying on an apron that read *Artist at Work*. "A little bird told me someone's been craving hamburgers." He winked at Amy. "If he hit the window this morning, he was fine by afternoon."

Amy washed her hands at the kitchen sink, trying to keep her emotions off her face. She'd mentioned burgers last week. Today, while she was out gallivanting after upsetting them both, he'd decided to make her a special supper. And spent part of his free afternoon on a grocery run.

With her back to Michael, Amy risked saying, "That's the sweetest thing anyone's done for me all week."

When she turned, he made an elaborate bow. "Sweeter than taking you on a pilgrimage today?"

She tipped her head to the side and stared. "No contest." Was this about competing with Ross? No way. Unless... The back of Amy's neck prickled. Unless Emilie's jokes were right and Michael really did want to isolate her from everyone else.

Emilie nudged her. "Pilgrimage?"

"What? Oh, a friend drove me to the crash site today. It was time to face it."

A smile played around Emilie's lips. "So who is he? Have I met him?"

"As it happens, it was a he, and you did meet in passing. Ross Zarin, a guy about Michael's age, who came to pick up a painting one other time you were here."

"Ooh, he's gorgeous. Way to re-enter the field!"

Behind Emilie, Michael opened the fridge and started pulling out ingredients.

Amy glared at the girl. "It's not like that. Ross will find a suitable, Muslim woman who won't mind him thinking he owns her. Not what I want, at all."

Emilie arched her eyebrows. "And what do you want?"

Amy kept from glancing at Michael. "It doesn't matter."

Below the pink-tipped hair, Emilie's eyes narrowed. "As long as it's not what I want, we'll be fine."

Amy reached for a cutting board. They might both die old maids.

Chapter 10

The next morning, as soon as Amy had dressed for the day and before going downstairs for breakfast, she settled in her bedroom chair with her phone and re-read the anonymous text. This was her one real clue, and she had no idea what to do with it.

The silent letters on the phone screen mocked her. Amy rubbed her forehead. Was Aunt Bay still praying for the truth to come out?

Amy stared out the window at the seagulls wheeling over the water. Circling, restless, like her thoughts. The gulls wanted food. She wanted answers.

Her stomach growled. Okay, she wanted answers and food. Amy frowned at the phone. Two could play the texting game. If she hadn't been so startled yesterday, she could have shot back a reply. She started typing. *You just proved it wasn't an accident. Who are you?* Her thumb jabbed the send button.

Amy slid the phone into her pocket and left the room.

Half a pot of coffee waited for her in the kitchen, where Beatrice lingered over the paper. The older woman looked up with a smile. "Did you sleep well?"

"Surprisingly, yes. I was afraid visiting the crash site might bring back the nightmares." Amy poured herself a cup of coffee and opened the fridge for some milk. "Aunt Bay, I didn't want to say it last night in front of Emilie, but I'm sorry I upset you yesterday. I didn't think it through."

"All's forgiven. We only want what's best for you."

"I'll go back with you if you'd like. Now I know I won't fall apart, I was thinking of planting some flowers or something. It looks pretty bare." Amy set her mug on the table across from Aunt Bay's newspaper and prepared a bowl of cereal.

Michael's aunt looked up when Amy slid into the seat across from her. "I'm glad to see you healing. You've been cocooned long enough."

Amy gathered her hair at the base of her neck and flipped the ends behind her back. "Butterflies struggle to break free, and if someone tries to help, it kills them."

"But humans weren't designed to fight alone. Either one of us would have gone with you, you know. Or both of us. We'd have counted it a privilege."

Amy focused on her cereal. "You're both so supportive. I just felt... I needed to go, and Michael doesn't understand I'm ready for these things."

"He can be a bit overprotective. I've lived long enough to see clearer, child. Next time, let me work on him." Aunt Bay folded the newspaper and set it aside. "Are you still troubled about that young reporter's sabotage theory?"

"I'm not satisfied it was an accident, but when I phoned the flight club, they wouldn't talk to me." Amy dropped her spoon in her bowl. Milk splashed across the table and she snatched a napkin from the holder to blot the drops. "The investigators didn't find anything out of line, and even Gilles' parents are satisfied there was nothing wrong. Who's going to listen to me?"

Aunt Bay reached across the table and squeezed Amy's hand. "I will. And God will listen to us both."

Heat prickled the back of Amy's neck. "He doesn't want to hear from me."

"He's heard our conversation. And He'd love to hear you

ask Him for help with whatever you think disqualifies you from His love."

Amy's head came up. Aunt Bay's eyes held no judgement, only concern. Amy shook her head. "It's nothing I've done, so I can't undo it."

"Child, we've all done things to separate us from God. We can't undo them, but He'll forgive us if we ask." The hand holding Amy's tightened. "If someone has abused you, Jesus is the only one who can truly make you whole again."

"What? No!" Thank God, no. Amy glanced at the ceiling. Would He mind her thanks? She looked back at Michael's aunt. "It's nothing like that."

The older woman's face relaxed. "I thought perhaps your reaction to your father's letter..."

"I need to answer him." Before he decided to phone. Amy slid her hand free from Aunt Bay's grip and crossed her arms. "He rejected me when I needed him, and now that I'm fine, he's asking for contact."

"He may have struggles of his own. Not that I'm excusing his behaviour, you understand."

Amy stared at a spot on the tabletop. The man had tried to explain. "So you think I should give him a chance?"

The corners of Aunt Bay's mouth lifted. "If the situation were reversed, what would you want him to say to you?"

Amy pushed back from the table. "I'll think about it after I catch up on the office messages. We got a little distracted here on Saturday, with Dafiq."

She cleaned up her dishes and walked through the house to the gallery and office. On a Monday in mid-September, they'd be unlikely to have any visitors to the gallery, but she unlocked the door and swung the sign to "open." After Amy finished the paperwork, she'd see if Michael had anything else ready for framing.

Saturday's coffee mug sat on the desk, still three-quarters full. Amy sighed and slid it aside. While the computer woke

71

up, she sorted the rest of the paper mail. From the email, she listed a few questions for Michael, replied to some general questions, and made a note to drop off more framed prints at one of their local consignment spots. Tourist season might be winding down, but early Christmas shopping had begun.

No reply from the mysterious texter. How many hours' difference between Halifax and Winnipeg? Her anonymous "friend" might still be asleep.

Emilie should be awake by now on a school day. Amy shot off a quick text. *Remember to ask your dad what he and Gilles fought about. Closure = good.* She added a smiley face for good measure.

The men's argument was all she had. Gilles' medical tag was the one thing to come back to her at the crash site, but he died from crash-related injuries. He must have wanted the EMTs to know about a drug allergy. The information had been nothing that could save him.

Amy logged off the computer, picked up her notes and days-old coffee. The chime on the gallery door would let her know if a customer entered.

She stopped in the kitchen to empty the mug into the sink and stick it in the dishwasher. No sign of Aunt Bay. Music drifted from Michael's studio upstairs. Amy followed the sound.

Michael perched on the edge of a high stool in front of an easel, canvas angled to catch the daylight from the enormous picture window beside him. He glanced up and flashed a smile. "Hi." His focus snapped back to his work. "Grab a chair if you can stay. If someone's looking for me, they'll have to wait until I finish this bit."

"Nobody's waiting. I just had a few office things to follow up on." Amy leaned against the wall, watching him work.

His painting clothes were old and comfortable. A moss-green shaker knit pullover with the sleeves pushed up to his elbows, and faded, paint-stained jeans. Eyes focused on the canvas, Michael's face bore the tiniest hint of a frown, as if he could see through it to the real-life scene he wanted to evoke. Could he hear it, too? Smell and feel it? Taste the salt air, if it was a seashore scene?

Often he played the water-themed relaxation CDs they used in the gallery, but today the music had words. Amy caught something about Jesus — it must be his Christian Internet station again. She wouldn't stay long. Some of the songs stirred a hunger for a world she couldn't be part of.

She gathered her hair in one hand and twisted it over her shoulder like a rope. This morning wasn't the first time Aunt Bay had invited her into their faith, and said it didn't matter what it was that held her back. Gilles had said the same thing, and he wasn't even a Christian. They'd talked a bit about God, since Gilles had claimed to be running away from Him. Amy's smile turned down.

Everybody loved Gilles. Of course he'd assume God did, too. That all he'd have to do was stop running, turn around, and be embraced.

Gilles had laughed at the idea that her birth excluded her from the kingdom, an expression he'd no doubt picked up from Aunt Bay. He said something about "original sin" and that everybody had to lay theirs down and let God adopt them into His family. Amy had longed to believe him, but Gilles' opinion didn't carry much weight against the church folk from her childhood. Those people knew their Bibles.

Michael squeezed more white paint onto his palette and cut some blue from one of the other dabs. Mixing them together with his knife, he shot her a grin. "Did you just stop by to gaze in adoration, or are there really some messages for me?"

A little from column A, a little from column B... "Didn't you get enough adoration this weekend with Emilie following you around?" Amy lifted her forgotten notes. "I do have a few things I need your input on, but they can wait for a break. You looked pretty focused when I came in."

"I'm past the tricky stage for now. We can chat. If it's something that needs too much thought, I'll ask to save it for later." Michael picked up his brush, but turned his full attention to Amy. "Emilie... you were joking, right?"

Amy gave him her best level stare.

Red crept into his face, and he squirmed as if the stool had picked up a mild electric charge. "Are you sure?"

When she didn't speak, Michael asked, "When did this start?"

"When did she first meet you? It was going strong when I came on the scene."

Michael hitched himself fully onto the stool and put his feet on the rungs, paint brush resting on his jeans. "She was my best friend's kid sister. I never thought—"

"You didn't see her, but she saw you."

He pushed his free hand through his hair. "Wow. Maybe ten years? Aren't crushes supposed to be short?"

Heat danced in Amy's cheeks now, but she maintained eye contact. "Not if they grow into love." She put on an impish smirk. "Or a fixation, I suppose."

She let that dangle for a minute while Michael sat shaking his head. "Seriously? I think she's in love with who she thinks you are. A guy who looks like you but parties like Gilles."

Michael's head-shaking picked up speed. "That was never me. Although we did get into some interesting adventures." His shoulders slumped and he met Amy's eyes. "That part of me died when he did. If not before."

Amy's heart twisted at his brokenness. She pushed away from the wall and plopped into the nearest chair, and summoned a teasing tone. "Aunt Bay said to ask you about fireworks."

The effect was priceless. Michael's jaw dropped, his eyes went wide, and it didn't take much to imagine a neon sign flashing the word *panic* across his face.

His gaze darted around the room. "Nobody knew!" The words came out in a whisper.

Amy's cheeks hurt from grinning. "This is one story I've got to hear. Do I need to wait for a statute of limitations to run out?"

Michael looked out the window toward the water. "Did you ever wonder why two complete opposites were such close friends? It's too long a story for now, but there's no harm in telling it." He seemed to remember the brush in his hand, and reached to dip it in the cleaner. He blotted it, dipped, blotted, then frowned at it and left it to soak.

He picked up a fresh brush and turned to Amy. "She never said a word."

"Did she need to? Or did you learn your lesson, whatever it was?"

His lips twitched. "If the lesson was don't listen to Gilles' crazy ideas, no. If it was fireworks, boats and a non-swimmer are a bad mix, then definitely." The smile left his face. "We almost died that night."

"But you lived."

"And it bonded us closer than brothers."

Until whatever separated them. When Amy had asked about it, Gilles was uncharacteristically sharp in telling her to let it go. He'd almost seemed relieved when Michael decided to move his business out of province.

Amy picked up her notes. "Okay. You paint, and I'll do the assistant thing. Question one. Do you want to donate something to the firefighters' silent auction?"

Michael applied his fresh brush to the paint and turned to his canvas. "Sure. Remind me this afternoon."

"Right. And Vannette's shop in Mahone Bay wants some more consignment prints."

Michael didn't reply, but Amy knew he'd heard. He studied the canvas, then made a few tentative dabs at it.

Another dip into the paint, and he fell back into a smooth painting rhythm.

Amy allowed herself to watch for a moment, then looked at her list. "We have an invitation for a new craft fair, the weekend you're at the Forum. If Aunt Bay wanted to help you there, I could do a table at this new one."

"Tell me more at lunch, but my instinct is to pass. New venture, same weekend as a major event... you could sit there all day and sell one, maybe two notepads. Besides, I'd rather have you with me."

"That's me. Indispensable." Amy couldn't keep the bitterness from her tone.

Michael brush stopped, then started again. "What's that supposed to mean? Do you want to waste your day in some two-bit craft market?"

"Not really." But it would be nice to think he wanted her company instead of her abilities. "One last thing. Would you do a portrait of a couple with their dog?"

"That's a new one. Did they say what kind of dog?"

"No, just that she's older, and not in great health. They want a memorial."

"Aw, how can I say no to that?" Michael wiped excess paint from his brush. "Send them a quote based on three people, and find out more about the dog. If they want to go ahead, set up a meeting for next week. I'd like to have the open house behind us first."

"Sure." Amy glanced around the room at the other canvases in various stages of completion. "Whatever happened to the portrait you were doing of me for Gilles?"

"His dad offered to pay me even without finishing it, but I couldn't take his money." Michael glanced her way. "Don't worry, you won't show up in an art gallery or online auction."

"Now that would be creepy. I—" Amy's phone buzzed. The phantom texter? "Excuse me." She slid the phone from her pocket and opened the message.

I knew Gilles well. He would want you to stay out of this. Please. You mustn't be seen asking questions or you'll be a target.

She snapped her phone shut and stood. "I'll put on fresh coffee. Are you ready for a break soon?"

"What's wrong?"

"Nothing. Just one of those no-name messages."

"Amy, tell me you're not still chasing sabotage theories. Next time I see Troy..."

"Troy won't even talk to me now. He's been warned off. Doesn't that tell you something? And what could I find out on my own?" Amy's hands clenched. "Gilles was your best friend. If someone killed him, shouldn't you care enough to make it right?"

She fled the room, ignoring Michael's call to wait.

Chapter 11

Amy skidded into the kitchen. The television was on in the living room, and hopefully Aunt Bay would stay occupied for a while. Turning to face the doorway, she cued a reply to the anonymous text.

No. She wanted to talk to this person.

She opened the back door and walked onto the deck. It was chilly despite the sun. Amy wrapped her free hand around her other arm and jabbed the call button.

The phone rang three times, then cut off. No voice mail, nothing. As if the other party had disconnected her. She tried again. Same result.

"All right, be that way." She fired back a text instead. *Someone murdered my fiancé and I want justice. Help me.*

The reply was almost instant. *I'm trying. If you involve yourself, you'll make it harder. No more contact.*

"Thank you." Amy whispered the words and held the phone to her lips.

Sudden fear stabbed her. This "helper" could be anyone — even the killer. What better way to silence her questions than by pretending to investigate?

Troy's instinct said the warnings were friendly, but instincts could be wrong. Had he tried contacting this person? Amy pulled up his number from her contacts list, but her call went to voice mail. She hung up, her thoughts too jumbled to form a coherent message.

When she stepped back into the kitchen, Michael stood at the sink, filling the coffee carafe. The warm room, plus the guilty heat of her parting shot at him, hit Amy like a sauna. Fanning her face, she pocketed her phone. "I'm sorry. I was coming to start that."

Michael poured the water into the coffee maker and slid the carafe under the filter. He closed the distance between them. "I would have sacrificed anything for Gilles. If I thought there was any chance this wasn't an accident, I'd do all I could to make it right. But I just don't see any evidence — or any reason for it."

Amy looked away. "I know you care. I'm just so frustrated that no one seems to believe anything's wrong, when something is."

Michael's hands settled on her shoulders. "Why are you so sure?" Warmth laced his tone, without accusation.

"I can't tell you." One glimpse of those texts, and his protective nature would go into hyper-drive. Not happening.

He slid his hands down Amy's arms and stepped back a pace. "I think you're right about needing closure. Visiting the crash site was a good start. Are you ready to try flying again?"

Amy gaped at him. "I—"

"Think about it, and see. We could find a local pilot to take us up." Michael spread his hands. "Like getting back in the saddle after being thrown by a horse. Not that either of us has likely been on a horse, but you know what I mean."

"We?"

"You want to heal. I want to help you. That makes we. Aunt Bay can come, too, if she'll get in a plane that small."

Amy threw her arms around Michael and squeezed. "Thank you." She darted back before he felt obligated to return the hug. "Did you put fresh coffee in the filter, before I push start?"

"I did."

She pressed the button. "While we're waiting, do you want to decide what goes to the shop in Mahone Bay?"

"Sure. Vannette said prints, right, not originals?"

"Yes. Ten to twelve." Amy followed Michael through the house to the office. A filing cabinet along one wall held prints of his paintings, page-sized and smaller, each one backed with cardboard and sheathed in a plastic sleeve.

He rooted through the drawers and stacked a selection on the desk. "We'll frame a few of these. Would you grab some of the notepads and cards? She might be interested in those too."

Amy had her hands full of cards when the phone rang. She cradled everything in one arm and picked up the handset. "Hello? Stratton Gallery."

"Amy?"

Luc's voice. With a definite hostile tone. Amy took a slow breath and carefully transferred the cards to the desk. "Luc, how are you?"

"Perhaps it's best to revert to Monsieur Renaud."

"All right, *Monsieur Renaud*, how can I help you?"

Michael turned from the filing cabinet, eyebrows raised.

Amy grimaced at him.

Luc's voice raised. "My Halifax dealership called. That reporter has been harassing my employees."

"Troy? He won't speak to me about his investigation, but I promise you, when we did the interview, I asked him to keep your family out of this." Amy stacked the packets of cards on the desk, and added a few notepads.

"This talk of sabotage has to stop. It was an accident. Leave it at that."

Amy's jaw tightened. "I have no influence over what Troy does or does not do. You may have noticed I've said nothing else publicly about the crash."

"But you used my daughter to pump me for information. Information you planned to pass on to your tabloid friend."

If looks could kill, Amy's glare would burn through the wall and straight to Luc's head office. And char him. "That is not true. I asked Emilie to ask you something—"

"Which was none of your business!"

"To ask you something which I hoped would help me find closure for my loss. At no time did I have any intention to reveal Gilles' personal information to anyone. Press or no press."

Michael had crossed the room to her side. Amy stared at the ridges in his sweater, desperate to stop the trembling before she broke into tears. Michael laid a gentle hand on her arm.

"You can direct any further communication through my lawyer. I want no more—"

"Luc, you listen to me!" Pain sliced Amy's chest with each breath. "Your wife shut me out of Gilles' funeral. She stuffed my belongings in garbage bags — *garbage bags* — and dumped them in my hospital room. The only memento I have of Gilles is my engagement ring, and that's only because your conscience finally kicked in. And you wonder why I still need closure?"

A sob tore from her lips and she thumbed the button to end the call.

Michael slid the phone from her grip and set it on the desk. He folded her into his arms.

Amy pressed her face into his sweater and let her agony flow. How could Luc be so cruel? He'd been the supportive one... at least when he could do it behind his wife's back.

The warmth of Michael's embrace, his solid strength supporting her, slowly worked into Amy's consciousness. The steady beat of his heart brought her back to herself. No matter what happened, this man was her one safe place.

Except he wasn't. Not the way she wanted. Not with the love her heart craved. Fresh tears slid down her cheeks. She opened her senses to store everything in this moment to remember in the lonely nights ahead.

Michael spoke into her hair. "I'll talk to him later and work this out."

Amy stayed in the circle of his arms, face buried, memorizing his heartbeat and the feel of his nearness. The faint scent of paint and cleaning fluid. The rhythm of his breathing.

The phone rang again. Michael jumped away from Amy and cleared his throat. "Stratton Gallery." He frowned. "Thanks, we've just heard from him. Troy, you're upsetting a lot of people for no reason. You need to lay off." Michael shook his head. "That's not enough, and you know it. It could be anyone — Gilles' family, someone from the flight club — anyone who's sick of this conspiracy hype."

He finished the call and put the handset down, flashing Amy a sheepish smile. "He was calling to warn us. You okay now?"

Amy rubbed her arms, missing his warmth. She must be blushing like crazy, but he'd assume she was embarrassed about crying on him. "They've hurt me in the past, but it's always been Honore."

Michael's mouth twisted down. "Luc's grieving too. But he doesn't need to overreact."

"Emilie did say he and Gilles were pretty heated about whatever sent Gilles away. I guess I shouldn't have asked about it."

"Funny Gilles didn't tell you. It must have been a family thing." Michael picked up some prints from the desk. "You can frame these, and we'll box everything up. But first, the coffee."

"We should have grabbed a box from the workshop."

Michael smacked his palm into his forehead and let out an exaggerated sigh. "Now she tells me. Come on. We'll leave the rest of it here for now." He carried his handful of prints out of the room.

They found Aunt Bay in the kitchen, pouring coffee. Michael dropped the prints on the table. "Hey, save some for me. You didn't have to use a bowl."

His aunt lifted an eyebrow and added milk to her ordinary-sized china mug.

When she set the milk down, Michael asked, "So when did Gilles tell you about the fireworks?"

She sniffed. "I knew the night it happened. If I acknowledged knowing, I'd have had to tell your parents."

"Aunt Bay, you are a treasure." He hugged her.

When he let go and reached for a mug, his aunt winked at Amy. "Don't you forget it. Why is your sweater wet?"

Amy's cheeks warmed again. Michael banged his mug onto the counter. "Luc phoned and upset Amy." He pulled out a second mug for her, and picked up the coffee pot. "Troy's causing trouble with his sabotage questions."

Aunt Bay carried her coffee to the table. "I'm not surprised."

"It doesn't mean he's wrong." Amy took the drink Michael handed her and settled beside his aunt. "The idea does keep coming up. Aunt Bay said that could mean something."

Michael leaned against the counter, holding her gaze. "Other than Troy's wacky theories, it's only coming up for you, and I think it's because you're still hurting. Like it's some kind of cry to finish healing. I'm not going to lie. I believe the investigators. But if you need to look into it more, we'll do that — in a way that doesn't send Luc into orbit. That's why I suggested the plane ride."

Amy stared into her coffee. Michael always had her back, but it would mean so much if he believed her. Should she show him the warning texts? Except then he'd bail on the flight and she'd lose her chance to talk to some of the regulars who might have been there the day Gilles did his final safety check. At least this way Michael would help,

83

even if not for the right reasons.

Michael grinned at Aunt Bay. "Would you like to join us?"

"If I wouldn't fly with Gilles, I'd hardly risk it with a stranger."

"Some people might suggest you wouldn't fly with Gilles because he wasn't a stranger. You knew his crazy streak."

"Aunt Bay?" Amy tapped her fingernails against the side of her mug. "Do you know why Gilles took his impromptu walkabout? Or anything about a conflict with his father?"

The older woman's eyes narrowed. "He came to see me before he left for Montreal that weekend, troubled enough to ask me to pray for him. He wouldn't say what about, and insisted I not say a word to Michael."

Michael shook his head. "He seemed fine to me. Until he phoned to say he'd be gone for a while."

Aunt Bay shrugged. "Whatever was bothering him, when he came back he said it was handled."

"But he didn't tell you what it was." Amy rested an elbow on the table. "I wish I knew what caused the fight with his father. And what he meant about running away from God."

Michael stared at the tabletop, lips tight. A deep breath lifted his chest. "I wish I could know he turned around before the end."

Amy nodded.

Aunt Bay went still, eyes fixed on Amy.

The sudden scrutiny made Amy squirm. "What?"

"You have no problem with the idea of Gilles' repentance being acceptable to God, even with the life he led, yet you're convinced your own baggage is insurmountable." The older woman's face softened. "Nothing is too hard for Him, Amy, and He could bring so much joy — and healing — to your heart."

Michael's face reflected a longing almost as deep as the one in his aunt's voice. Or the one in Amy's soul. "She's right. And she won't let go. Talk to either one of us — please. More than that, talk to God." He set his empty mug on the counter. "I'll go back upstairs in case you want to say anything private to Aunt Bay. If she can keep the fireworks incident to herself, no secret of yours will pass her lips."

His aunt swatted his arm as he passed. "You have a good heart. Even if your mouth needs work." She focused on Amy, but didn't speak until Michael's footsteps reached the top of the stairs. "Someone does need to help you give whatever you're carrying to God. I'll tell you this — your past might shock me, even disappoint me, but you cannot change my regard for who you are today. I won't reject you. Neither will God."

Amy's eyes welled. "It sounds so silly, and Gilles said it was nothing, but—"

The lines deepened around Aunt Bay's eyes. "What did that boy do? He didn't pressure you into an abortion, did he?"

The weight grew in Amy's chest. "You, too?"

"I'm not judging, child. I'm sympathizing."

"You're assuming. Just like everyone else." Amy thrust the hair back from her face. "First his mother accused me of trapping him into marriage by getting pregnant — because of our short engagement. After Gilles died, she demanded I let her and Luc adopt their grandchild and give up all right of contact. When time proved I wasn't pregnant, she accused me of aborting the baby out of spite."

Breathing hard, Amy stared at her clenched hands on the table. If she could hold onto the anger, she'd drown out the soul-hollowing sense of loss. "Hateful woman."

Amy dropped her face to her forearms, tightening her fists until her fingers ached. If she'd carried Gilles' child, would the baby have survived the crash? Would she now have an impish toddler to heal her heart, or would the Renauds' lawyers have snatched even that connection?

Aunt Bay's chair legs scraped nearer, and her arm slid across Amy's shoulders. "Honore is grieving too. It's a pity she can't do it without poisoning everyone in sight."

"That family has hurt me beyond belief." Could Aunt Bay even make out Amy's muffled words? "It's almost enough to make me wish I'd never met Gilles." Almost. A smile twitched Amy's lips. Gilles had loved her. Truly loved her. And his parents could never take that away.

Amy rested in the shelter of Aunt Bay's hold another minute, then looked up at the older woman. "So, no. Gilles knew what God has against me, but it's not that. Would you honestly still accept me if I'd ended an innocent life?"

Aunt Bay sat back but kept her hand on Amy's shoulder. Her gaze pinned Amy's. "Yes, I would. You are more than what you've done — good, bad, or ugly. You're God's precious creation, and He loves you. I'd be hurt, and God would have been hurt at the time, but rejecting you wouldn't make it better."

She squeezed Amy's shoulder and let go. "Forgiveness is what makes it better, and for that, you and God need to do business about whatever's keeping the two of you apart."

There had to be more to what Aunt Bay was saying, but Amy's head hurt too much to puzzle it out. This was bigger than someone like Gilles quitting the party scene and deciding to follow the rules. Forgiveness, of something as irreversible as an abortion?

Amy's breath stopped. If God would do this, then forgiving her unacceptable birth couldn't be impossible. She clutched Aunt Bay's hand. "Can you prove to me that God forgives even things that huge?"

The gallery door chime cut off Aunt Bay's reply. She huffed and pushed back from the table, disengaging her hand. "I'll go. Michael won't hear that, and you'd frighten the person away. We'll talk later." She bustled from the room.

Hope tingled in Amy's nerve endings. Aunt Bay sounded so sure. She'd been in church long enough to learn these things.

Casual fling. Mistake. Conceived in sin. Whispered judgements from her childhood shrank Amy in her seat, covered in prickly shame. Those had been the church people. The ones who knew God's requirements.

Amy moaned. How dare she think one old lady's interpretation of the Bible could negate the others?

She fled for her room before Beatrice could return.

Chapter 12

Amy pleaded a headache at lunchtime. She lay in her darkened room, under the plush throw blanket Michael had given her on her first Christmas here. If only she hadn't asked Aunt Bay for proof — proof she didn't dare believe. This was what came of longing for the impossible.

She stared at the faint square of light glowing through the curtains and listened to footsteps on the stairs. Michael, going back to his painting?

A tap came at her door. The handle turned and a crack of light appeared. "Amy?" Aunt Bay.

Amy pulled a steadying breath. "Yes?"

The door pushed wide and Michael's aunt entered, closing it behind her. She carried a tall glass on a tray. "Michael made you a smoothie. There's a sandwich here as well."

Amy hitched herself toward the headboard and propped her pillows behind her back. "Thank you."

Aunt Bay set the tray beside Amy on the bed. "Michael told me about Luc's call. Between that and thinking about how Honore treated you, it's no wonder you have a headache. Rest now, and we'll talk later. I can tell you God loves you, but you'll never be sure if you don't experience it for yourself."

Throat suddenly tight, Amy swallowed hard and shook her head. She reached for the glass.

Aunt Bay studied her for a long moment, then left the room.

The icy feel of the glass and the straw's vertical position in the red-purple mixture said Michael had used plenty of frozen fruit. Amy drew in a mouthful and held it briefly before swallowing. She set the glass back on the tray and swung her legs over the side of the bed. A little background music would help her relax better than lying here brooding. Amy flipped open her laptop and cued the mellow jazz playlist.

Might as well use this private time to ask Troy's opinion about the anonymous texter. How could they know if the messages were legitimate? Amy slid back onto the bed with the laptop and turned on her bedside lamp.

After she sent the email, she laid the machine aside and lingered over her lunch. This afternoon would be about framing those prints and answering messages. That should be enough to postpone Aunt Bay's heart-to-heart.

When the worst of the tension had faded, Amy carried the tray downstairs. Music still seeped from Michael's studio. Aunt Bay was nowhere in sight, and Amy breathed a little easier.

The prints were gone from the kitchen table, but Amy found them stacked on the counter near the workshop door. She collected them and headed for the basement.

It didn't take long to pop them into empty frames. Amy wound bubble wrap around each one and nestled them in a box big enough to hold the rest of the order. She carried it upstairs and through to the office.

The desk lay as cluttered as they'd left it, so likely this morning's visitor hadn't needed any paperwork beyond a simple receipt. If they bought anything at all. Often tourists only wanted to look around.

Amy filled the box and set it against the back wall, where it wouldn't trip anyone. Michael's gallery didn't do a lot of business, but it gave him a showroom when needed. Increasing the portion of his home used for business helped at tax time, too. She settled behind the desk and whipped through the follow-up Michael had given for his messages.

Snatches of the soothing water-themed music drifted from the gallery. Here in the quiet was a good chance to draft a reply to her father.

Instead, Amy stood and pulled the duster from on top of the filing cabinet. She drifted into the gallery, humming along to fragments of the music. A place like this needed cleaning before it looked dirty. When she finished dusting, she checked email for the gallery and for herself. Nothing. Troy may have been warned off, but would it kill him to acknowledge her message?

Who was this mysterious texter? Was he — or she — genuine? Or just trying to make Amy and Troy stop raising a cloud of suspicion? It could even be a local person who bought a cheap phone and set up a Winnipeg number.

Amy sighed and opened a new document to start a letter to her father. She had to write this now, before he phoned. What would he say if Aunt Bay or Michael answered?

They'd been so caring while she healed, but this was different. They'd know Amy could never fully belong in their world. Could she face their pity?

She glared at the blank screen. The man's story made sense, and if Amy were someone else's child she'd sympathize with him — with her mother — with his wife. People made choices, which sometimes backfired to hurt others.

He hadn't asked Amy's neighbours to whisper about her mother and her. Definitely hadn't suggested her classmates taunt her. Those words all reflected on him as well. Except he hadn't been there to hear them.

Give him a break, Amy. He didn't know you existed.

That was the problem

Amy left the desk and grabbed the broom. She swept the little office, raising dust until the grit stung her eyes. Her mother had explained her reasons in the letter she'd left for the lawyer to send when Amy came of age. And her father's reaction when she did contact him proved the original decision wise. The knowledge did nothing to soothe the child's wistful yearning that still lived in Amy's heart.

She moved into the gallery, not caring that the broom undid her earlier work, jabbing it into corners, under display fixtures.

"Hey, don't tear the place apart." Michael's voice came from behind her.

Amy squealed and dropped the broom. She picked it up and turned to face him. "I didn't hear you come in."

"I can tell." He tipped his head to the side, studying her. "Aren't you worried about bringing your headache back?"

"Stress cleaning. To keep it away." With the tip of the bristles, she herded a dust bunny toward the other sweepings.

Michael stepped nearer. "You've had a rough day, and the weekend was packed. Not what you needed after a road trip, and with our open house coming up. Why don't you take the rest of today and tomorrow off? Lie low and recover?"

And write to her father. Avoid Aunt Bay. Poke around in a few more online flying forums. Amy spread her hands, still holding the broom. "My mind's a whirlwind right now. If my body stops, the thoughts will only speed up."

"Then should I see if we can book a plane for tomorrow, or would that stir things more? We could deliver that consignment order and prowl for some more water images instead."

"If the weather's good, I'd like to fly. Maybe you're right, and it'll settle things a bit. But it needs to be a calm day, and dry. I don't want to freak out."

Michael's eyebrows twitched. "I'm sure the pilot thanks

you for that. I'll go phone. For now, do you need to do something as intensive as cleaning, or might we go over the plans for the open house?"

Amy leaned on the broom, trying to remember details. "I think everything's in place, but let's double-check. I'll finish here and pull up the files."

"I'll be back in fifteen minutes. With some strawberry tea."

Her favourite. "You are the best boss ever. And the smoothie was great."

"I sneaked in some chia seeds. That's where your energy burst came from."

Amy hefted the broom. "I'm pretty sure it was stress. But thanks." She swept the dust and fluff into a pile and moved to attack the last corner.

Behind her, Michael's footsteps faded toward the kitchen. Such a caring man, and a good friend. How could he be so sensitive to her needs and yet utterly obtuse about her — and Emilie's — feelings toward him?

How could Amy point him in the right direction, without frightening him away?

Chapter 13

Amy's pulse kicked into double-time when Michael turned the van into the flight club parking lot the next morning. The hangar buildings, the office, the runway on the far side of the fence... nothing had changed. Except her.

Her body knew that light aircraft could crash. Amy tried to work enough moisture into her mouth to swallow.

Beside her, Michael turned off the engine. "You okay?"

She nodded.

"We don't have to fly today. Want to just look around a bit? Maybe sit in the plane?"

Amy cleared her throat. "I want to do this." Her hand shook as she opened her door.

When they walked into the office, a middle-aged man in a stained blue shirt nodded at them and held up his index finger, his attention on the phone pressed to his ear. Amy glanced around the room while he finished his conversation, taking in the bright posters and overflowing message board, the faint sound of a machine shop coming from another part of the building.

The sharp tang of oil brought bile to her throat. She swallowed hard, eyes casting wildly for the bathroom. If she threw up before they even reached the plane, Michael would never let her fly.

Amy's chest burned. She gulped a cooling breath, then another. Michael's eyes seemed to read her fear.

For Gilles. She had to do this, for Gilles. Defy the physical reactions. Get into the plane. Remember a clue, anything she could use as proof.

Her smile felt wobbly. "I'll be okay once we're moving."

Brow creased, gaze searching, Michael reached for her hand. "Amy—"

The man behind the counter put down the phone. "Sorry about that. What can I do for you?"

Michael's mouth firmed. He was going to back out. Amy's eyes welled. "Please."

He stared at her for a long moment, then released a half-heard sigh. He turned to the flight club worker. "We're here to meet Rafe Bisson for a sightseeing flight. I spoke with him yesterday."

Sharp black eyes scanned them both and checked the schedule in front of him. "Stratton? Rafe's doing his aircraft pre-flight. He'll be right in. I'm Grady."

"Michael Stratton and Amy Silver."

The black eyes narrowed, looking daggers at Amy. "You've been told to mind your own business."

Michael raised his hand like a traffic cop. "My friend and I wanted a safe flight, to help her let go of the crash memories. I would think that is her business."

Matching Grady's glare, Amy gritted her teeth against the words boiling on her tongue. Her chin lifted and steel replaced the trembling in her core.

His glare intensified. Could he tell from her smile that he'd helped conquer her panic?

Behind Amy and Michael, the door banged. "Mr. Stratton?"

Michael turned, stepping between Amy and her accuser. "Rafe?"

"That's me." Rafe was on the short side, stocky, with a ruddy complexion and deep laugh lines. He strode toward them, hand out to shake. "You two ready to go?"

Michael jerked his head toward the counter. "That's up to your boss, here. He doesn't think my friend deserves another chance at flying." He gestured to Amy. "Amy Silver, survivor of the crash two years ago that killed Gilles Renaud."

Rafe's eyes widened, and he held out his hand to Amy. "I'm sorry for your loss."

Her hand felt small in his. He barely squeezed, as if Amy might still be fragile. She smiled. "Thank you. Will you take us up?"

He shook Michael's hand next. "This guy's not my boss, and I'll fly who I like. Grady, you oughta be waiving her fees, a young woman brave enough to take another flight after that last one."

Grady spat a curse. "This Silver chick is nothing but trouble."

Michael stiffened, but Amy silenced him with an elbow and a look. She took a slow, deep breath, eyes locked on the man behind the counter, watching his face darken. Her lungs held the air, and when she released it, her words flew like arrows. "Would you like some trouble? Or would you rather apologize?"

The man's Adam's apple twitched. Finally he shrugged. "I was out of line. But so is stirring up rumours and gossip. The investigators' report clearly marked that crash as an accident. We run on a shoestring budget, lady. If people start thinking our planes aren't safe, that could put us under."

Amy shook her head. "I never said your equipment was unsafe. I just want to know what happened. What if someone did sabotage that plane? Wouldn't you want to stop them doing it again?"

"The investigators—"

"Might have missed something. That's what the case in the US says."

Michael put a hand on her shoulder. "But that's not why

we're here today. This is about healing. Moving on." His eyes warned her to let it drop.

"Right. And we're wasting flight time." Amy turned to Rafe. "You've done your walk-around, but could you show me again, just so I'll feel safe?"

"Of course." He led them to the aircraft, a white Cessna single engine plane with red accent paint. "I filed a basic sightseeing flight plan. Was there something specific you wanted to see, or an area you wanted to avoid?"

Like flying over the crash site. Amy shivered. How easy was it to change a flight plan? "I didn't think about that. Let's go with what you have."

Watching Rafe's inspection felt surreal, as if he were re-enacting Gilles' final flight. Saliva flooded Amy's mouth and she choked it down. Focus on the details. Detach. Pretend it's not real. Remember any clues.

She mustered a smile for Michael. "It's okay."

Caution shadowed his eyes, but he nodded.

Rafe swung open the passenger door. "Who's my co-pilot?"

Amy glanced at Michael. "Could we both sit in the back? In case I need some moral support?"

Rafe chuckled. "I won't take it personally." He helped them climb into the craft, and shut the door.

The sharp click of the latch made Amy flinch. She tried to cover it by adjusting her seat belt while she brought her body back under control. She could do this. For Gilles.

While Rafe settled into the pilot seat and prepared for takeoff, he ran through a safety briefing. Then he spoke into the radio and waited for clearance.

Michael pulled an airsickness bag from the seat pocket ahead of him and offered it to Amy. "Gilles told me when you're nervous, just holding one of these helps. Plus, if you need it, there's no time to dig it out. Not that I think you'll need it."

Amy took it without protest. The last thing she wanted was to spew all over the inside of the plane, and she'd die if she were sick on Michael.

The engine revs increased, the roar vibrating through her body like a rising current. The little plane trundled onto the runway, bucking at every seam in the tarmac.

Heart pounding almost loud enough to deaden the sounds around her, Amy clenched her teeth and reached for Michael's hand.

Outside, the ground rushed past. Then they were airborne. The plane lost its awkward motion and lifted, as if drawn upward by a thread.

The band around Amy's lungs loosened enough to let her breathe. She pulled in as much air as she could. Fainting now, or hyperventilating, would ruin everything. She closed her eyes and concentrated on Michael's gentle touch. Her lifeline.

When Amy felt the plane level out, she opened her eyes. The bright sky made her blink. Still gripping Michael's hand, she peered out the side window at the ground below.

So far, so good.

Rafe glanced back at her. "Doing okay?"

"I'm fine." It felt like they were floating over the earth.

Rafe flashed her a thumbs-up and turned back to the controls.

Amy smiled at Michael. "I'd forgotten how much fun this is."

He squeezed her hand and let it go. "Remember this. This is what Gilles wanted to give you."

The plane followed the shoreline, high enough that the ocean waves were lines of white skimming dark blue water to the shore. Outside of the city, houses became sparse, bordering the narrow road that snaked the coast. A few cars inched along the grey strip.

Visibility was perfect, with a high cloud cover that

protected their eyes. Over the engine noise, Rafe called, "I'll take us over Peggy's Cove next. It's a whole different view from up here."

Gilles had done the same, not because he cared about Nova Scotia's most-photographed lighthouse, but to show Amy more of the province where they'd live until he convinced his father to reassign him to the Montreal dealership. He'd looked at the Halifax position as a proving ground. If his performance pleased his father, Luc might give him the assistant-manager spot in Montreal, until Luc retired and let Gilles run the show.

The thought of impulsive, unrestrained Gilles in an expensive suit, directing the high-end car sales establishment always made Amy smile. He'd done it, and his charisma brought results, but she preferred the side of him that she'd known so briefly.

She stared out the window. Below, the enormous rocks of Peggy's Cove looked like slabs of grey-brown modelling clay pushing out into the ocean. The red and white lighthouse looked like a toy.

Michael pointed past her. "The gallery's that way."

Amy craned her neck without any hope of seeing the house. Rafe turned inland and soon they flew over dark evergreen forest mixed with the lighter greens of different leaves. From this height, Amy couldn't see the occasional traitorous leaf that had already turned yellow, orange, or red. She'd seen them from the ground, though.

The plane jolted downward. Amy screamed. Cold swept her skin, iced her heart. Frosted her sight.

"Sorry about that." Rafe sounded perfectly calm. "Air pocket. We're safe."

Safe. Amy pulled a shuddering breath through clenched teeth and fought memories of the crash. See the sky. They were still airborne. Smell the cockpit scents. No burnt wires. No blood or fluids. Hear the roar of a healthy engine. The propeller whine and assorted rattles. Feel the vibration of the little craft pushing through the sky.

They were not falling.

Her mind believed it, but her body shook. Her throat felt ready to explode. Or erupt.

Michael stroked the back of her hand — when had she grabbed his leg? The fingers of her other hand clutched the armrest.

"Amy, it's okay. Just keep breathing. Nice and slow. See outside... everything's fine." He spoke in her ear, soothing, coaching. "You can do this."

Rafe looked over his shoulder. "I can't guarantee we won't drop like that again. Are you good to finish, or should I radio for clearance to head back early?"

"I want to keep going." Amy bent to retrieve the paper bag from the floor. She stared at it for a minute before pulling the water bottle from the pocket in front of her and twisting open the cap. Her throat muscles were too tight to let much pass, but a trickle of liquid went down. She took another sip.

Rafe nodded. "Good girl."

Amy glanced at Michael, her face suddenly warm. "I didn't mean to grab you."

"That's nothing. Aunt Bay once latched onto a total stranger on a commercial flight." He rubbed his thigh. "I'll have a nice set of bruises."

The heat in her face flared. "I'm sorry."

"That's why I'm here. Look down there — see the river?"

A winding strip of blue lay among the textured green forest as if someone had dropped a ribbon. Amy concentrated on the terrain beneath them and tried to regain the peace she'd felt at first. Here and there a house appeared, and ahead the trees gave way to farmland.

Slowly her heart rate dropped and the plane's vibration loosened her muscles. Before she was ready, the green changed to urban sprawl, roadways, and a few parks. Then Halifax Harbour stretched below them, with its twin bridges and port traffic.

A tiny island slid past, the plane banked, and Rafe called, "Landing in a few minutes. Everything's good."

Eyes twinkling, Michael held out his hand to Amy. "Use this instead of my leg? I need to walk to the van."

The shakes were back. Amy took his hand, wedged the paper bag between her knees so she couldn't lose it, and gripped her armrest with her other hand. Breathe. Concentrate. Planes landed all the time. They'd be fine.

The ground rushed to meet them. At the last instant, Amy shut her eyes and hid her face against Michael's shoulder. He tightened his grip on her hand.

With a dull thump, the wheels caught tarmac, and they were down. Amy lifted her face and slid her hand free of Michael's. "Thank you. I'm sorry for getting in your space."

His patient smile said it didn't matter. "Did this help?"

"I think so." Not with clues, but with closure.

Rafe taxied to a stop and went through the shut-down procedure. "That wasn't so bad, was it?"

Amy unfastened her seatbelt. "Thank you so much. I'm sorry I screamed."

"You did great. You weren't even sick." Rafe opened his door and jumped out. He extended a hand to help Michael and then Amy.

The ground felt good under her feet, if a little wobbly. A gentle breeze lifted the ends of Amy's hair and filled her nose with warmth and the smell of aviation fuel. She gave Rafe a shaky hug. "Thank you again."

His sun-weathered face creased in a smile that deepened his laugh lines, but his eyes stayed serious. "Gilles logged a lot of his practice hours with me. He was cocky on the ground, but he took the aircraft seriously. I'm sorry for your loss."

Amy nodded. "Today you gave me back a connection to him. I lost it in the crash."

His eyes held hers. "You're not the only person to question the investigators' findings. But you're not the one to be asking. Sabotage means enemies, and Gilles would want you out of danger."

"I don't even know what to ask." Amy passed her tongue over her lips. "Troy Hicks, the journalist who raised this in the paper? Would you talk to him?"

Rafe squinted at the sky as if searching for an answer. Finally he pulled out his wallet and passed Amy a card. "Have him call me, but tell him not to get his hopes up."

Michael passed Rafe a handful of bills. "Thank you."

"Thank you. Since I retired, I take any excuse I can to fly. It was a pleasure meeting you folks. Anytime you want to go up again, give me a shout." He stuffed the bills in his pocket and sauntered toward the office.

Amy turned to Michael. "You heard what he said about the investigation."

A patient look settled in Michael's eyes. "I did, but it's only speculation. Even if it could have been deliberate, that doesn't mean it was. There's still the whole motivation thing. Gilles had no enemies."

Amy remembered the warning texts. "None that we know of."

Chapter 14

Amy glanced behind as Michael steered the van out of the flight club lot. Was Grady glaring at them through the office window?

If Michael wanted to fly again, he'd better call the pilot directly. His name would be beside hers now on the club's blacklist. "Thank you for today. It was healing, and it was a lovely break from regular life."

"Do you have to give Rafe's contact information to Troy? If there's nothing to find, all he's doing is upsetting Luc and causing trouble for the flight club. You heard the man in there."

Amy sniffed. "Warning Troy off implies there's something to hide. I just wish I knew what it was." She turned in her seat. "You were going to settle things with Luc. Did he say anything helpful?"

Michael switched lanes to pass a city bus pulling out from a stop. "I gather there's a lot of stress with the company right now, and bringing up Gilles was the last straw. You really need to go easy on him."

"Me go easy on him? Didn't you hear him on the phone?"

"Amy, we're all grieving for Gilles. But Luc's... broken." Michael's hand flexed on the steering wheel. "No parent should have to bury a child. This is not the same man I knew, and I think he's getting worse."

"So he should take it out on me?"

"Of course not. But you shouldn't take it out on him, either."

"I don't—"

"You do." His lips turned down. "Luc and Honore treated you badly, no question. But sometimes I think you rehearse the hurt and allow it to keep hurting. Part of becoming whole again involves letting go of the memories and of our right to be angry."

Amy stared at her clasped hands. "As in, forgive them." And forgive her father.

"It doesn't mean they were right. It frees you from the power of the past." Michael stopped at a traffic light and turned to Amy. "Gilles would be furious with them over this. But he wouldn't want you to let it make you bitter."

"I'm not bitter... am I? Okay, don't answer that."

The van moved forward, and Amy watched older homes and the occasional storefront pass. The engine revved as they turned onto a crosstown connector highway. So she was bitter. There'd been some major lemons in her life. Hadn't there been good things too? Enough to sweeten the proverbial lemonade?

Amy's mother, embittered in her own way, had not only kept her unplanned child but had loved her fiercely until the end. And provided for her after that. Gilles had poured more light and happiness — and love — into Amy's life in their few months together than she could have imagined. Since then, Michael and Aunt Bay had been kindness personified.

Michael... she peeked at his profile. Life with Gilles had been tempestuous and exciting. At times it seemed like their relationship would flare out and die. She hadn't admitted it to herself then, but she could now. But this man beside her? Amy had no trouble seeing herself with him into their senior years. Her heart twisted. If he ever noticed her.

He caught her staring. "Luc said their argument was personal. No clues there."

103

"It does sound crazy, doesn't it? Except someone wants Troy to stop." Amy leaned against the headrest, remembering today's flight and the one two years ago. Gilles hadn't been nervous or expecting trouble. But how could he have enemies willing to kill, and not know it?

She spoke with her eyes closed. "I'm sorry about my attitude. I have so much to be thankful for."

"Jesus can help with that, when you're ready. Trust me, it's easier than going solo."

Amy tensed. *Nobody knows who the father is. Sinful. Mistake.* The church ladies' pseudo-sympathetic whispers from her childhood had twined deep roots in her psyche. Michael and Aunt Bay would agree, if they knew.

"Amy, whatever it is, He's big enough to deal with it. And He loves you enough to want to. Just talk to someone. It doesn't have to be me or Aunt Bay. Let me introduce you to our pastor, or to one of the women from church."

"I'm sorry, Michael. I've already been diagnosed and found wanting." The words hurt her throat. Amy stared through the windshield. They were on the highway now, nearly home.

A gentle hand touched hers, then let go. "That's the point — we're all wanting. And the only One entitled to throw stones would rather show mercy. He's our only hope."

"Despite what Safia and Ross believe?"

His sigh sounded sad. "I'm afraid so."

"I can't meet the entry requirements."

"Come dirty. He'll clean you." Michael's words didn't sound glib. Just impossible.

Ahead on the pavement, a big crow pecked at a bit of roadkill. It flapped away when the van approached. Amy's lips twisted. "No matter how stained. Or how big the barricade."

"No matter."

Her peripheral vision caught his nod. "You know this for

sure."

"I do."

"So what's the biggest thing He's had to do for you?"

Michael's mouth snapped shut. His Adam's apple bobbed and he kept his eyes firmly on the road. The engine revs increased. "I can't tell you."

Amy's face heated. "I'm sorry. It's none of my business. It's just — I need proof, and you seem so clean. I didn't realize I was asking too much."

Almost five minutes passed before Michael spoke. "Of course you need proof. And I am clean — God cleans me daily. More often, most days." His laugh seemed forced. "What first kept me from Him wasn't very exciting. Poor self-image and an inflated trust in my own abilities. I didn't think God would want me, and I was sure I didn't need Him running my life." He signalled and slowed for the exit ramp. "I was wrong on both counts."

"That doesn't sound very sinful."

Michael stopped at the top of the ramp, signal light clicking, waiting to turn left onto the overpass. "Maybe not, but it was enough. The point is, no matter how big or how small the obstacles, how dirty or damaged the person, we all need Jesus and we can't earn His acceptance on our own. But He reaches out to us."

Not to Amy.

On the two-lane road, Michael slowed behind a lumbering dump truck. "I hope this guy's turning off soon, or it'll be a long drive home."

Safer conversational ground. Amy allowed herself to relax. "It always feels long, especially coming off the highway. No wonder Aunt Bay misses her condo in the city."

"She likes being in the thick of things. We're near enough for me, and it's nice to have fresh air and less noise."

"I agree." A sudden pang hit Amy. "When she moved

back in with you, it was supposed to be a short-term thing. I'm way past well enough to move out. Then Aunt Bay could have her life back."

"We don't want you to go." Michael's words came fast. Hard.

Amy blinked at him.

Colour swept his face. "We don't. But I have no idea where that tone came from. I'm sorry."

"Okay... but would Aunt Bay tell either of us if she needed a change? I could get a room nearby and keep working in the gallery." How long could she do that, when half her pay was in room and board? But how long could Amy impose where she was?

"Aunt Bay says she's fine. She's on the go a lot anyway, and she likes driving."

The dump truck finally turned onto a side road, and Michael sped up. They drove in silence until he pulled into the local bakery. Let's pick up some sandwiches to take home."

Amy's frugal nature couldn't fight the thought of thick, fresh bread. She and Michael crossed the parking lot while he phoned to ask for his aunt's order.

From the bakery, it was a short drive home. They carried the food into the kitchen just as Aunt Bay poured boiling water into the teapot. She turned to greet them. "Perfect timing."

Over lunch, Amy and Michael shared their morning. Minus the hostile man in the flight club office. Michael lamented his "injured" leg with enough drama to equal anything Emilie could offer.

Aunt Bay skewered him with a look. "You're mocking us both, young man, and it ill becomes you." She turned to Amy. "I'm sure he told you my story."

"He did." Amy picked up her mug. "We need something on him. Tell me about the fireworks."

Michael choked on his drink. When he caught his breath, he said, "How did you know, Aunt Bay? And why didn't you send someone to help us?"

His aunt swallowed a mouthful of sandwich. "Anyone with half an eye could see you were planning something. Old Karl Jolivet, God rest his soul, had his life jacket on, all ready to launch his boat, when the two of you surfaced. He kept watch in case you ran into more trouble, and I beat it home to feign ignorance." She winked at Amy.

Michael let out a low whistle. "Mr. Jolivet. Did the whole shoreline know?"

"Just the two of us. I—" The ringing phone cut her off. She crossed the kitchen and picked up the handset. "Stratton Gallery." She stiffened and glanced at Amy. "One moment." Aunt Bay covered the mouthpiece and held it away from her face. "Amy, a Neal Williamson."

Amy's head was shaking, fast. She raised her palms to push him away, but he wasn't in the room.

Aunt Bay's lips thinned. She raised the handset. "Miss Silver's not free at the moment. Is there a message?" She listened, thanked him, and set the phone back on its base.

Concern shone in the older woman's eyes. "He'll be in Halifax next week on business, and he'll phone then. You don't have to see him if you're not ready."

Amy released a breath she hadn't known she held. Giving Aunt Bay the chance to interrogate her father was a horrible idea, but her own self-preservation came first. Apparently the man didn't want to share their story any more than Amy did.

Michael leaned forward on the table. "Amy, who is this guy?"

Amy stared at the crumbs on her sandwich plate. Cue the ominous music. "He's my father. He wrote last week. I guess he wants to meet me — somewhere." *Not he wants to meet me. Wants to meet me somewhere.* Her eyes flicked to

Michael, then Aunt Bay. Back to the plate's safety. "Aunt Bay knows... after the accident, I asked for help and he refused. Now he's had some kind of change of heart and wants to reconcile." Amy raised her gaze to Aunt Bay. "I don't know what to do."

Michael's aunt nodded. "He'll have no access unless you say so. Think about it, though. There may come a day when you'll wish you'd spoken with him."

A day? She'd had years of wishing to meet her father, to spend time with him. When the lawyer forwarded her mother's letter on Amy's twenty-first birthday, even though the message requested no contact except in an emergency, the paper had been special because it bore her father's name. Amy had slept with it under her pillow for a week. She'd learned everything she could find online. Even though the man didn't know she existed, he filled a gaping hole in her identity. Until his words of rejection shattered her dreams of a "someday" reunion.

What changed his mind? And did she want to throw her heart under the bus again to find out?

~~~

Tuesday evenings Michael attended his men's group at church. From what Amy understood, it involved Bible study, prayer, and snack food. He said it was his safe place. Amy was loading the last of the supper dishes into the dishwasher when Michael stepped into the kitchen.

"If you want to give me the pilot's card, I'll pass it on to Troy."

"Thanks. I'll get it." She closed the dishwasher and went to fetch the card from her purse. When she came back downstairs, Michael stood by the front door, zipping his coat. Amy handed him the card. "Thanks. Especially since you don't want him to have this."

He tipped an imaginary hat brim. "At your service, ma'am. Should I ask him to sign for it?"

"I'll trust you. This once." She lowered her voice, although Aunt Bay wouldn't hear her over the television. "Does your group know about — what I shouldn't have asked?"

Michael's smile fled. "Troy does. And a few others. We pray for one another when we're struggling." He held out a hand as if to touch her, but let it fall to his side. "Amy, please don't imagine some deep, dark secret. I'm not going to snap in the night and kill us all. You won't find bodies if you dig in the basement. Or porn if you search my computer. This is a personal... situation." He shrugged. "Someday it'll resolve. One way or the other."

The weariness in his voice wrung Amy's heart. "God should listen to you. You're a good person."

"It's not about how good we are. It's how good He is, and how needy we are. But yeah, that qualifies me. For now, He's teaching me to wait and trust Him. It's one of those universal lessons." Michael lifted his Bible in salute. "See you in the morning." The door closed behind him.

Amy stared at it for a minute. Most Tuesdays, she and Aunt Bay watched a travel show or something on Discovery Channel. Hopefully that'd keep the older woman from bringing up God... or Darth Father. Amy sighed. That wasn't fair. Okay, the man had shot her down in flames, but he must have a good side or Amy's mother wouldn't have fallen for him. His letter of apology seemed sincere.

So where did that leave her now? Brush him off? Meet him, exchange awkward conversation, and say goodbye? Try to build a bridge long-distance? Amy sighed. She should at least find out if there was any medical history she needed to know.

She wandered into the living room and plopped into a chair. Lush greens glowed on the television, and the chatter of exotic birds filled the air.

Aunt Bay looked up. "Brazilian rainforest again. But it's pretty."

Amy unzipped the tote bag beside the chair and pulled out her knitting. She'd been working on a sweater for Michael for Christmas — for last Christmas, actually. Tuesdays were the only nights she made progress. Knitting alone in her room did not appeal. She held up the first three inches of the final sleeve. "The end is in sight."

"If you'd chosen thicker yarn, you'd be long done. But he'll get more use out of the lighter weight."

"As long as it doesn't become his new painting sweater."

"Agreed." A half-completed sock dangled from Aunt Bay's set of double-pointed needles, which kept a rapid pace with only occasional glances from their owner. Aunt Bay churned out sturdy socks year-round for a homeless shelter in the city, grey to camouflage any dirt, but always with cheery bright stripes on the cuffs. This one sported emerald green.

Michael's great-aunt had never married. She claimed a husband would only slow her down. Until retirement, she'd taught high school and spent the summers abroad, often on a mission tour.

"Aunt Bay, why don't you travel anymore?"

"Hmm? I suppose it's been a while."

A particularly piercing bird call came from the television. Amy flinched and nearly dropped a stitch. "Is it me? You're staying to be a chaperone for Michael and me?"

Aunt Bay's knitting slowed. "I moved back into the house because you needed care, and yes, for appearance's sake, but I don't feel shackled or denied the chance to go."

"Have your travelling friends given it up?"

"Mercy, no. I was just looking at the photos one of them posted on Facebook from her trip to Iceland."

Did Amy detect a hint of wistfulness? "I told Michael I

should move out. Let you have your life back."

Aunt Bay snorted. "I'm sure that went over well."

"But I'm cramping your style."

"Child, if I wanted to go, I'd go. I might, in the spring. A few of my friends are planning a cruise. It wouldn't be hard to find someone else to stay here in my absence — as long as it wasn't Emilie. I wouldn't put either of you through that."

Amy finished the last few stitches in her row of knitting and turned the needle. "Michael didn't know she has a crush on him."

"Why did he think she acts like she does? He can be so dense about women."

Amy's sigh earned her a probing look. She pretended to study her knitting pattern.

Aunt Bay didn't question her. "Emilie's wasting her time. She's too much like her mother, and Michael saw the manipulations Gilles had to dodge."

With a final squawk, the nature program rolled into its closing theme. Amy's phone buzzed in her pocket, and she jumped. She'd started carrying it around in case the mystery-texter tried to reach her. She pulled it out. "Hello?"

"Amy? It's Ross, just checking in. No bad dreams or ill effects from our visit to the crash site on Sunday?"

"No. Thanks for asking. And for driving."

"Michael wasn't upset about you going out with me?"

Amy pushed down the remembered guilt. "I do get time off."

Ross' chuckle was rich, deep. "I'm sure of that. No, I've been talking with Gilles' sister and she has some... concerns that your freedom might be somewhat restricted. I'm glad that's not so."

"It's not so at all. Emilie makes things up."

Aunt Bay's needles stilled and she turned to Amy.

Amy mouthed *Ross Zarin* and kept talking. "It's her creative streak."

111

"She's also afraid you're becoming fixated on Gilles' death and looking for sinister intent in your accident. I was able to reassure her that Sunday helped with closure — and that you seemed perfectly sane to me."

"Thanks for the vote of confidence." The anonymous texts had warned Amy to ask no questions. How many other people had Emilie spouted off to? The room suddenly felt chilly.

Chapter 15

Amy spent Wednesday morning in the basement workshop preparing frames. She'd declined Michael's invitation to go with him to deliver consignment prints to the Mahone Bay store. It wasn't a long drive, but they'd taken a half-day yesterday for the flight, and before that, the road trip to the Ontario exhibit.

The gallery open house was this Saturday. After that, they had maybe a month before the Christmas craft fairs took off. Even though they worked year-round to prepare enough inventory, Amy would like to have more framed prints on hand. Especially with the increased consignment sales this year.

Michael's art had received some excellent press and his reputation was growing. Despite his concern that she not overwork herself, the more Amy did on this end, the more time he could put into his originals.

If anyone came to the showroom door, the chime would sound through the baby monitor they kept on one of the workshop shelves. Drop-ins were increasingly rare this late in the season. Another few weeks, once the leaves changed, the tourists would all be heading to Cape Breton instead of past the gallery door to Peggy's Cove. Rocks and stunted evergreens couldn't compete with the vibrant colours along the Cabot Trail.

Frames of different sizes spread across the newspaper-lined worktable, propped on little cubes of scrap wood so Amy could finish to the very edges without them drying to the paper. This batch had a clear finish to emphasize the wood grain. Michael used these the most, but she'd do others in various light stains and paint finishes as well. Her favourites were the frames built from weathered wood and painted to accent the distressed look.

Amy set down her brush and stretched the kink from between her shoulder blades. Brush in hand once more, she stroked a thin layer of finish onto the wood. From upstairs, she heard voices and footsteps. Michael must be back.

Her phone buzzed a text alert. She pulled it from her pocket. *Yesterday's flight was a bad idea. Don't do anything else to attract attention.*

A quick swipe finished that edge of the frame. Amy set the brush down and keyed a reply. *I met someone else who thinks it wasn't an accident.*

Buzz. *Stay out of this. Please. I'm trying to keep you alive.*

The workshop door opened and Michael started down the stairs.

I'm not IN anything. Your warnings are the only proof I have of sabotage. Amy slid the phone back into her pocket and picked up the brush. "How'd it go?"

"Mission accomplished." He surveyed the frames. "Those look good. Are you about ready for a break?"

"Just these last two and I'll go upstairs while everything dries."

"Who's the pain today? Emilie or Luc?"

"Hmm?"

"That was a pretty fierce scowl you tried to send with your text."

Amy kept painting. "It's nothing."

"Only if you've turned cranky in your old age." Michael stepped nearer. "Want me to talk to one or both of them?"

"I can stand up for myself."

114

"I know. But I don't like them harassing my best framing staff."

She lifted an eyebrow. "Your concern is commendable."

"Boss of the year, that's me. Seriously, Amy, which one is it this time?"

"Neither." Amy dipped her brush and tapped off the excess against the lip of the can. "It's okay. Really."

Michael frowned. "If it's your father, he has no business pressuring you to see him."

Amy stopped. She tipped her head and looked at him. "He's right to make contact. I need to at least hear what he has to say. But this wasn't him, and I don't want to talk about it. Please?"

He raised his hands. "I'm sorry to pry. I've tried to create a safe place for you to thrive, but lately there's more irritation than peace."

"I'm not a plant in a garden, Michael. Don't overprotect me." Amy stuffed the frustration down. Fighting would hurt his feelings. "Look, I admit I didn't handle Luc very well the other day when he called, but even that was good for me. Letting out more of the hurt, confronting him about how they treated me — it needed to happen. I'm stronger now."

A little smile played at the corner of Michael's lips. He nodded. "You've definitely come a long way since the crash. I'm glad." He turned to the stairs. "See you in a few minutes. I'll put the kettle on."

Amy finished her work and took time cleaning her brush. She pulled her hair free of its ponytail and slipped the elastic onto her wrist. Michael had looked almost proud of her progress. Did that mean he might release her from his mental rehab and see her as whole? Attractive? Open to be loved?

Yeah, right. Amy blew out a sigh. She buried those thoughts and went upstairs.

In the kitchen, Michael and Aunt Bay had set out mugs. A

115

basket of thick-sliced brown bread rested on the table beside a small jar of homemade blueberry jam. Amy's stomach growled. She'd been smelling that bread all morning. "Aunt Bay, you spoil us."

Aunt Bay nodded. "Help yourself. Do you want tea or coffee?"

Amy thought for a minute. "I feel like Darjeeling."

Sun streamed in the window. Michael poured himself a cup of coffee. "Let's have our break on the deck. We won't be able to do this in another month."

Packet of tea leaves in hand, Amy said, "You may earn that boss of the year award yet."

Aunt Bay pulled a tray from the cupboard and loaded it with the bread and jam and her own coffee.

Amy's cell phone rang. Her free hand pulled it from her pocket. "Hello?"

A scratchy hiss grated her ear. "Amy Sssilver." The voice was unrecognizable. Inhuman. "Go back where you came from. You are not sssafe here. Leave. Now." *Click.*

Amy stared at the phone.

Aunt Bay's tray clattered to the counter beside Amy. The older woman touched her arm. "What's wrong?"

Michael let the back door slam. He reached Amy in an instant and slid the phone from her unresisting hand. "Hello? Hello? They've gone." He thumbed buttons. "Unknown name and number. Typical."

Amy blinked at the mess of tea leaves strewn across the counter. She didn't remember dropping the package. "I — that was weird."

On the stove, the kettle reached a boil. Aunt Bay scooped some of the tea leaves into the drawstring bag Amy had laid out, and popped it into the smaller teapot. While she poured the water, Michael led Amy outside to a wooden deck chair in the sun.

"Close your eyes for a minute and breathe. When Aunt

Bay comes out, you can tell us what happened."

Amy nodded, clutching the arms of the chair. Warmth caressed her palms, and the sun painted the inside of her eyelids red. She breathed the fresh air of fall, rich and tree-scented, with a hint of the cold winds to come.

The door banged. Aunt Bay's quick footsteps rapped across the boards of the deck. "Do you want a glass of water while your tea's steeping?"

Amy opened her eyes. "No, thank you." She shivered. Looking from one concerned face to the other, she said, "Someone threatened me. I think."

Michael's brows pulled down. "You think?"

"Well, it could have been a warning. Like the texts. I—" *Didn't mean to mention the texts.* Amy braced for her listeners to pounce.

Aunt Bay set the tray on the round wooden table, and she and Michael drew chairs closer to Amy. "Take pity on an old woman and start at the beginning." Her blue eyes shone clear and alert.

Amy's gaze bounced between her two interrogators. She drew a deep breath. "The caller told me to leave. By name. Said I wasn't safe here." Memories of the voice raised the hairs on her scalp. "The voice was the worst. Hissy, slithery."

A giggle burst from her mouth, but she felt closer to tears than laughter. "The crazier plane crash theories blamed 'the reptilian elite' — some kind of aliens that are apparently running the earth in secret." Amy's fingers tightened on the chair arms. "That's what it sounded like, a reptile. I couldn't tell if it was male or female."

Michael scraped his chair across the wood until he could take Amy's hand. His eyes held hers. "Voice distortion. Something mechanical, or an app, or computer program. Whoever this is, he — or she — is human."

"I know that!" Amy's lips quivered. "I'm sorry, Michael."

117

He waited, never dropping the eye contact. Concern furrowed his brow, but his eyes weren't tight with any offence.

Amy concentrated on slow, deliberate breaths to settle herself. "I didn't mean I thought it really was a reptile. That's just the sound. It creeped me out. And the words. I've never had a call like that before."

Aunt Bay huffed. "I should hope not."

Michael squeezed her hand. "Did the caller say why you're not safe?"

Amy shook her head. "Just to leave now. It has to be about the plane crash. You were right, I shouldn't have asked questions, but doesn't this prove there's something behind it?"

His lips quirked, as if he were trying to form the right words. A wariness in his eyes suggested he feared the wrong ones would trigger a backlash. "What about the texts?"

Heat crept up Amy's neck. "I didn't tell you, because I didn't want you to worry."

"Please, tell us now. I don't want to invoke boss privilege and demand to see all texts exchanged on company time." His eyebrows mashed together and his lips pushed out in an exaggerated mock-stern expression.

Amy flashed a smile she almost felt. "That's only half the story, anyway." She pulled her phone from her pocket and brought up the message history. "Troy and I both got warnings from the same number, with a Winnipeg area code. They've never tried to frighten me, just keep saying not to get involved because it's dangerous. The sender claims to be a friend of Gilles who wants to help. I don't know what to think." She handed the phone to Michael.

He read rapidly, then seemed to start over and process with more care. Then he stood and took the phone to Aunt Bay. Once she returned it, he dropped back into his seat and dug out his own phone. "I'm going to call the police."

"Proper thing." Aunt Bay poured Amy's tea and carried it to her along with a lavishly-spread slice of bread on a napkin. "Eat. Get your strength back."

"Thank you." Amy concentrated on the wind in the pine trees and tried to ignore Michael's low conversation.

When he ended the call, he said, "They'll send someone later for a statement. It could be a while, where there's no immediate sign of danger."

Amy swallowed her last bite of bread. "Time to get back to work."

Aunt Bay frowned. "Surely you can take time to recover."

"I need to get that voice out of my head."

Chapter 16

It was late afternoon when the sound of a vehicle in the gallery's horseshoe drive reached Amy in the office. She saved her work on the computer and pushed back from the desk. Time to stretch anyway, whether this was a customer or the police. Through the showroom window she saw a police cruiser. Would the officer come to the gallery entrance or the home door?

A stocky woman in uniform stepped out of the car and strode up the walkway to the gallery.

Amy met her at the door, which Michael had insisted she keep locked today. "Come in. I'm the one who received the call — Amy Silver."

"Constable Marsh." She gave Amy's hand a brisk shake. "Is Mr. Stratton available, too?"

"This way, please. Thank you for coming, Constable." Amy led her through the hallway to the main house. "Michael?"

"Be right there." The music from his studio cut out, and his footsteps crossed the upper hallway. He hurried down the stairs.

Amy still couldn't believe Michael had allowed her to be alone in the gallery after the call.

His aunt joined them from the living room, and Amy understood. Aunt Bay had been keeping an ear out for trouble from here. Amy pressed her lips together. It was hard to be cross with people who wanted to protect her. Especially when some unknown person had other plans.

Michael led them into the kitchen to sit around the table.

After brief introductions, Constable Marsh met each one's eyes and then settled on Amy. Once she'd heard Amy's account and read the texts, she asked, "Do you have any enemies, Ms. Silver? Any dissatisfied customers here at the gallery? Angry ex-boyfriends?"

"Not personally, not that we know of, and no. Except someone doesn't want me stirring up interest in the plane crash that killed my fiancé."

Constable Marsh looked at her notes. "I gathered that from your text conversation. Yet the crash investigators ruled it to be an accident." Her eyes flicked to meet Amy's. "I did my homework at the station."

"Then you know it's possible to sabotage a small plane without being detected."

"I know that's what they claim on the Internet."

"My reporter friend has confirmed it with people in the industry. Pilots and mechanics." Amy sat taller in her chair. "If our crash was an accident, why am I getting warnings — and threats?"

A patient, closed look spread across the officer's face. "It could be any number of things. Friends or family of the deceased who dislike the implication that he had enemies."

"The deceased had a name — Gilles Renaud. And a life, until someone took it."

Marsh didn't even blink. "Someone at the flight club who thinks it's bad for business. Or someone with something against you personally, who sees this as an opportunity."

Amy pressed her palms against the tabletop. "I've told my story, you've seen the texts. Do I need to sign anything?"

Constable Marsh shook her head. "I have all I need. Ms. Silver, this doesn't give us much to go on, but we'll be in touch. Be extra vigilant, and if you receive any further threatening communications, let us know at once." She picked up her hat from the table and stood. "Thank you for your time. I'll see myself out."

Michael followed, but Amy stayed in her seat until their voices faded. "Excuse me, Aunt Bay. I need some air."

She shoved her feet into a pair of muddy shoes she'd left by the back door, and clomped across the deck and down onto the grass. She didn't stop until she reached the rocky stretch by the water.

Here under the trees the air was chilly, but anger could keep her warm for a while. A few of the rocks were big enough for seats. Amy perched on one, elbows on her knees, and stared at the ripples on the bay.

Wind. Tidal forces. Invisible to the eye, but their effects proved their presence. Why wouldn't the authorities accept that the backlash to the idea of sabotage proved the possibility? Amy burned to phone Troy and insist he write an exposé about their wilful blindness.

She glared at a seagull bobbing on the water. Nobody'd print something like that. Except perhaps the local tabloid, and Troy likely didn't want his byline showing up there. Would an online article get enough attention? From normal people, not the lizard-fearers?

Amy scuffed the toe of her shoe in the dirt. It wouldn't matter anyway. Troy believed the warning texts. He wouldn't do anything to put her at risk. He'd still investigate, as long as there were leads to chase. Had he talked to the pilot?

Gilles' unnamed friend wanted to help from a distance. It wasn't like everyone had abandoned Gilles. Amy sighed. Not everyone. Just those in authority. Plus his family and most friends.

"Good thing she's not a doctor." Aunt Bay's voice behind Amy nearly startled her off the rock.

Amy twisted her head to look at Michael's aunt. How

long had she been standing there?

Aunt Bay stepped forward and carefully lowered herself onto another of the big rocks. "Constable Marsh. Terrible bedside manner. But she may be very good at her job."

"Is antagonizing the victim a requisite skill?"

Aunt Bay's lips twitched. "I'm sure it comes in handy at times. If the victim has something to hide, which in this case you do not." She looked out over the water. "Did you notice she didn't actually say there was no sabotage?"

"Yes, she did."

"No. She quoted others, and offered alternate suggestions."

"Well, she implied it." Amy's hair had fallen forward over her shoulders. She gathered it in a brisk motion and flung it behind her back. "Sometimes I think it's me. I'm small and nondescript. People treat me like a child."

"Not those who know you."

"You call me a child!" Amy studied the bare ground between her shoes.

"I call most people 'child' if they're younger than me. Especially if I want to rattle their chains. But I hope I treat you as the responsible adult you are." Aunt Bay reached out and took Amy's hand. "You, Amy Silver, are very precious to me. I'm proud of how you've rebuilt your life and how you're standing up to this challenge. And how you push Michael beyond the boundaries he likes to set."

Amy's head came up. "I feel like he's closing us all in. Like overprotecting me has become a habit, and as a guardian he only dares go out when you're home. Between that, work, and a bit of church stuff, he doesn't have a life. No guy events, not one date that I can remember since I moved in." Okay, that was a good thing. Seeing Michael in love with someone else would kill her. But still… "Don't you worry about him?"

The older woman's lips twisted. "Somewhat, but I expect

it will work out in time. He does see you, Amy. But Gilles casts a long shadow."

"I—" Amy looked away. One more thing she didn't want to talk about with this too-perceptive woman. "You were very quiet with the constable, Aunt Bay. You didn't even challenge her to pronounce your name."

A quiet chuckle said Amy's diversion was temporary at best. "I suspected the officer might be lacking the necessary sense of fun. Besides, it's always good to try new things. Quiet elderly people — and those of petite stature — are often overlooked, which provides the chance to observe and learn things that speakers wouldn't ordinarily reveal. In this case, I picked up on Marsh's noncommittal handling of the sabotage question."

"So what does it mean?" A squirrel raced across the ground in front of Amy and shot up a nearby tree.

Aunt Bay shrugged. "She knows more than she's telling."

"And that helps us how?" The squirrel chattered a tirade at whatever had frightened it. Amy smiled. "I guess I was a bit like that with the officer. I cannot stand being talked down to."

"I'm not sure she meant to have that effect. Although she may have. That one's more calculating than she appears."

"Well, I hope she uses her smarts to find the truth, instead of swallowing the politically-correct group-think."

Scattered pine needles drifted to the ground. Amy looked up to see the squirrel dash outward along a branch and jump to the outstretched branch of the next tree. A few more needles rained down in its wake. It stopped, scolded again, and took off.

Aunt Bay stood. "This rock makes a hard seat."

Pain had been growing in Amy's hip. Movement would hurt, but staying longer would only make it worse. She braced a hand on her own rock and pushed to her feet. "Remind me next time I storm out for air to take my cane."

The older woman held out a hand. "Lean on me."

Amy took her arm. "You like having me around because I make you look younger. Don't deny it."

"It's a fringe benefit." Aunt Bay matched Amy's slow pace across the grass. "People talk down to senior citizens too, as if grey hair and wrinkles are a sign of regression. I could let them define me, or get angry about it, or I can be myself and not worry about their short-sightedness."

"Come on, I've seen you put people in their place." Like poor Troy, on his first visit.

"I can be forthright, yes, but it's a deliberate choice. I don't let people goad me into it." She chuckled. "It's more effective that way. The trick is to not allow them to make you angry. You'll turn into someone you won't like."

Amy stepped on a fallen pine cone, and it crackled underfoot. "I feel like that's happening already."

"You have a lot on your mind, with this sabotage possibility, and your father, And Michael says Luc's been giving you grief." Aunt Bay stopped before stepping onto the stairs to the deck. "When God is stirring our hearts, things get messy at first. I know you're not ready to talk about it, but trust me. The longer He stirs, the more 'stuff' floats to the top. And He can't help you clean it up until you ask Him to."

Mistake. Should never have been born. God made the rules. This was beyond cleaning up.

~~~

Michael had the microwave running when they entered the kitchen, and the scent of warm spices set Amy's mouth watering. The oven light was on. Were those biscuits she saw through the glass?

He turned from the sink. "Everything will be ready in about five more minutes, or it can wait if that's too soon.

125

Aunt Bay, I wasn't sure what time you wanted to leave tonight."

His aunt glanced at the wall clock. "There's plenty of time. I'll go wash up. Are you hungry, Amy?"

Amy drew in a deep breath. "I am now. Is that the rest of the stew I smell?"

Michael grinned. "It's best after it's mellowed for a day or two."

Aunt Bay left the room. Amy heard the bathroom door close. She stepped nearer to Michael. "I'm sorry if I embarrassed you this afternoon. Maybe I'm not as ready to take on the world as I think."

His lips twitched. "Or too ready." He rested his hands on her shoulders and stared into her eyes as if looking for wounds. "I wish you wouldn't push yourself so hard, but I know sometimes it's easier to work than to stop and think."

Amy nodded, soaking up the warmth of his touch. "That phone call was scary."

"Hence the comfort food." Michael's smile told her all was forgiven.

It took all Amy's self-control not to launch herself into his arms. A hug would do her so much good right now, even a bittersweet, brotherly embrace. But she'd cried on him once already this week. She would not turn into a drama queen like Emilie.

Instead, she left the room to wash her hands.

When she returned, Aunt Bay had the table set and was filling water glasses. "How's your hip?"

Amy grimaced. "Better than it should be after sitting on that cold rock. How are you?"

"Fine. I'm the spry one, remember?"

"Well, thank you for coming after me."

Michael carried a plate of steaming, golden biscuits to the table. "Amy, would you get the butter, please? I'll bring the bowls."

After they were seated and Aunt Bay said grace, Amy asked, "Where are you off to tonight?" The older woman didn't often go out in the evenings.

"There's a special speaker at church, talking about forgiveness." Aunt Bay split a biscuit and extended her knife for some butter. "I wish you could go. It might give you some perspective with your father. Even on God's desire to overcome whatever's keeping you from Himself. But you've had enough excitement today."

A talk on forgiveness would count as excitement?

Michael's brows drew together. "Bad idea, Aunt Bay."

Aunt Bay locked his gaze. Her features sharpened. "Are you vetoing me?"

"I want what's best for Amy."

"So do I. That's why I'm disappointed she's not going this evening."

Amy glanced from one to the other and tried to keep herself calm. *Don't turn into someone you don't like.* "Do I have a say in this?"

Michael sighed. "You don't want to go. Trust me."

"How do you know?"

Something like worry flickered in his eyes. "The speaker is the last woman abducted by Harry Silver. The only survivor. She convinced him to turn himself in."

Aunt Bay touched Amy's hand. "I wanted you to hear the forgiveness part. But her ordeal must have been terrifying. You don't need to be thinking about that this evening."

Amy stared at the older woman. "Harry Silver is my cousin."

The faintest pink suffused Beatrice's face. "I didn't know."

"Remember I told you we met my cousin Carol at the Toronto show? He's her brother. I thought Michael would have told you."

He shrugged. "It was yours to tell. And it wasn't relevant

127

until this came up."

Aunt Bay stared into her stew for a long moment before looking at Amy with pain-filled eyes. "Is that what holds you back from God? You said it was outside your control. Something your cousin did to you?"

Amy shook her head. "I only knew him by reputation — first as a racing star, then as a monster."

The older woman's expression cleared. "That's close enough for any of us. One of his victims was our speaker's niece. I want to hear how she could forgive that, and then forgive God for allowing her to be abducted, herself."

"Aunt Bay!" Amy's hand flew to her mouth. How could a believing person speak that way?

Michael's aunt nodded, as if she heard Amy's thoughts. "We should never blame God for what happens. But when you know He could have prevented something, it can be a struggle to accept that He didn't."

Amy twirled the spoon in her stew. "She forgave Harry for what he did to her niece. Why?"

Aunt Bay huffed. "It's hard to imagine, isn't it?"

"But why?"

"I don't know the full story. That's why I'm going tonight. God does tell us to forgive others. It doesn't mean they're not guilty, but it frees us to be whole. That's why I hoped you'd come with me. But not today."

"I want to go." The words left Amy's mouth before she knew they'd formed. She blinked. Thought about it. Turned to Michael. "I do. Not to defy you or to prove my independence. It's — I don't know." Amy pressed her palm to her chest, fingers wide. "Something inside says to go. Maybe because Aunt Bay's been pestering me about my father."

The older woman slid the plate of biscuits closer to Amy. "Pestering, indeed."

"Well, you do. And we love you for it." Amy looked from

Aunt Bay to Michael. "If this woman had been threatened first, it could be too much for me tonight, but Harry's crimes were a different thing altogether. I'll be okay. And I won't tell anyone he's a relative."

Michael studied her for a long moment, as if measuring what she'd said. He nodded. "If you think you should go, I hope it helps."

Amy spooned a mouthful of stew. Church. What had she gotten herself into? But if this woman could forgive the unforgivable, Amy might pick up a way to let go of her father's hurt — and of the long absence that hadn't been his fault.

Chapter 17

Aunt Bay steered her little four-by-four into the church parking lot and found a space not too far from the door.

Amy's hip twinged as she stepped from the vehicle. Maybe leaving her cane at home was a bad idea, but she didn't want anything that would draw attention. Slip in, hear what she needed to hear, and stay anonymous. She glanced at Michael's aunt. Well, as anonymous as possible.

Her steps slowed. Aunt Bay stopped, and turned to wait for her. The older woman smiled. "They don't bite. I promise. Neither does God."

Amy stiffened her spine and picked up her pace. *Hello, God? I hope You can ignore me coming into Your house. There's something here I need.*

Stepping through the door felt like facing a spiritual version of a security scanner. Every muscle tight, Amy held her breath until she was safely inside. Of course no red lights flashed, no sirens blared. The woman who'd greeted them didn't suddenly demand some sort of church-approved ID. Still, Amy found herself taking shallow breaths as if to minimize the impact she made on this place.

For all Aunt Bay's outspokenness, the older woman seemed to respect Amy's hesitancy. She led the way to aisle seats at a safe distance from the front, and while she waved and greeted her friends at a distance, she didn't plunge Amy into conversations with strangers.

130

Amy squeezed Aunt Bay's hand and whispered, "Thanks for making this easier." From the aisle, she could escape if need be, and she wouldn't feel trapped in a crowd of God's accepted people. Would He mind less, this way?

She leaned nearer to Michael's aunt. "I'm sorry I didn't tell you about you-know-who. I figured Michael would tell you, once he knew."

Aunt Bay raised an eyebrow. "You came to us with no family. I was happy you found your other cousin, and that your father wants to reconcile, as difficult as that is for you right now. This one, you'll do better without."

Amy dropped her voice even lower. "I still can't believe he turned himself in. I hope she talks a bit about that tonight, too."

Aunt Bay nodded. She filled the next few minutes pointing out her friends and describing the different groups where she'd met them, and giving Amy an overview of the congregation's history.

Safe chatter, and Amy didn't need to retain it or respond. Before long, a middle-aged woman in a burgundy blazer and sharply-creased black pants stepped behind the podium and picked up a microphone.

Amy rubbed a hand across her jeans.

Aunt Bay spoke in her ear. "She always dresses for a board meeting. You fit in fine with the rest of us."

Amy flashed her a grateful smile. True enough, Aunt Bay and most of her friends had come in their regular clothes.

The woman at the front surveyed the room. "Welcome, everyone. It's good to see so many new-to-me faces among our regular family. For those who don't know me, I'm Irina Banks and I coordinate women's ministries here at Seaview Point." She stretched out her free hand. "Gentlemen, we're especially glad to see you here this evening, because I promised our speakers it would be a mixed event."

Speakers? Plural? Amy glanced at Aunt Bay. The older

woman shrugged.

Irina continued, "Ruth and Tony Warner were in the news a few years ago when Ruth was mistakenly abducted by escaped convict Harry Silver. God had called her to pray for the man after his arrest, but only a wild coincidence — or as I like to say, God-incidence — brought them together. Ruth and I have been friends for many years, and I've appreciated getting to know Tony as well. In their daily lives, Ruth is on staff at Harrington's Fabric Hut, and Tony's principal of Halifax West High School. Ruth and Tony worship at The Beacon Church, and they've been sharing their story with local congregations. Now, please join me in welcoming Ruth and Tony Warner."

She gestured to the side as an ordinary-looking couple walked toward her. The women hugged. Irina passed over the microphone before leaving the platform.

Ruth Warner stood taller than Amy, but not by much. Her husband carried an extra fifty pounds or so. If they felt under-dressed compared to Irina, it didn't show. Ruth placed some paper on the podium and replaced the mic in the holder. "There. Now if I get flustered, I won't drop pages everywhere."

She smiled. "It's good to be here. Some of you may have heard my story before, and if so I thank you for your kindness to come again tonight. We're going to give you the basic overview of events, but instead of focusing on what I can only call our ordeal, we want to share what we learned — about God, prayer, and forgiveness."

Beside her, Tony nodded. "God willing, nobody in this room will endure what we went through. But the lessons we learned apply to stressful situations in general." He paused. "We will all have stress."

A ripple of quiet laughter swept the room. Ruth faced the crowd. "This is not my comfort zone, although I'm getting used to it. It took almost as many nudges from God to get me talking as it did to get me praying for Harry in the first place."

She glanced at her notes. "Harry Silver escaped from prison after being convicted of a series of rapes and murders, all targeting young, blond women with long hair."

Ruth touched her brown curls. "I don't fit on a couple of counts. I was in the wrong place at the wrong time, and he grabbed me instead of the young woman he wanted. What you may not know is that the last girl he killed before his arrest was our niece, Susan."

One hand gripped the edge of the podium. "I hated that man. But God told me to pray for him, gave me a deep concern for his soul." She moved nearer to her husband. "Tony was furious."

His beard twitched in what might have been a grimace. "I wasn't a believer at the time."

A shadow crossed Ruth's face. "And you were hurting. We both were. Anyway, long story short. Abducted. Terrified. Harry couldn't handle my connection with Susan, or the fact that I forgave him to his face." She shook her head. "Only God could help me do that. So my part of tonight's talk is about forgiveness — why it's important, and why we can't do it alone."

Tony leaned toward the mic. "I was an agnostic, with a vague trust that Ruth's prayers would be enough if there really happened to be a God somewhere. I didn't want her preaching at me, and I actually forbade her to pray for Harry Silver. When he took her, I fell apart. God put me back together again once I let Him in." He slid his arm around Ruth. "And He protected my wife and gave her back to me."

Someone in the back of the room let out a piercing whistle that raised every hair on the back of Amy's neck. A grin split Tony's beard. "I agree."

Ruth leaned into him for a second, then straightened. "God wouldn't let up on me until I surrendered and started praying for Harry. He showed me how much His heart breaks to see a soul lost — even one as dark and damaged as Harry's. Then I couldn't stop, even at the risk of losing my marriage."

She flashed Tony a private smile. "I thought it was about me, about my healing, and I did heal. But in hindsight, God was using those prayers to mitigate what He knew was coming. If you take one thing home from me tonight, let it be this — if we refuse to forgive, we wall ourselves in with the hurt. And we wall ourselves away from God's healing. We also lock the offender into a place that makes it harder for him or her to experience God's goodness."

Amy dropped her eyes to avoid contact as Ruth gazed around the room. Not belonging to God, she didn't have the option of His healing. It made sense that forgiving her father would cut off his rejection's power to hurt her, though. It didn't need to hurt now, because he was trying to retract it. The issue there was, did she want to lay down the grudge?

She twisted her hands in her lap, as if she could twist out from under the weight of Ruth's message. Was carrying that grudge hurting her father somehow? If so, did it matter?

Childhood dreams welled, the fantasies she'd created about this man whose absence was a never-healing wound. He was a soldier, or a spy, on a dangerous mission. A scientist working on a top-secret cure for disease. An astronaut. He loved her, and missed her terribly. As soon as he could, he'd come home, sweep her into his arms, and never leave again.

A tear tracked Amy's cheek. She brushed it away. Just like she'd brushed away those dreams in her teens. Yet the ache remained.

If the child-Amy had the chance now to meet her father, she'd run to him. She'd never hold back, or throw resentment between them.

But the child-Amy hadn't been threatened with a

restraining order if she contacted him again. Amy fished a tissue from her purse and blew her nose.

Aunt Bay shifted closer.

Amy leaned into the older woman's shoulder. Even though Neal Williamson didn't fit her childhood imaginings, he was her father. Enough of her dreams had attached to this man. She couldn't refuse to meet him, lock him out of her life when he finally wanted in. It was too great a risk.

Rejecting her was wrong. Her father knew that, now, and he was trying to make things right. Forgiving him would be Amy's step. With the decision, a weight seemed to slide off of her chest.

Amy tried to tune back into Ruth's words, but her father's face intruded. She knew what he looked like from the Internet, but not his mannerisms. His voice. They'd missed so many years together. Could they ever become close? Would they even like each other? Her father was willing to try. She'd try, too.

A change in the flow of sound brought Amy back to her surroundings. Audience members were asking questions. Amy scuffed her feet against the carpet. She'd come to learn, and then ignored what was said. But she'd forgiven her father. Perhaps she'd heard enough.

Amy listened to the interplay of questions and answers. "How do you let go of an offence that huge? How did praying for someone like Harry Silver change you? Tony, how could you forgive a man like that for what he tried to do to your wife? Did you ever blame God?"

Honest questions. Ruth and Tony gave honest-sounding answers, even if they didn't all make sense to Amy. Not knowing the ins and outs of a relationship with God, she stretched to understand how a person could know what He was saying to them.

From the side, a man's voice called, "A question for Ruth. You said God gave you a concern for Harry Silver's soul. I get how praying helped you heal, and even influenced his decision to turn himself in instead of going through with his plans. But did you really believe God could save a man who did what he's done?"

Ruth's face lit up. She flashed a grin at her husband. "I am so glad you asked. We wanted to share this tonight, but I told God I needed a go-ahead from Him. You're it."

"Look at that, Clayton, you're an answer to prayer!" The call came from the back. The same guy who'd whistled earlier?

Clayton turned in his seat and shot back, "Be sure to tell my wife." Around Amy and Aunt Bay, people laughed.

Smiling, Ruth waited until the noise died before she spoke. "I've felt led to share my story, again for my own healing but also because I believe so strongly in the importance of prayer and forgiveness. And I've seen the hand of God in action. I've told my story. Harry's is his own."

She shifted from one foot to the other and back, as if she couldn't keep still. Tony stepped to the side and turned to watch his wife. The love and pride on his face were everything Amy longed to see in Michael's. Amy shut out her heart and focused on Ruth's words.

Ruth continued, "The details will come out in the next *Canadian Christian* magazine, probably next week. You can get it at the Christian bookstore or online, or wait for his television interview in October."

Amy didn't recognize the name of the magazine or the television program. Why would Christian media talk with Harry, or he with them? She scuffed her fingertips against the weave of her jeans. Harry had no more likelihood of reconciliation with God than she did. Not after what he'd done. Conversation hummed around her.

Ruth spoke louder. "I can tell you Harry Silver went back to prison as a Christian. Forgiven, saved, and likely to spend the rest of his life in our highest-security institution in solitary confinement."

Amy's senses sharpened. She whispered to Aunt Bay, "How could that be?"

Did the older woman's narrowed eyes mean she disagreed? Or was she considering the possibility?

Aunt Bay's lips pressed into a line, then curved to a smile. She nodded. "A miracle, that's how. That's how it is for any of us, just not usually so spectacular. The Bible says that anyone may come to Jesus." She held Amy's gaze. "Even you. No matter what. And even Harry Silver. The miracle is that he'd want to."

Why would a dangerous offender decide he wanted to belong to God? And how could he know God accepted him?

The noise brewed for another minute, before Ruth raised her hand. "If we could have quiet, please. Quiet?"

She waited until the buzz decreased. "What I just said has offended some of you. Feel free to take that up with God. But I encourage everyone to at least hear Harry out. Criminals with his level of guilt have been saved before. How can I believe it? I saw the change in him. And in communicating with him since he went back to prison, Tony and I have seen consistency in his words and spiritual growth. There's no benefit to him to pretend about this — it's not like he'll get out early on good behaviour. He's in custody until he dies."

She paused. "Then he'll be in Heaven. With you and me."

More mutters from the crowd. Aunt Bay whispered, "That'll twist some of them into a knot."

Amy shifted sideways in her seat. "But you believe it?"

"Ruth and Tony believe it, and they'd know better than I. He's convinced the people who interviewed him, too, or they'd never release the story. Which, by the way, I intend to check out."

"But how could anyone be sure?" And how dare her

criminal cousin take a step Amy couldn't take? He was a serial rapist-murderer. She was simply a victim of her circumstances.

"Child, we have to talk. Soon."

Amy's thoughts whirled. The condemnation — disqualification — from her childhood said she had no chance with God. Without knowing the details, Aunt Bay promised she did. A handful of Christians versus one. Here tonight, Amy saw different opinions too.

She needed more than an opinion. She needed proof.

Conversation continued for another half hour, mostly Ruth and Tony expressing certainty that God had accepted Harry, with some in the crowd celebrating the news and some arguing. As people began to leave, Amy asked Aunt Bay for directions to the washroom.

As she'd hoped, when she came back only a few stragglers remained. Aunt Bay stood chatting in a knot of women.

Projecting all the confidence she could, Amy approached the front of the room, where the speakers and a few others lingered. She caught Ruth's eye. The dark-haired woman excused herself from the conversation and approached Amy. "Hi. You look like you have something on your mind."

Amy stuck out her hand. "Amy Silver." She snapped her mouth shut. Heat flooded her face. It was her standard professional greeting, but with Ruth, of all people, she'd planned to hide her connection with Harry.

Ruth's eyes widened. She took Amy's hand. "It's good to meet you, Amy. Silver's not a common name. I expect it's hard to share it with a dangerous offender."

"He's my cousin. We've never met."

She held Amy's hand a little longer, then released it. The gesture didn't look like it cost anything, but to Amy it was the difference between yet another rejection and acceptance.

Ruth's face was open. Friendly. "Harry mentioned his

sister and her son, but I didn't know he had any other family."

"His sister lived with my mom and me for a few years. He probably doesn't know I exist."

"You're quite a bit younger than Harry." Ruth seemed to brace herself. "How do you feel about his coming to faith?"

"I need to ask how you can be sure."

Her face softened. "I saw the change, Amy. He couldn't have faked it, and the man who abducted me wouldn't have faked it. He was as God-hostile as they come." She smiled. "You need to hear his story, but I promise you, he's been transformed. Only God could do that."

"But why?"

Ruth's brows drew together. Her head dipped nearer to Amy's. "Why what?"

"Why would God do that? Accept him, after all he's done?"

Ruth's laugh carried delight, not scorn. "Because He's God, and He wants to save us all. Plus, it shows how powerful He is. Most of us don't think it takes a lot of effort on His part to clean us up. Someone like Harry? People sit up and take notice."

"How can you know? That He wants to save us all? Aren't there limits?"

"Walk with me." Ruth led her to the far end of the front row of seats. She sat, and beckoned Amy to join her. "I'm guessing you don't know the Lord too well yet."

Mistake. Sinful. What a shame. The words crashed into Amy's thoughts. She shoved them away.

When Amy didn't speak, Ruth asked, "If God saved Harry, what could keep Him from saving you?"

"But what if it's not true?"

Ruth nodded gently. "As in, what if you risk it and the bottom falls out?"

Amy stared at her hands, clenched in her lap. "Beatrice —

my friend who brought me — says what you say, that God can forgive anything. But that's not what I was told as a child."

"Amy..." Ruth's voice was soft, motherly. Her arm slid around Amy's shoulders. "Tell me what it is. It cannot be worse than what Harry did."

"I need proof. If I trust people's opinions but God thinks different—" The dam burst. "I'm illegitimate." She braced for Ruth's reaction.

The other woman shifted a bit closer. "And...?"

Amy stared at her knees. "My father went home to his wife. Mom never told him. They weren't married."

"And you've felt cut off from your Heavenly Father because of your parents' decisions."

"It wasn't my sin — how could I confess it and be forgiven?"

"I see."

Amy's muscles tightened into a shield. Inside, hope bled out.

Ruth's arm left Amy's shoulders and she shuffled a few inches away. "Amy? Look at me, please."

Jaw tight, Amy forced her tear-blurred eyes to make contact. To meet this verdict head-on. The compassion on Ruth's face nearly undid her.

"Sympathy will just make it worse." Could Ruth even hear her broken words?

Ruth's expression didn't change. "The Bible has many names to show God's character. One of them is 'Father to the Fatherless.'" She took Amy's hands. "He adopts us. He knows we can't earn our way into relationship with Him, so He does it for us."

A ringing started in Amy's ears. "Can you show me that? In the Bible?"

"Of course." Ruth pulled out her phone and tapped the screen.

Released, Amy's hands felt chilled. She tucked them under her arms. "Fatherless. I've been called that before. And worse." The labels queued on her tongue, but she held them back.

"Here it is." Ruth scrolled through text, then back to the top. "Psalm 68. It's a bit long, and some of it won't make sense to you, but listen to verse five. 'A father to the fatherless, a defender of widows, is God in His holy dwelling.'" She passed Amy the phone to read for herself. "I can show you in my print Bible, now that I know where to look."

"Please."

Ruth walked away. Amy stayed focused on the text, tiny black words on a white screen. *A father to the fatherless, a defender of widows, is God in His holy dwelling.* She read verse six as well. *God sets the lonely in families, He leads out the prisoners with singing; but the rebellious live in a sun-scorched land.*

There was more, but Amy's eyes snapped back to that one, heart-stopping phrase. *Father to the fatherless.*

Ruth settled beside her and extended her opened Bible, pointing to the text. "Sometimes seeing things in print makes them more real."

Amy took the book. She slid her finger over the words on their smooth page. "Can I trust this? I've heard about people using the Bible to justify whatever they want."

"You can trust it. People do take things out of context, and this is just one verse out of I don't know how many in the whole Bible. Once God adopts you as His own, the journey really begins. Spending time with Him, reading the rest of this book... it's a lifetime's learning."

After a minute, Amy looked up from the text. "So I have to take it on faith, and experience will prove it?" Or experience would prove she'd made a disastrous mistake. Would God actually zap her with lightning? Could she risk losing her half-life with Michael?

"Faith in God, yes, and in His word. Not faith in my opinion." Ruth scanned the room. "You said you came with a friend. Is she still here?"

"She'd better be, or I'm walking home. But she doesn't know about my parents."

"Will she hold it against you?"

"Not unless she thinks God does."

Ruth nodded. "Then let her be your second opinion about that verse. If you're ready to tell her."

Amy turned in her seat. Aunt Bay stood with her back to them. The two friends with her also faced away on an angle. "The church ladies when I was a child made it sound so terrible — so final. Even if Aunt Bay agrees, how can I be sure you're right and they were wrong?"

"Amy, sin is anything that separates us from God... what we do, what we don't do, our words, our attitudes. It can literally be anything. Sometimes Christians will get hung up on one or two pet sins and try to judge the whole world through that lens. That's sin, too, although they don't see it. Your parents' choice was outside of God's rules for healthy living. So was mine, to hate Harry when I found out what he'd done. So were some of the choices you've made. Nobody's perfect. But God promises to forgive us when we ask, and to receive us as His own if we'll accept Jesus as our Lord and Saviour."

Ruth lifted the Bible from Amy's hands and set it, still open, on the seat beside her. "Do you want me to get her for you?"

"I'll go." Amy stood. "I'm sorry to take so much of your time. If you need to leave, I'll ask her to look up the verse at home."

Light danced in Ruth's eyes. "Are you kidding? I wouldn't miss this for the world. You are so close to being adopted by the King of the Universe. He's drawn up the agreement. It

143

just needs your okay."

The current of excitement in her voice tickled Amy's waking hope. "I'll be right back."

As soon as Amy started toward Aunt Bay, the woman on the right touched Aunt Bay's sleeve. She and her friend stepped back, and Michael's aunt turned to Amy, gentle questions on her face.

Amy beckoned.

Aunt Bay spoke quickly with her friends, then hurried to Amy's side. "I wasn't ignoring you."

"Yes, you were, and it nearly killed you." Amy set her shoulders. "Ruth believes like you do, that God can forgive anything."

"Wise woman."

"She showed me a verse. I want you to see it. To see if it applies to me." Amy's feet braced and her knees bent, as if preparing to physically lift the weight of her secret. "I'm illegitimate. My father planted the seed and left."

Aunt Bay swept her into a bone-crushing hug. "You silly, sweet child, God doesn't care about your pedigree. He cares about you."

Hope buzzed in Amy's heart, like cicadas on a summer night.

Aunt Bay squeezed tighter, then released her. "Let's check out this verse."

They walked back to Ruth, and Amy introduced the two women. Aunt Bay shook Ruth's hand. "Thank you for your message tonight. And thank you for talking sense to this precious child who won't listen to an old lady."

Amy slid her foot sideways to tap Aunt Bay's. "Don't play the age card. The truth is worse. I was afraid you were wrong."

Aunt Bay sniffed. "I'm wounded."

Ruth picked up her Bible. "Beatrice, did Amy tell you her background?"

"Just now."

"So when I call God 'Father to the Fatherless,' based on Psalm 68:5, and I tell her that He adopts us into a new heritage that makes the old one irrelevant, what do you think?"

Aunt Bay ignored the outstretched Bible and focused on Amy. "It's true, child. Jesus died — and lives — to save us all. Everyone who asks."

"Even me." Weight fell from Amy like a concrete cast that had broken. She looked from one woman to the other. "I've always believed in God, but thought His rules kept me out. How do I ask Him to accept me?"

Smiling, Ruth waved her Bible at Aunt Bay in a "you-lead" gesture. "You two have a history."

Aunt Bay's eyes glistened. "I — Amy, you're a child of my heart and this can't make me love you more, but I'm bursting with pleasure. You're aware that God is holy and we can't earn His acceptance."

Amy nodded.

"And that you're separated from Him by your own sins and imperfections, not just the circumstances of your birth?"

"Ruth explained that."

"Do you believe that Jesus' death and resurrection is enough to pay for your sin so that nothing will separate you from God the Father?"

"There's a lot I don't understand about that, but yes."

Aunt Bay took her hand. "There's a lot I still don't understand. We'll study together. For now, you need to invite Him into your life, to clean and adopt you. It means living His way, not yours, from now on. He'll help you with that. Don't worry about praying fancy. He knows your heart."

Ruth joined hands with them and gave Amy's an encouraging squeeze. "You can do this. He wants to say yes."

Amy shut her eyes. "Hello, God? I believe Your words. I am fatherless. Will you be my Father?"

The pressure on Amy's hands didn't ease when she finished. Should she say something else? "Oh. Amen."

Aunt Bay and Ruth took turns praying for her. Hope bloomed in Amy's spirit, watered with words of love. Finally Aunt Bay said, "Amen."

They dropped her hands, only to envelop her in hugs. Eventually, Ruth pulled away. "Will you keep in touch?"

"I'd like that." Amy fished in her purse for one of the gallery's cards. She wrote her name and cell number on the back. "I don't always have my cell on, but the gallery number is good."

Ruth took the card. "Oh, Stratton Gallery. We've been there, but not for years."

Aunt Bay held out a scrap of paper and a pen. "We have an open house on Saturday, if you'd like to see Amy in her natural surroundings."

Ruth wrote her contact information and handed it back. "I'll see if Tony has plans. You're near Peggy's Cove, right? If it's fine, we could stop at the restaurant for gingerbread." She hugged them both. "One way or another, I'll talk to you soon."

She picked up her Bible and went back to her husband.

Aunt Bay nudged Amy. "We should get going, before Michael comes looking for us. He frets worse than an old woman."

Amy fell into step beside her. Michael. "He'll be so excited to hear this. Do we have to tell him what kept me away?"

"Child, it's a non-issue. You need to believe that. Michael won't care, but keeping secrets gives them power to poison us."

Chapter 19

The fourth time Amy opened her eyes, pale dawn light had finally seeped into the room. The house lay silent. Amy swung her legs over the edge of her bed and sat up. Her alarm wouldn't sound for another hour or so. She turned it off. If she did fall into a decent sleep now, she'd wake in such a stupor that she'd be useless all day.

She fetched her bathrobe from the hook on the bedroom door. The laminate floor was cool against the soles of her feet, but not as cold as it would be in a few months. The temperature, and the smooth surface, made a soothing contrast to the sticky, tangled mess of her dreams.

Amy positioned the rocking chair to face the window and opened the blind. She sat, drawing her fluffy robe tight around her middle. Outside, a crow cawed. A few sweeter-voiced birds answered. As light spread across the sky she watched gulls soaring over the water.

Maybe Aunt Bay and Michael had been right about the evening being too much after that frightening phone call. Dream fragments echoed in Amy's mind, most in the distorted voice from the phone. Threatening, mocking, rejecting her in front of rooms full of onlookers.

Her criminal cousin sat with Ruth and Tony, all three wearing old-fashioned judges' wigs. Gavels banged. Fingers pointed. Heaven thundered.

Aunt Bay threw up her hands in defeat.

Michael turned away.

Motion outside the window pulled Amy's thoughts into the present. A squirrel dashed along a tree branch. Amy followed his progress, thankful for the distraction.

The little creature sprang to the next tree's branch, raced to the trunk, and scurried to the ground. Whatever his errand, Amy envied his simple life. Eat and avoid being eaten. Harsh, but without the mind games that turned humans into such wrecks.

Becoming a child of God should make her feel better, not worse. The peace that had washed her had been stolen in the night. Amy replayed the conversation with Michael when they came home. The joy on his face. The way her explanation only made him hold her tighter. She'd never seen him speechless before.

The rocker creaked as she stood. Maybe the mindless routine of her physio exercises and a shower would banish her mental discord.

The house was still silent when Amy crept downstairs, dressed for the day and desperate for caffeine. A light in the kitchen warned her she wasn't the only one up. The sharp scent of coffee pulled her into the room.

Aunt Bay sat reading the paper, wrapped in a red plaid robe. The paper rustled as she set it down. "Good morning. You're up early."

Amy put on her brightest expression, but her beeline for the coffee pot would tell Aunt Bay the truth. "I may turn into a zombie by noon." Clutching her mug, Amy shuffled to the chair opposite Michael's aunt. "What's the latest?"

The older woman snorted. "You'd have to ask Google. This is out of date by the time it's printed and delivered."

"But you read it every day."

"I don't mind a time lag." Aunt Bay flipped back through a few pages and spun the newspaper to face Amy. "Our friend Troy is at it again."

Did Crash Investigators Ignore Evidence?

Amy slid the paper nearer and focused on the article's small print.

> *Investigators may have overlooked evidence pertaining to the fatal crash of a private aircraft on a Nova Scotia road two years ago. Speaking on condition of anonymity, a reliable source suggests that in the absence of visible motive, investigators may have ruled certain details extraneous due to the "statistical improbability" of sabotage in the case.*

> *A potentially suspicious car was seen on club grounds prior to the disastrous flight. Key security footage was indecipherable, and the night guard's report had gaps big enough to fly a commercial jet through.*

> *With the recent findings from the crash in Maryland, these and other grey areas are enough to prompt this reporter to call for a second investigation. A man may have been murdered. Do his loved ones not have the right to know the truth, one way or the other?*

At least he hadn't mentioned Amy's name. Or the pilot's. "None of this sounds very solid, but it's too much to have ignored in the first place. How can they find evidence this long after the fact?"

Aunt Bay rotated the paper on the table and returned to her previous page. "I don't know. I still can't get my head around someone trying to kill the two of you. What could they possibly gain?"

"That's the question." Amy dropped her forehead into her palm, nose wrinkling at the tang of newsprint. She had no answers on a good day, let alone after a night like the one she'd just endured. "Luc is going to be livid."

"Let me answer the phone if he calls."

"I can't expect you to fight my battles for me."

"Not all of them. This one. For today."

Amy straightened and reached for her coffee. "Today, it would be most welcome."

"You made a big decision last night, after a crazy day. It's no wonder you didn't sleep well."

The first sip of coffee woke Amy's taste buds and warmed her throat as she swallowed. She leaned on her elbows, mug supported in both hands, and filled her nostrils with the potent aroma. "I had terrible dreams. Does that mean God didn't want me after all?"

Faded blue eyes studied her. "What do you think?"

"I think I should believe what I saw in the Bible, not what I feel."

"Good answer. The old you will fight to stop the new you that God wants to grow."

Amy savoured another mouthful of coffee, then set her mug down and rocked it gently on the table. "What Ruth and Tony said last night helped me think through the whole thing with my father. I can forgive him. And I'd like to meet him while he's in town."

"You've never met?"

Amy shook her head. "He found out about me the hard way, when Gilles invited him to our wedding."

"No wonder he had issues."

"I know, but that didn't make it any easier when I needed him."

The older woman tapped a finger on the newspaper. "You could invite him here, for safety. Michael and I could stay out of the way. Then he could join us for supper if you decide to ask him."

Michael stepped into the kitchen. "Supper when? Who?" He pulled a mug from the cupboard and grabbed the coffee pot.

His aunt spoke to his back. "Amy's father. When he

calls."

As Michael poured, he said, "After yesterday's threat, I'd feel better if he came here. Any man could pretend on the phone, and lure you somewhere. Besides, I'd like to meet him."

Amy pushed her chair out from the table and stood. "I might as well get an early start on the office work, since we lost part of yesterday with our friendly, neighbourhood police officer."

Michael turned. His eyes held hers. "Leave the door locked unless a customer knocks? Just in case?"

"I won't even put up the 'open' sign this early." Amy hurried from the room before he could ask about her night.

By mid-morning her eyelids were scratchy and drooping. Time to get the blood pumping some oxygen to the brain. Another cup of coffee wouldn't hurt, either. Amy stood and stretched.

As she passed through the gallery, a shadow at the door made her flinch. She took a second look as the person knocked. Ross!

Amy hurried to let him in. "Hi. How are you?"

He walked into the showroom, casually elegant in a tailored leather jacket. His dark eyes, always unreadable, searched her face. "Perhaps the question is, how are you?"

She flipped her hair behind her back. "I had a bad night, that's all. Were you looking for Michael, or is there something I can help you with?"

"I was in the area and thought I'd see if you were free for an early lunch." He stepped closer. "Granted Emilie has an active imagination, but I've been concerned about you. Perhaps rightly."

Amy moved to the nearest display rack. Her fingers straightened already-straight packets of greeting cards. "Everyone has troubled dreams sometimes." She tried to keep her voice light. "Aunt Bay and I were out late last night, and I didn't unwind well enough before bed. Honestly, it was nothing to do with my life here — or with the crash. But thank you for caring."

"You've suffered so much. I'd hate for anything else to go wrong." His voice carried warmth. Sincerity.

Amy felt her defences go up. Michael. The unnamed texter. She didn't need a third protector hemming her in. Mouth closed, she brushed a fleck of dust off the wire rack. She didn't need to alienate one of Michael's clients, either.

Ross trailed his fingers through the tabletop fountain. "I saw another article today about your plane crash. That reporter is another person with a flair for the dramatic."

Was Ross the phantom texter? He could afford a second, throw-away phone to keep his privacy. The question stuck in Amy's mouth. Whoever it was, the person didn't want to disclose his — or her — identity. "He's been asked to keep me out of his investigation."

"Wise move."

"But if you read what he wrote today, don't you think he raises some fair questions?"

His brows came together. "The investigators know their job. I make it a point not to waste time on areas outside of my expertise. It saves me much trouble."

Footsteps sounded in the hallway, and Aunt Bay walked into the room. "Oh, hello, Ross. I was just wondering if Amy needed any help."

"Miss Rockland, a pleasure to see you. Perhaps you'd convince Amy to let me take her to lunch. A break can do wonders."

"It can, indeed. I'll watch things here if you'd like to go, Amy."

Amy shook her head. "Thank you both, but the best break for me today will be a nap."

Ross lifted his palms. "Another time, then, for lunch. I don't give up. Have a pleasant day, ladies."

Aunt Bay locked the door after he left. "A fine young man."

Amy nodded. "He didn't need me falling asleep in my salad. If you don't mind, I'll go lie down for a bit now. This afternoon Michael wants the three of us to go over the weekend plans."

The open house would be fun. Amy always enjoyed observing patrons react to Michael's work, and hosting here gave her a sense of personal pride. The entire main floor would be open to guests, with Michael's art on display throughout. The spacious, eat-in kitchen made a perfect gathering point for drinks and finger food. Michael's arrangement with the local bakery meant professional-quality refreshments that were an art form in themselves.

She clutched Aunt Bay's arm. "What if whoever phoned makes trouble? I didn't leave like they wanted, and Troy's article will only provoke them."

~~~

Amy's alarm woke her from a forty-five minute power nap. She couldn't say the snooze energized her, but at least she'd be able to string coherent thoughts together for the meeting. When she left her bedroom at noon, faint music from Michael's studio said he was still painting.

She found Aunt Bay pulling coffee cake from the oven. "Smells good in here."

Michael's aunt set the pan on a cooling rack. "I thought we could all use a treat."

The front doorbell rang. Amy grinned at Aunt Bay. "Someone knew you were baking." She hurried through the house to the entrance.

When she pulled open the door, Luc stood on the step. Amy hadn't seen her intended father-in-law in months. He spent most of his time in Montreal, and when he was here, it was easier to stay off his radar. Gilles had been their only real connection.

In those months, the man had aged years. Lines trenched his face, and his eyes peered out from dark caves. She caught his arm and drew him inside. "Luc, are you well?"

Aunt Bay bustled toward them. "Luc Renaud, you can be polite to Amy or you can leave."

"It's okay, Aunt Bay." Amy kept a hand on his arm. "Come and sit down. Can we get you a drink?"

"No, thank you." Even his voice was thinner, although his most recent call proved he could still be forceful when roused. Luc allowed Amy to take his jacket and followed her to the living room.

Aunt Bay joined them. "I apologize, Luc. After you upset Amy on the phone the other day, I thought you were here to do it in person."

He flapped a hand. Dismissing the apology, or the presumption of his intent? His eyes sought Amy's. "It was never my aim to hurt you, chérie. Gilles loved you so much." He sank into the couch. "The loss of my son destroyed me, and you see the wreckage today. This talk of the plane crash, of sabotage..."

Luc paled as he spoke, but his eyes burned. "You have questions. I have questions. But asking them is dangerous for my family."

Family? Amy studied the shell of Gilles' father. A successful businessman would have rivals, but enemies who would target his children? What kind of trouble was Luc in? She sat beside him, angled to see his face. "What are you going to do?"

His eyes, once so like his son's, blinked rapidly. "Nothing. And I plead with you to do the same."

"But the police—" Would do what? The investigators had signed off. The case was closed. Amy squeezed Luc's hand. "If we found some proof..."

"No." Again the forlorn head shake. "What is done is done. I can't bear to lose any more. It's possible that our intrepid reporter will draw enough attention to himself that he will pay the price. We must say nothing."

Aunt Bay huffed. "Luc, you need help. This is too much to face alone, but you can fight it."

He closed his eyes for a long moment. "These are powerful men, Beatrice. Ruthless. Unstoppable. They must believe they have won. It's the only way we're safe. Now, because of Amy's earlier questions and even her recent flight, she and this household are also under scrutiny." He touched Amy's cheek. "For Gilles, I tried to keep you safe. I distanced you, but it wasn't enough."

Amy frowned. "I thought you agreed with your wife's opinion of me."

"Chérie, you were Gilles' missing piece. I had never seen him happier, even under the darkness. For that I am forever grateful. Honore may have seen it in time, but I knew from the beginning. You were no mistake. You were a gift."

The words seared Amy's mind. Luc's lips still moved, but her ears sang with what she'd heard. *No mistake. A gift.* He meant for Gilles, not a comment on her birth, but the words spun and grew, eclipsing his smaller meaning. And perhaps he did know it all. Gilles might have told him.

A tingling sensation wrapped Amy like a soft, static-charged blanket. Like a divine hug, from the inside. Warmth flooded her and poured out in tears. This wasn't pain, or hurt. This was... healing.

She shaped her trembling lips into a smile so Luc wouldn't worry. He reached for her, then hesitated.

Aunt Bay thrust a box of tissues into Amy's lap and rested a hand on her shoulder. "Let it out, child. You've carried too much for too long."

Amy sniffled and grabbed a handful of tissues for her face. "Luc, what you said means more than you can know.

Thank you. And I'm sorry. About the mess. About misjudging you. And about stirring up danger for you. I didn't know."

Michael stepped into the room. "What's going on?" His gaze tracked across Amy's face to pin Luc, and his face darkened.

Aunt Bay pressed Amy's shoulder. "Nothing you need concern yourself with just now. We've been having a heart-to-heart."

They locked eyes, until Michael looked away. "I just had a call from Troy. Someone lured him out into the country about the plane crash, and ran him off the road. He's okay, but his car's totalled."

Amy went cold. "He could have been killed."

Aunt Bay turned to Luc. "The reporter."

Luc's face set in grim lines. "As I feared." He looked at each one of them. "Gilles discovered the hold they have on me, and it cost his life. Please. No questions. Keep yourselves safe."

Michael opened his mouth, but Aunt Bay cut him off. "I'll explain later." She turned to Luc. "Amy had a threatening phone call yesterday. Someone wants her to leave."

Luc spread his hands. "They have an extensive network, across Canada and internationally. You can't hide from them."

"We're not going to give in to threats. And after what happened to Troy, we're not going to even think about the plane crash. Any of us." Michael stood with his feet spread, arms folded tight across his chest. His eyes pinned Amy. "It's too great a risk. I loved Gilles too, but we have to trust Troy to convince the authorities to do their job."

Amy swallowed hard. "You're leaving Troy to the wolves."

Pain flickered in his eyes. "Journalists don't back down. That's his choice. Mine is to keep you safe."

Chapter 20

Luc's words left Amy subdued but with a warmth in her chest like a glowing coal. She wanted to sit alone and study it. Instead, she sat under Michael's watchful eye at the kitchen table with Aunt Bay, eating soup and sandwiches.

Michael's pen retraced the words on his weekend list, darkening the letters. "Amy, are you sure you're up to this? You're a great hostess, but this has been a killer week. And a spiritual rebirth can have ripple effects."

"If I can sleep, I'll be fine." She rested one foot on a chair rung. "I love these events, and the social side doesn't tire me like it does you. We have all day tomorrow for setup, and Saturday morning for the last-minute things. Plus, you can bet Emilie will show up to help."

Michael tugged at his collar. "What am I going to do about her?"

Aunt Bay gathered their empty dishes and carried them to the sink. "Find yourself a girlfriend."

Heaviness settled in Amy's stomach. She forced a laugh. "Playing nursemaid has cramped your love life. But I'm better now."

Above the hiss of water as she rinsed the dishes, Aunt Bay scolded, "Stop blaming yourself for other people's circumstances. Luc spoke truer than he knew when he said you were a gift, child."

Michael's eyes tightened. "Too bad he couldn't have

remembered it on the phone the other day. Was that why he came, to apologize?"

Aunt Bay dropped back into her seat. "He saw Troy's latest article. You heard the gist of his warning."

"And we need to obey it. Nothing ever fazed Luc. Anything that can ruin him like this is more than I want to take on."

Aunt Bay frowned. "Luc needs to take what little he has to the authorities. I never thought I'd see the man cave like that."

Amy rubbed the ring of condensation her glass had left on her place mat. "Is that something we can pray for? Peace for Luc, and wisdom? Courage? If God can change my convict cousin, He should be able to get through to Luc."

The older woman tapped her fingers on the table. "Of course we can."

Michael held up a hand. "I'm out of the loop, here. Did they say something last night about God changing Harry Silver?"

His aunt's lips twitched. "I did invite you."

He took a slow breath. "So what happened?"

"They said he turned to Christ before going back to prison. There's supposed to be an interview in the next issue of *Canadian Christian*. Do you know anyone who gets that?"

"I don't think so." Michael tipped his chair back. "Wow."

"That's what made me ask for myself." Amy leaned her elbows on the table. "Ruth was sure God accepted Harry, and I thought maybe Aunt Bay was right that He'd accept me too."

"Maybe Aunt Bay was right." The older woman's singsong mimic made them all laugh.

Amy slid her soup bowl to the side. "Carol and Joey must have known, when we were there. She said they'd been in touch. From what Ruth said, everyone's been waiting for him to decide to tell his story."

"It'll be worth hearing." Michael picked up his list. "I'd better get going. Speaking of stories, are you going to tell Carol and Joey yours?"

"I think they'd like that." Amy stopped, and let out a huff worthy of Aunt Bay. "Carol knew Mom was unmarried. She was still pointing me to God. Why didn't I put it together that she meant it wasn't too much for Him?"

Michael's smile was a caress. "You've put it together now, and I can't wait to see what He does with you." List in hand, he headed for the door.

Aunt Bay took Amy's hand. "I'm glad I had the privilege to be part of your spiritual birth. One by one, the Lord is answering my prayers."

"What's next?"

"Keeping us safe from whoever crashed your plane. After that?" A mischievous grin stretched Aunt Bay's face. "I'm not telling."

"Well, I hope it's good." Amy pulled her hair into a ponytail with the elastic from her wrist. "I need to move, or I'll fall asleep. Want to help me set up some of the easels and display stands for Saturday?"

"We'll do the bigger ones, and then I'd like a lie-down, myself."

Together they carried the collapsed stands from the basement. Nothing was terribly heavy, but the tall easels were awkward without a second person.

Amy reached the top of the stairs on their fourth trip as the phone rang. Behind her, Aunt Bay said, "We'll drop this in the kitchen. And let me get the phone, just in case."

Not another call like yesterday. A shiver chased down Amy's spine. Aunt Bay stepped off the stairs and they laid their load on the floor. The older woman hurried across the room and picked up the ringing phone. She frowned at the call display and hit *talk*. "Stratton Gallery, good afternoon."

Her posture relaxed, but not completely. "Just a moment."

She turned to Amy and held the phone down by her side. "Your father."

Amy's mouth went dry. A jolt rocked her stomach. Fear? Excitement? She licked her lips and reached for the phone. "Okay." She cleared her throat. If her words didn't come out any better than that, it wouldn't be a long conversation.

Aunt Bay passed over the handset. "Just be yourself."

Amy lifted the phone. "Hello?" She walked out of the kitchen.

A deep voice spoke. "Amy? It's Neal Williamson. Thank you for taking my call. Do you have a few minutes?"

"I can take a break now. How was your flight?"

"Not bad. Long."

They exchanged brittle pleasantries that made Amy cringe. Did he feel the same, dancing around what they needed to say but not knowing how to get there? Amy settled in one of the living room chairs and curled her feet up under her. The room wasn't cold, but she drew a blanket over her knees.

Finally, she blurted, "I got your letter. I needed time to think."

"That's fair." His question hung in the silence.

"I — I do forgive you. It was a mix-up. Gilles didn't tell me what you'd said to him."

"I shouldn't have said it, no matter how surprised I was." He recapped what he'd sent Amy about his wife, and about her mother.

Amy listened, twirling the blanket fringe in her fingers. Hearing about her mother, young, carefree and in love, brought back the happier days of her childhood. Mom had made home a safe, loving place. Even when she got sick, they'd hung out together and watched old movies. And eaten popcorn. When Mom's body couldn't tolerate it, she'd insisted Amy make a batch to "share" — Amy eating, and her mother enjoying the scent.

She told Neal about that, and about the good times. "Mom wouldn't tell me anything practical about you, even your name, but she'd talk about how kind you were, and how you made her feel alive. When I was little, it helped me imagine you. Until I grew up enough to realize you were never coming back."

Through the window, she saw a car drive past. Like her childhood dreams of her father, always passing, never stopping. Except now he'd stopped. He was near.

"Even if I'd known, I couldn't have come back. I had to stay in one world or the other. But I wish I could have been there for you. Does that help at all?"

"Not really." Amy scrunched the blanket in one hand. "Look, Neal... Father... I don't even know what to call you. We can't change what was. But what do we want now? What do you want? Should we meet, shake hands, and go back to our lives? Or should we try to build a relationship as adults?"

"Call me Neal for now. Honestly? I'd like to get to know you. I'm getting older, and I have no other children. You're a gift." His laugh came out harsh. "A gift I refused and have no right to claim. If you never want to see my face, or only want a one-time meeting, I'll respect that."

Childhood dreams tumbled through Amy's mind, colliding with the labels she'd worn for so long. Clear as pure light flashed the sudden awareness that she was no longer fatherless — and it had nothing to do with the man on the phone. She had a new Father, who loved and accepted her.

Amy's breath hissed inward, and her shoulders lifted. The old accusations, any new ones, none of them mattered. She belonged. And her Father might not be a spy, soldier or astronaut. But He was a King.

"Amy?" Neal sounded worried, like he expected to be turned away.

The feeling of light glowed in her now, melting the last of her tension. "Sorry. I was thinking. Are you free tomorrow? You could join us for dinner. The gallery's in a house, and we all live here — my boss, Michael, his aunt and I. They've been like family to me since the crash, and they're curious about you."

"Nothing like a trial by fire."

"If that's too much, we could do something on Sunday. Saturday there's an open house here and I'll be busy."

"I have meetings all day tomorrow, but I'll cut out early. You're what, forty minutes from the downtown core?"

"Give yourself an hour in Friday afternoon traffic."

"Would six be okay? If I can be there earlier, I will. And, Amy? You deserve a perfect father, but I'll be learning as I go."

Amy had a perfect Father. Neal Williamson couldn't match that standard, nor could she. She smoothed the blanket in her lap. "Mom did the hard parenting stage. I think we should aim to be friends."

"I'd like that. See you tomorrow."

"Goodbye." Amy disconnected and stared out the window. That hadn't been as rough as she'd feared. "Thank You, God. And thank You that I can talk to You."

Her father was coming to dinner, and she didn't have to hide the fact that they'd never met. If Aunt Bay fired off a few direct questions, Neal was a former hockey player. Hopefully he'd still have the reaction time he'd need to think on his feet.

~~~

The phone showed voice mail, but when Amy checked, both calls were hang-ups. She took the handset back to its dock and pulled the dry mop from the closet. Better to go over the floors before positioning the easels.

She'd barely started on the entryway when the phone rang again. "It figures!" She leaned the mop handle against the wall and scurried back to the kitchen.

Call display showed the number from the warning texts. Amy clutched the phone. "Hello?"

Click.

Why call the gallery land-line when the mystery person had Amy's cell number? The cell was in Amy's pocket, and it hadn't buzzed. She double-checked that it was on. Should she text back?

Growling, she wedged the handset into the waistband of her pants and went back to her mop. Gilles' unnamed friend claimed to be on her side, but that didn't mean Amy had to play his or her mind games.

By the time she'd finished the floors and started positioning the smaller display stands, she'd taken another dead-air call from the same number.

Aunt Bay came down the stairs. "How was your conversation?"

"We found things to talk about. He said he'll come to supper tomorrow." Amy grinned. "You can grill him, but not too hard. We're going to try to build a relationship."

"I'm glad. Don't mind Michael if he's a bit tense."

"What do you mean?"

Aunt Bay's eyes narrowed. "He doesn't want anything to hurt you, and none of us knows this man."

Amy shifted the display stand to the side. "I feel okay about it. I don't have any great hopes that we'll become instant best buds." She stepped nearer to Michael's aunt. "This may not make sense, but now that I have God as my true Father, I don't have to have any big expectations about my biological father. I hope we'll become close, but I'm not looking for him to meet all my childhood emotional needs."

"That sounds like a healthy—" The ringing phone cut her off.

Amy whipped it out of her waistband. Same Winnipeg number. She thrust it toward Aunt Bay. "Will you try? They hang up on me."

"Stratton Gallery, how may I help you?" Aunt Bay huffed. "No answer."

"That's the number that sent the warning texts. Right now they're just making me mad."

Michael's aunt carried the phone to the kitchen. "Let it ring, next time. While I'm here, let's set up these bigger easels and get them out of the kitchen."

The two women had everything in place when Michael arrived with shopping bags and a fistful of mail. He passed an envelope to Amy. "This one's for you. Everything else is junk or for the gallery."

Amy ripped open the envelope with a finger and pulled out a single sheet of paper. Unfolded, it read *AMY SILVER, GO HOME*. She dropped the page and turned over the envelope. Just her name and address and a postmarked stamp. "Michael?" She couldn't keep the squeak from her voice.

He turned from his unpacking. One look at her face, and he snatched up the letter. "I suppose we've ruined any fingerprints."

"What now?" Aunt Bay crossed to Amy's side and planted a hand on her shoulder before reading the message. "You *are* home, child. Don't let this change anything."

Amy shut her eyes and leaned into Aunt Bay.

Michael's voice came out flat. "Yesterday's phone call started a file with the police, and this letter will add to it."

Aunt Bay squeezed Amy's shoulder. "Perhaps we'll have a friendlier officer this time."

"I hope so." Amy picked up the page again. "In old movies, there'd be a wonky letter and the detective could trace it back to a specific typewriter. Or there'd be a unique watermark in the paper. This could have come from anyone's printer."

The phone shrilled again. Michael reached for it, and Amy rattled off the texter's number. He shot her a puzzled look. "Who is it?"

"Gilles' friend with the warning texts, but he won't speak when we answer. We've both tried."

Michael jabbed *talk*. "Who is this?"

Rapid, indecipherable sounds. Michael's knuckles whitened on the handset. His face paled to match them. One glance at Amy, and he left the room.

From his few, one-syllable responses, he hadn't gone far. She couldn't sneak past to listen on another phone.

When Michael returned, it took him three tries to line the handset up properly in the dock. He turned toward them, back pressed against the counter. His face was the colour of old wax. "I have to go out. Aunt Bay, will you follow up with the police about that letter?"

"Of course. What's this all about?"

The shake of his head was a tired old man's. "When I come back." He plucked the van keys from their hook and hurried out.

From the coat closet, hangers jangled. The front door slammed.

Everything was still, as if the house itself were holding its breath. Amy remembered to breathe. "What just happened?"

Aunt Bay matched her whisper. "I don't know. I'll call the police about the letter. But first, we pray."

165

Chapter 21

Amy locked the door behind the police officer. He'd been kinder than the first one, but he didn't sound hopeful of finding fingerprints or being able to identify them if they were present. Still, he'd listened, made notes, and taken the letter and envelope as evidence.

"Michael, where are you?" His mad dash from the house had scared Amy far more than the letter. What had Gilles' friend said on the phone?

Despite the warmth of the room, Amy shivered. She'd never seen Michael that off-balance. Nor had Aunt Bay, from the woman's urgent prayer when he left.

She wandered into the kitchen. Aunt Bay was pulling leftovers from the fridge. Amy's stomach quaked. "I can't eat, not while Michael's out there somewhere."

Aunt Bay shot her a sharp look. "He's not lost in the woods. He went to meet someone who's been trying to help you."

"Someone anonymous who claims to be helping. Michael's so protective that sometimes he doesn't think straight. What if it's a trap?"

"If it was a trap, wouldn't they target you? You'd have gone, too, without a second thought." Aunt Bay took a plate from the cupboard. "I need to eat. There's plenty here when you're ready, and for Michael when he comes home."

One of the knives in the wooden block stuck out farther

than the others. Amy nudged it into place. "You make me feel like I'm overreacting, but you saw him too."

Michael's aunt snorted. "Child, if I thought you were overreacting, I'd straight-out tell you. I'm not afraid for his safety, but I'm concerned about whatever he learned. Until there's something productive I can do, I choose to keep calm and go about my business. For now, that means food."

The phone rang, and Amy dove for it. Caller ID showed Safia's number. Swallowing her disappointment, Amy tried to sound cheerful. "Hello."

"Amy, it's Safia. Is everyone all right? I just got in, and Dafiq says a police car was there. He's sulking because his father wouldn't allow him to run over to see it."

Amy grinned. Obviously the boy hadn't seen the previous cruiser. "We're okay, thanks. It wasn't a break-in, or anything else to concern the neighbourhood. More like hate mail."

"But why?"

"Someone's mad I asked questions about Gilles' and my plane crash. If I wasn't suspicious before, I would be now."

"Oh, Amy, be careful. Keep your security system on, just in case."

"We will. Give Dafiq a hug for me, and another one for Aunt Bay." Amy replaced the phone. "Dafiq saw the police car."

"Why am I not surprised?" Aunt Bay put her plate in the microwave. "It wouldn't be overreacting to text Michael and ask how long he'll be."

"And if his answer reassures me that he's okay, so much the better?"

"Naturally."

Michael's answer didn't reassure either one of them. *Don't wait up. And don't worry.*

They did wait up, but Amy tried to follow Aunt Bay's example and not worry. Finally they went to bed.

Michael came home well after midnight. Amy made herself stay in bed, but she heard Aunt Bay call out to him. He grunted something indistinct and went straight to his room, footsteps heavy.

Amy woke the next morning thick-headed and parched, with a sour taste in her mouth. Only exhaustion from the previous night had let her sleep. Whatever she'd dreamed before waking cast a heavy dread over her spirit. Dread and a fear for Michael, even though her brain knew he was home.

The house was silent. Amy flung back the covers and slid out of bed. Silent half-prayers flitted through her mind, with the more practical thought that Michael would need a good breakfast.

She was puttering in the kitchen when the alarm console by the front door beeped. Aunt Bay, deactivating it to fetch the newspaper? Moments later, Michael's aunt walked into the room. She sniffed appreciatively. "I could get used to this."

"There are cheese scones in the oven, and I'm about to start the bacon. How did you sleep?"

"Short and sweet. You?"

"I slept." Amy slit the bacon package and placed the first strips on the grill. "Do you want to wait for Michael, or should I start your eggs now?"

Aunt Bay poured herself a glass of orange juice. "I'll wait." She settled at the table with the paper.

When Amy heard the sound of running water from upstairs, she made fresh coffee. Bacon sizzled and popped on the grill. What wasn't eaten this morning could be crumbled in salads or added to pizza. Amy's taste buds popped. Homemade pizza sounded good. Maybe for Sunday, when they could unwind after the open house.

A while later, Michael came in. "What's this? I figured you two would be mad at me, and here you are, making a feast."

His eyelids drooped, and even a shower and a shave couldn't make him look energetic. What had Gilles' friend said? And how could it have taken so long?

His aunt spoke first. "Amy knows you'll talk better on a full stomach."

Michael shoved a hand through his hair, leaving damp tufts sticking up every which way. "It was definitely sabotage. Gilles was the intended target. The man I spoke with has people he can ask for help. Until we hear from him, one of us stays with Amy at all times and we leave the alarm on, even during the day. Except for the open house, but I'm hoping to hear from him before then."

Amy took the frying pan off the heat and shut off the burner. The eggs could wait. "There's more to it than that. You were gone a long time."

A strange expression crossed his face. "I can't tell you any more."

Amy lodged her fists on her hips. "Says who?"

"The guy. His name's... Nathin. Nathin Ayon." Michael scowled. "From what he said, I agree."

Aunt Bay stood and crossed to the cabinets. "And you're sure we can trust him?" She snagged a mug and passed it to Michael.

"Absolutely."

A sharp scent stung Amy's nose. She spun and grabbed a flipper just as Aunt Bay unplugged the grill. Four black shapes of what used to be bacon lay crisp and stiff. Amy chipped them up and dropped the pieces on a plate to cool before disposing of them.

Aunt Bay cranked open the window. "Michael, I don't care how much this fellow talked, there's no way you spent all night listening. Where were you?"

"I learned something about Gilles." He focused on pouring his coffee. "I needed some space."

Amy still held the flipper, and her fingers curled tighter around it. "What did you learn?"

Michael didn't look her way. "I can't tell you. I'm sorry."

"He was my fiancé. I have a right to know."

"I agree. But for now that's how it is."

~~~

Paintings brightened the walls throughout the main floor of the house, along with prints of all sizes, framed and unframed, on easels and display stands. Amy ran her fingers along the edge of a white, wooden frame showcasing a dew-laden spider web sparkling against a deep blue sky. If Michael pronounced his newest painting ready in the morning, they'd hang it here and move the spider's strands to a secondary position.

Judging by the volume of his music, things weren't going well in the studio. No wonder, after the upset of yesterday and his late night. Still, this was his biggest event of the year, and the show would go on. With or without the image of melting snow dripping from red winter berries that he felt still needed "something".

Amy wandered through the artwork, adjusting an angle here and a display stand there. She double-checked the office. Tidy. The living room had been emptied of their personal items and turned into an intimate salon, displaying small and mid-sized prints of Michael's originals.

Later tonight, they'd clear the kitchen. In the morning, the caterers would roll in. Amy swiped her palms on her jeans. First, dinner with a perfect stranger — her father.

She scurried upstairs to change out of her work clothes. Michael had done most of the lugging, but she'd picked up dust marks and even a stain from somewhere. She stared into her closet. What to wear, to impress a man whose opinion had her heart skittering? Objectively, it shouldn't matter at all. Practically, it turned her into a six-year-old.

Four-thirty already. She had at least an hour, but he'd said he'd be here as soon as he could finish his meeting. Amy's hand shot into the closet and pulled a flowing, emerald-green blouse from a hanger. She loved how the silky material felt against her skin. Sensible black pants and shoes would keep it from looking like she was trying too hard.

Amy frowned into the mirror. There wasn't much she could do about the dark circles under her eyes. She undid the functional ponytail and gave her hair a good brushing, then let it fall free against her back.

By the time she walked downstairs, Amy had achieved a calm-and-collected look. Inside, a butterfly migration was in full swing. She poked her head into the kitchen. The roast smelled delicious. Aunt Bay stood at the sink peeling carrots.

Amy peeked into the pot on the stove. Chunked potatoes, resting in water so they wouldn't discolour. Her mom used to do that, too, when she wanted to prepare ahead. "So, what, you don't want to miss anything once he arrives?"

"Or I want to go upstairs so I won't eavesdrop. Although Michael or I will have to turn on the vegetables when it's time."

"Do you want me to cut up the carrots?"

"Sure. My hands are pretty good today, but why do them in?" Aunt Bay took a final swipe at the carrot in her hand, and laid it down on the cutting board.

"Sliced or diced?" Amy pulled a bib apron over her head and grabbed a hair elastic from the junk drawer.

"I was going to slice them, for a honey-ginger glaze."

"Sliced it is."

Aunt Bay spread an autumn-leafed cloth on the table and set out cutlery and glassware.

When Amy finished the carrots, she hung up the apron and released her hair. "Do you think this top is too much?"

"What do you think?"

Amy grinned. "I like it."

"Then it's perfect. And you look gorgeous. They'll both think so."

"They? Michael never notices what I wear."

"Child, he's an artist. He's hard-wired to see beauty." Aunt Bay's eyes narrowed. "But as we've observed today, he can be very closed-mouthed."

"Amen to that. Will you wait with me for my father, or do you have things to do?"

"Nothing I can't do once he gets here."

They settled in the living room, Amy watching the driveway. She tried to respond to Aunt Bay's conversational cues, but her thoughts bounced from her father to Michael's secret about Gilles and back.

Finally a car crept along the drive and stopped by Aunt Bay's purple SUV. A jolt of adrenaline shot Amy from her chair. "He's here."

"So it would seem. I'll get Michael, and give you a minute alone. Then if you could introduce us, we'll fade into the woodwork until it's time to cook those vegetables."

Amy gave the older woman an impulsive peck on the cheek. "Thank you."

Aunt Bay left the room first. Amy perched on the edge of her chair, waiting for the doorbell. Pulling the door open ahead of time would look too eager. She scuffed a toe against the laminate floor. After all the moving around today, leaving her cane in her room wasn't the wisest choice. But she didn't want to play on Neal's sympathy. If he liked her, let it be for her strengths.

The bell pealed. Amy gulped a deep breath. The zinging sensation in her stomach had upgraded from butterfly wings to swooping birds, but she made herself walk sedately to the entrance.

The cool metal doorknob grounded her. She turned it,

swung the door inward. And stood face to face with her
father.

Chapter 22

Neal Williamson was taller than Amy had expected, and a bit heavier than his online photos showed. Amy's gaze swept pale blond hair cut short around the ears, a florid complexion with a long nose that broadened at the tip. She met his eyes, blue and somewhat wary. Was he regretting this?

She stepped back to let him in. "Neal. I'm glad you came." Her voice carried a flutter, as if one of the birds had escaped.

A cardboard cake box dangled by its strings at his right side. He set it on the floor and extended his hand. "It seems stiff to shake hands with my daughter, but shall we?"

His grip was strong, his palm dry. Not nervous after all? But he was, by the tightness around his eyes.

Amy liked his direct approach, and the slow smile that crept out of hiding when their hands clasped.

Neal picked up the cake box and offered it to Amy. "The hotel desk clerk said I couldn't go wrong with a dessert from the Seaport Market."

"You didn't need to bring anything, but their bakery choices are amazing. Thank you." Amy reached for the box.

"And I found this outside the door. A child must have dropped it." Neal held out a fashion doll in a glittery wrap.

"That's odd. Our neighbours have a little boy, but no girls." Amy turned at the sound of footsteps on the stairs. "Neal, I'd like you to meet Beatrice Rockland and Michael

Stratton. Michael, Aunt Bay, Neal Williamson. My father."
They knew that, but it felt good to be able to say it — to
acknowledge the relationship and to not fear their
judgement.

Amy watched the hand-shaking and tested the tones of
their greetings. What if they didn't like one another?

"What do you have there?" Aunt Bay's sharp question
came out of nowhere.

"Just a doll I picked up from the step. Amy says there are
no little girls around, though." Neal held it out. "I've heard
of duct-tape dresses, but never aluminum foil."

Michael's aunt took it, frowning. The doll's head popped
off, long hair trailing as it bounced across the floor. Aunt
Bay shrieked and jumped back.

When was the last time Aunt Bay let anything startle
her? Amy tried to catch Michael's eye, but he had ducked
under an easel to retrieve the errant head.

Neal apologized. "I tried to put it back on."

Aunt Bay stared at the slim figure in her trembling hand.
"Michael?"

He handed her the head, sliding the hair through his
fingers. His face had taken on the waxy tint from the other
night.

Amy went rigid, limbs frozen. "It's — me. Isn't it? Hair
like mine. Silver clothes."

Michael took the cake box from Amy's unresisting
fingers and handed it to Aunt Bay. He pulled her into his
arms in a grip that barely let her breathe.

Cold, so cold... but his warmth enveloped her. One hand
pressed her head against his chest, caressed her hair. Amy
caught a few of his whispered words. Praying. Michael was
praying. For her. She burst into tears.

Behind her, Aunt Bay's clipped tones informed Neal what
had been happening.

His voice rose in protest. "Amy, come home with me. It's

not safe here."

Michael's arms crushed Amy's ribs. He spoke over her head. "They'll find her anywhere."

"She's my daughter. I want to help."

"She's my—"

Michael's face pressed into Amy's hair and his hold relaxed enough to let her breathe. Her heart banged against her ribs, so hard and fast that he had to feel it. Would he think its pace, her arms' frantic grip, was only fear? Did she want him to know the rest, since he clearly didn't share the emotion?

He cleared his throat. "My responsibility to keep safe."

Whatever he'd been going to say, these words didn't carry much clout. Amy could practically hear the electric charge of the two men's eyes meeting over her head.

Aunt Bay's approaching heels clicked on the tile. "That's enough testosterone. There'll be an officer here shortly. In the mean time, shall we sit? Amy, Neal, it's a shame your first meeting had to be spoiled like this. You go into the living room and I'll make us some coffee. Michael will help me." Her tone made it an order.

It felt like Michael pressed a kiss into Amy's hair before releasing her. Her lips twisted. Wishful thinking on her part.

Her arms didn't want to let him go. "Thank you," Amy whispered, drying her eyes on her sleeve. The tears turned the silky green fabric almost black.

She turned to her father, staying as close to Michael's side as she could. "I should have told you on the phone, instead of waiting to see you in person. Thank you for not bolting straight out the door. It's not your fight."

His face settled into grim lines. "When you accepted me into your life, it became my fight." He tossed out a laugh that didn't fool anyone. "I never backed down from a scrap on the ice, and I'm too set in my ways to change now."

A long look passed between Neal and Michael. Then

Michael stepped forward, one hand trailing across Amy's back until he lost contact. The other hand reached for Neal's. "Then we're on the same side."

Neal gave a crisp nod and took his hand. "The police should take this seriously now that it's escalated to a physical threat."

Aunt Bay huffed. "I certainly hope so. What about Gilles' friend and his contacts?"

Michael pulled out his cell phone. "He'll be furious. But he needs to know. Excuse me while I make this call." He walked into the gallery.

The office door clicked shut. Did he really need that much privacy? They all knew what had happened. Amy rubbed her palms against her upper arms for warmth. "I guess now we wait for the police. Again."

Amy led her father to the living room. She dropped into her favourite chair and elevated her leg to ease her hip. Her other foot tapped the floor.

Neal stood with his back to the window, feet wide and hands clasped behind his back. "No one knows we're connected. Fly west and stay at my place until the authorities solve this. Come back to your job and your life here when it's safe."

So far away... Would absence make Michael's heart grow fonder, or would she slip his mind entirely? "This is our busiest time of the year with exhibits and shows."

"I'm sure they'd rather hire a fill-in worker than see you hurt."

Amy's toes tapped faster. "Michael said they'd find me anywhere."

"Assuming he's right, it would give the authorities more time to catch them first. I don't like this contact who'll only speak with him."

"He started by texting me to stop asking questions. Maybe I made him mad by not cooperating."

"Apparently you inherited a touch of my bullheadedness." Neal rocked back and forth on his heels. "Use it wisely."

Amy smiled. "It's come in handy so far."

Aunt Bay poked her head in the doorway. "Coffee's ready, if you're interested."

Neal straightened. "I'll come and get it. No need to deliver. Amy?"

"None for me, thanks."

He returned with a mug of coffee and a tall glass of water. "Beatrice thought you might like this."

"Thanks." Amy cradled the glass carefully in her lap. Maybe the focus on not spilling it would slow her still-jittery pulse.

After a few false starts, Amy and Neal fell into an exchange of stories about her mother, Isobel. Neal's memories spanned a brief time, but they helped Amy see her mother differently than she had as a child. Her own anecdotes brought smiles.

They'd somehow progressed to comparing cancer caregiver experiences when the doorbell rang. Amy placed her half-finished drink on the side table. "They'll probably join us in here." Would this be good cop, bad cop, or new cop?

Aunt Bay ushered a uniformed officer and two others in civilian dress into the room. The lead officer held a clear plastic bag with the broken doll.

Michael followed, carrying chairs from the kitchen. "Excuse the art on display everywhere. We have an open house tomorrow." He glanced at the man in uniform. "Unless you tell us otherwise."

Amy took her foot off the stool. "You've worked too hard to cancel."

Michael still looked pale. What had Gilles' friend said? "Your safety comes first."

The officer scanned the room. "I'm Constable Arnsberger. My associates, Finn and Kane, bring some special expertise to the case. They'll make the call on the event going ahead. Which one of you discovered the doll?"

Neal lifted a hand from the arm of his chair. "Neal Williamson. I found it on the doorstep when I arrived. I assumed it was a neighbour's lost toy, and brought it inside."

"You were unaware of the previous warnings?"

"Correct."

Aunt Bay told the rest of the story and fixed a stern eye on Constable Arnsberger. "How are you going to stop these people and keep Amy safe?"

"Ms. Rockland, I can assure you we will do everything in our power to ensure the safety of each one of you. Ms. Silver is clearly the primary target, but it may be that those close to her are in danger as well." He gestured to Finn and Kane. "With your permission, I'd like to ask my associates to go through the house and assess your security."

"Michael?"

"Of course."

Once they left, Arnsberger settled in one of the kitchen chairs and dropped the bagged doll at his feet. He opened a notebook. "We know essentially what happened, but I'd like to hear what each of you has to add. Impressions, related incidents, anything that comes to mind. Most of it won't be connected, but sometimes what looks like an insignificant detail can be critical."

All eyes turned to Amy. She focused on Arnsberger. "It has to be about the plane crash. I've had warning texts from this guy who claims he was Gilles' friend, and flak from Gilles' father. A phone call, a letter, and now this doll. And Troy — the reporter who started the sabotage idea. Someone ran him off the road."

Arnsberger made a note. "We couldn't be sure that was connected. I'll take another look."

Amy shifted in her chair. "Gilles' father knows who's behind this." And he'd kill her for saying so. "He's terrified. But we can't let them win."

Michael pressed his lips together and stared at the floor.

The officer glanced at him, then back at Amy. "Would you give me his contact information?"

"He may be too scared to talk to you. What if they find out?" She brought up the contact list on her phone and read off Luc's phone number. "I don't know if he's still in town. He shuttles between here and Montreal."

Aunt Bay didn't have much to add. Michael spoke even less. Arnsberger's gaze made Amy feel vaguely guilty, but she had nothing else to offer. And this problem wasn't her doing.

Finn joined them. "Everything is as secure as it can be in a private dwelling. Keep your doors and windows locked as a precaution, and let your security system provider know there's been a threat."

Arnsberger stood. "Maybe they're just trying to scare you enough to stop asking questions, but we can't be sure of that. Call if you encounter anything suspicious." He picked up the evidence bag. "Is Kane nearly done?"

"Almost."

Amy kept her eyes averted from the doll in the bag. "What about the show tomorrow? Can we go ahead?"

"There's been no clear threat connected with the event. Whatever they plan, they won't want to have witnesses. I see no need to cancel." Finn's grim tone did not inspire confidence.

"Thank you." Michael rose and shook both officers' hands.

As everyone stood and filtered toward the door, Amy found herself beside Arnsberger. She hesitated. "Constable, I know you're busy, but would you have time to let my neighbour's son have a look at your cruiser? He's seen them here a lot lately, and he's only four. It'd be a big deal for him."

Constable Arnsberger checked his watch. "I think we could fit that in. Let me lock the evidence in the trunk. He doesn't need to see that."

"Thank you. I'll phone them."

Safia and Dafiq arrived in minutes. The boy's brown eyes shone, and if his grin grew any wider, his face would split. Arnsberger showed him around the car and even let him sit behind the wheel. A siren pierced the air. Amy jumped, then giggled at the embarrassment on Safia's face.

The car door opened, and the boy zoomed to his mother's side. "Didya hear? He let me do the siren!"

Arnsberger followed, smiling. "He was careful to ask before he touched anything." He squatted beside the boy. "It was good to meet you, Dafiq. You take good care of your mom, now."

Dafiq seemed to grow visibly. "I will. Daddy too. I wanna be a police officer when I grow up. I've been watching for bad guys."

Arnsberger raised an eyebrow. "Have you seen any?"

"There was someone sneaking around Mr. Michael's house today." His high-pitched voice stopped the other conversations.

Still crouched to Dafiq's eye level, Arnsberger looked up at Safia. "I'd like to hear that story."

Chapter 23

Amy looked around the table. Nothing like a little danger to accelerate the bonding between her and Neal. If thinking about the broken doll didn't make her shiver, she'd almost want to thank her unseen enemy.

The officers had finally gone, with a side-trip to Safia's house so Dafiq could tell his story with his father present. Safia had whispered a promise to phone if he saw anything else.

Hungry and with the ice definitely broken, Amy, Neal, Michael, and Aunt Bay had talked their way through dinner. Amy made her slice of hazelnut-spice cake last as long as she could. She licked the crumbs from her fork. "Neal, this was amazing."

"I took a chance. Your mother loved spice cake."

"I have her recipe somewhere."

Michael raised a hand. "I volunteer to taste-test it."

Aunt Bay swatted his arm. "You already work this girl too hard."

"I do not. House rules. Everyone takes a turn in the kitchen, and what better way to spend it than making cake?"

"Listen to yourself. If you ate as much as you talked about it, we'd have to roll you up the stairs at night."

Neal drained his coffee cup and pushed back from the table. "It's been good to meet you all." His eyes lingered on Amy. "Especially my daughter. I should get out of your way and let you recover from the unwanted excitement. Please think about coming home with me until this settles?"

He directed a sharp look at Michael. "In the meantime, keep her safe. And keep me in the loop."

Michael nodded, face grim.

Amy walked him to the door. As Neal turned to leave, she seized her courage and gave him a quick hug. "Thank you. This means more than you know." She retreated, face burning. What if he wasn't a hugger?

Neal's throat worked. "It means a lot to me, too. I'm proud of you, Amy Silver. Stay safe. And have a great show tomorrow. I'll phone you on Sunday." He stepped out into the night.

Amy locked up behind him, and pressed her palm against the door. "Good night... Dad."

She went back to the kitchen to help with cleanup. "Thank you both so much for welcoming my father." *And for not judging me.* How could she have feared that for so long? But wasn't that what children did? Accepted the labels adults — and sometimes classmates — attached to them?

Aunt Bay looked up from wiping the table. "Neal seems like a good man. I wish we could have met without the drama."

At the sink, Michael made an affirmative-sounding grunt. He tackled a suds-filled roasting pan with a scrub brush. "Are you glad you found one another?"

"I am. He's nothing like I'd dreamed as a child, but he's real. I think we hit it off okay. I feel... I feel like I belong."

Michael concentrated on scrubbing the roaster. "You already belonged. With us."

"I value that too, Michael. But there's something about your own flesh and blood... I knew the hurt is greater if they reject you, but I didn't know the other side of it. How good it feels when they choose you." Amy snagged a tea towel from the hook and picked up the smaller pot from the dish drainer.

"So you're going to let him take you away."

"What?"

Aunt Bay returned her cloth to the sink. "Michael, we all want what's best for Amy. If that means we let her go, then we let her go. With our blessing."

The scowl he aimed at the roaster should have blistered its finish. He rinsed it and plunked it in the drainer.

Amy half-turned toward him and leaned her hip into the counter. "You need to dial back on your protective streak. I am petite, but I'm all grown up. I won't be taken anywhere I choose not to go. I've gotta say, right now you're not making me want to stay." Except leaving — permanently — would break her heart.

She grabbed the roaster and spun away from him, wiping it with energy that matched Michael's scrubbing zeal.

Behind her, Aunt Bay chuckled. "I expect you had to dish out that petite-grown-up line more than a few times in the corporate world."

Amy turned to face her. "You have no idea. If I wore heels and makeup, the guys in the branch thought it was an invitation, and if I wore flats and dressed low-key, they treated me like a child. They were fine with the other women, but I earned every scrap of respect I built there. Sometimes the customers were worse than my co-workers."

She set the roaster on the counter, warmed by a sudden memory. "Although I met Gilles in the bank." She smiled. "He stepped into my office, claimed he had an appointment, and insisted I go to lunch with him before he'd discuss his needs. I said no. Every day he returned with a gift... chocolate, an aloe vera plant, a little plush beaver with a note that said I worked too hard... a framed photo of himself for my desk."

Aunt Bay arched an eyebrow. "Very Gilles."

"Anyone else would have been labelled a stalker. My

manager offered to ban him from the premises, but Gilles didn't cause trouble, and he never hung around to bother me. By the second week, my co-workers all thought he was a great guy. Some had even gone for drinks with him. That Friday's gift was a bright red journal and pen. He'd already written in it — a list of reasons 'Why I need to date Gilles Renaud.' His list filled the first page. Some of it was pretty out-there. He numbered the lines on the next three pages and left them for me to fill out. I looked at it all weekend. Monday, we went to lunch."

"He was one of a kind." Michael shook his head, a pensive smile on his face. "So, did you finish the list?"

Amy nodded. "By then he'd changed the title to 'Why I need to marry Gilles Renaud.' It sounds like a bad movie, but Gilles made it magical. And real. Michael, remember when he phoned you to vouch for him?"

He laughed. "Suddenly I'm talking to this strange woman and giving a character reference. And she says Gilles asked her to marry him." Pain filled Michael's eyes. "He didn't deserve what happened."

"We're all agreed on that." Aunt Bay took the tea towel from Amy and hung it to dry. "I'm glad we've had you here with us. If you need to go, I hope you'll come back. Especially since you and I were about to start looking into the Bible together."

Amy's shoulders slumped. "I don't know what to do."

The doorbell rang. Amy stiffened, but Michael was already leaving the room.

His aunt called after him. "Use the peephole."

Male voices sounded from the entrance. A minute later, Michael returned with a swarthy, heavy-set man with a bushy, black moustache. "This is Del. He works with Gilles' friend, Nathin. When I phoned earlier, Nathin said to text when our guest had gone, that there'd be a package for us."

Del extracted a brown bag from a cavernous pocket in his

coat. He looked at the table. "May I sit?"

"Please." Michael and Amy joined him.

Aunt Bay reached for the kettle. "Would you like some coffee or tea?"

"No, thank you, Ma'am. This won't take long."

Aunt Bay took the fourth seat, peering at the bag.

Del produced three identical black objects, each smaller than a compact flip cell phone. "Keep these on you at all times. Or within reach, if you're in the shower. My organization is working with the local police on this, but out of sight. We don't want to spook our targets now."

He slid a unit toward each of them. "Amy, I wish you'd taken Nathin's first warning to stay out of this, but it may work out for the best. You've agitated these people. That may lead to mistakes on their part. Unfortunately, now you're in the line of fire." He blinked rapidly. "So to speak. We don't anticipate any shooting."

Amy's heart dropped. She met Michael's eyes. "What have I done?"

He reached for her hand. "None of us expected this. You were right that Gilles deserved justice."

"But I've put you both in danger and we still don't know why."

Del leaned on the table. "I know why. And we will bring an end to this. For the next few weeks, I want you to act like everything's normal, but be vigilant."

"Few weeks?" The squeak was back in Amy's voice. "What if I left? I have a place I could go."

Above the huge moustache, Del's eyes were compassionate. "Amy, if you have to run, be sure to let us know where you'll be. I can have someone liaise with you there. Ideally I'd prefer to keep the three of you together. You can watch one another's backs."

Aunt Bay prodded the black device with her index finger. "What do these do, and how do we use them?"

"Basically they're stripped-down cell phones with preset speed dials. Hit number one, you'll reach my team. I want to know anything that seems unusual, anything that makes you nervous. Don't second-guess, just call. Until this is settled, you're allowed to be paranoid."

He spread one hand on the table, palm down. "Play things very casual, and say nothing more about the plane crash. Another of my team is having this same conversation with the reporter who started it all."

Amy picked up the little phone. "Troy won't back down from an investigation."

"He will for the sake of three innocent civilians. Or at least to be first in line for the story when it breaks." Del pulsed his thumb on the table. "We're lining up our evidence. If you don't make any more waves, best case these people will think they've scared you enough and they'll leave you alone."

"Worst case?" Aunt Bay asked the question on Amy's lips.

"Worst case, if you can't even phone us, watch this." Del picked up Michael's device. "See this slider here on the side? Push it in and slide it this way, and it'll send an alarm signal to my team. This is for extreme situations only. We don't want to draw attention to you by scrambling a rescue force unnecessarily."

Amy's imagination flashed a picture of soldiers in flak jackets, hefting enormous rifles. Her skin felt suddenly clammy. "But you think we'll be okay."

"I think so. But I'm not a fortune teller." Del's smile was as big as his moustache.

It didn't comfort Amy at all.

Chapter 24

Emilie showed up at ten on Saturday morning, yawning and clutching a take-out coffee, offering to help set up. Aunt Bay lifted an eyebrow at Amy. They'd been up since six for a sturdy breakfast and last-minute clean-up. The displays were carefully positioned, without Michael's newest painting. Amy had heard him in his studio late last night, but he hadn't found the final element of serenity he needed for the piece.

Amy fingered the security device in her pocket. This didn't feel real. How could a simple question about their plane crash plunge her into danger — along with Michael and Aunt Bay? Without even the satisfaction of answers?

She grinned at Emilie. "Love the orange hair."

"It's good for autumn. I'll match the trees."

Michael came out of the kitchen. "Hey, Emilie. Thanks for coming. The caterers will be here soon, but until then we have a few quiet minutes. You three chat for a bit. There's something I need to check on."

Aunt Bay followed him toward the stairs. "I'm going to have a brief lie-down while I can. Getting old is a pain."

"You'll always be young at heart." Amy went into the living room and sank into a chair. Her hip had a long day ahead. At least with Del's promise to mingle with the visitors, she didn't feel too unsafe.

They'd agreed not to tell Emilie about the danger, or

about Del's investigation. If something spooked the girl during the open house, who knew what she'd do? Plus, if her father found out, they had no guarantee he could keep it from his enemies.

Emilie surveyed the art arranged around the room, sipping her coffee. "Michael does such good work." She settled across from Amy. "You look terrible. No offence."

Amy bit her tongue. Who looked their best in the middle of setting up for an event? "I'll change and do my makeup once I see if the caterers need help with anything."

"No, I mean it. Are you sleeping okay? Nothing's going on, is it?"

"This hasn't been a great week for sleep, but I can make it. I'll crash tonight."

"Can you sleep late while Michael and his aunt go to church, or will you be scared again?"

"That was one time. But as it happens, I'm going with them." Not that Michael would leave her home alone now, security system and special phone or not.

Emilie's carefully-shaped eyebrows pulled together. "Are you sure that's a good idea?"

"Em, I want to go. They joke sometimes, but neither of them would really pressure me about it."

Emilie's mouth turned down. "You don't see how much Michael is influencing you."

This from the girl with the long-term crush on him. Amy kept her tone level. "I went with Aunt Bay during the week, and I want to go back. I've always wanted to know God better. I was... afraid."

"Of what? Being bored out of your mind? My parents dragged us to mass at Notre-Dame Cathedral once. It was painful."

"Never mind. How are classes?"

"One of my profs looks like he died years ago and nobody noticed. But I'm learning some event management things that can kick Michael's promotion up a few notches next year." Instead of elaborating, Emilie switched to an animated description of a prank they'd pulled on the "dead" prof.

Amy reclined her chair and settled in to enjoy the tale. Gilles' sister shared his storytelling gene, although her accounts often had a more acidic edge.

In mid-sentence, Emilie set her coffee on the floor beside her chair. With both hands free to gesture, her story spilled faster. Another bubbled out behind it.

They were both laughing by the time Emilie stopped and picked up her cup for another drink. Again, her eyes pinned Amy. "Something is definitely wrong. You're on guard, even when you laugh. You can tell me. It's Michael, isn't it?" She glanced at the door and lowered her voice. "You need to get out from under his control. While you still can."

Emilie's guess couldn't be more wrong, but her ominous tone stirred Amy's uneasiness. Amy tucked her feet up on the chair and hugged herself. "It's not Michael."

"Then what is it?"

Amy picked at the hem of her shirt. "You're not the only one who wants me to leave. I've had some nasty... messages this week."

"Hey, I never said I wanted you to leave! I'm concerned about your wellbeing if you stay in Michael's protective bubble. It's like you're another display in his exhibit of life."

Could Miss Drama Queen be the one behind the messages? Amy shook her head. The first two, maybe, if Emilie considered her a rival for Michael's affection. But not the death threat. Plus, Del and his team connected the threats to Gilles' murder.

Murder. Amy hadn't thought of that starkly before, but whether they'd planned to kill him or simply scare him, Gilles had died. A wave of sorrow pressed her into her seat.

She would not go there now. Not with Emilie, and not hours before Michael's open house. He needed a poised, collected hostess, not a red-eyed wraith. Imagining how eager Emilie would be to take her place drove back the sadness and lit enough of a fire to enable Amy to smile and meet the girl's appraising gaze. "You should be writing novels. Or plays. His exhibit of life?"

"You know what I mean. But you said someone's sending nasty messages. Who?"

Amy lifted a shoulder. "No idea. Ever since I started asking questions about the plane crash, people have been upset. Your father's right, I need to let it go."

Emilie peeled the lid from her take-out cup and drained the last drops. She stuffed the lid inside and bounced the empty cup on her leg. "It could be Michael."

"What?"

"It sounds crazy, but listen. He wanted you to stop, didn't he?"

"Along with your parents, the flight club and who knows how many other people?"

The cup tapped faster. "If he could scare you into stopping, he'd increase his hold on you. The next time you want to do something and he objects, he can remind you what happened. Send you another threat if you try anyway."

Amy stood. "I don't have time for this." Emilie adored Michael far too much to believe he'd behave this way, but now was not the time to call her on her unsubtle attempt to clear the field. Amy started for the door.

Emilie gasped.

The sound turned Amy without conscious thought. "What's the matter?"

Eyes wide, fingers pressed to her mouth, Emilie stared long enough that Amy glanced back at the doorway.

It was empty. Amy released the new phone she hadn't known she gripped. She slid her hand from her pocket and ran it over her hair. "You scared me."

Emilie blinked. "I just realized what it is. Michael took

you in, but none of us expected you to stay so long. He can't ask you to go, so he's doing this weird passive-aggressive thing. Overprotecting you so you'll feel trapped and want to leave. Using anonymous threats since he can't speak it directly. Amy, you're in the way and he's too sweet to tell you."

The vibration of an approaching engine saved Amy the need to reply. The caterers' van drove past the window. "Excuse me." She hurried from the room.

~~~

Amy stood for a few minutes looking out the kitchen window at the peaceful evergreens and the light glinting off the bay. Behind her, the catering duo bustled with the efficiency of a well-choreographed routine. Clothing rustled, plates clinked, and their light chatter never faltered.

It wasn't like her to be nervous about an exhibit. That was Michael's turf. Hers was to smooth the waters, if she could allow herself that little pun. Today, with the week's threats, meeting her father, and now Emilie's blatant manipulation, Amy's own "water" was choppy.

Hello, God, my adopted Father? Thank You for caring. Please help today to go well for Michael, and keep us safe. Amen.

She needed time to learn about prayer, and more about God's love and plan for her life. A little shiver of anticipation zinged through Amy's spirit at the thought of church tomorrow. To the people, she'd be a stranger, but to God, she was accepted.

The thought lifted her shoulders and brought her back to what mattered now. Michael's work. Supporting him and Aunt Bay. The troubling, extraneous influences would keep for another day.

Except for Emilie, here in the midst of it all. Amy turned

from the view and went back to the living room. Spotless. Emilie hadn't forgotten her coffee cup. Amy plumped decorative pillows in the two chairs and slid a finger along the left edge of one of the wall paintings to straighten it. She'd be doing that all day, especially once patrons started touching the frames.

She walked through the entryway into the gallery, assessing and making minute adjustments.

Michael emerged from the office, Emilie chattering at his back. Amy flashed him a sympathetic grin. Poor guy, he didn't need this, especially now that he knew the girl's feelings. He wouldn't want to hurt her, but the reddish tinge to his ears showed his frustration.

Amy checked her watch. "Emilie, if you need a drink or a snack, now's the time."

"I'm good, thanks." Emilie caught Michael's arm. "Wait a minute. Your hair." Deft fingers straightened hair that had been less out of place than the pictures Amy'd been adjusting.

Couldn't Emilie see the way he tensed? Amy cringed for him. Michael might never love her, but he deserved someone who'd complete him. Emilie would only chip at him, marring what she tried to polish.

Emilie reached for his collar, and Michael twitched visibly. She pouted. "Stand still. Don't you want to look your best?"

"This is about the art, not about me." His eyes pleaded with Amy, but what could she do?

Any perceived interference would only push Emilie to greater extremes. Amy lifted empty hands and mouthed *Suffering for your art.*

Michael rolled his eyes. "Emilie, please. I can dress myself."

"I'm just trying to help." Her voice throbbed with emotion. She turned away from him and took a few tentative steps toward the exit. As she passed Amy, the girl's eyes shone with hope, not hurt.

Michael opened his mouth but Amy shook her head in a quick *no*. He frowned for a second, then relaxed. "The caterers are ready?"

"I just came from the kitchen. Everything looks great."

Aunt Bay called from the main part of the house. "Where is everyone?"

Amy turned and nearly tripped over Emilie. The girl hadn't fled far at all. "Sorry!"

By one-thirty the happy buzz of conversation filled the house and gallery. The caterers wove among the guests, offering water in long-stemmed glasses and trays of cold finger food.

Amy mingled, enjoying the ambiance. Ruth and Tony arrived mid-afternoon, and Amy felt herself glowing as she introduced them to Michael. Was she proud of him, or grateful to Ruth? Or both? He thanked them warmly. "We've been encouraging Amy for so long, but sometimes a person has to hear it from strangers."

A few minutes later, walking into the living room display, Amy noticed Del chatting with a woman in blue. Her smile felt suddenly brittle. How had she forgotten the danger?

Chapter 25

Amy tidied the note cards in the display rack. Seeing Del had brought back her anxiety. She paused in front of the nearest easel, pretending to adjust the picture. Her eyes drew on the stillness of the scene, and her lips slid into a more natural smile. Michael loved Hemlock Ravine Park in Halifax, but he said the hike to the actual ravine would be too much for her hip. Instead he'd taken her to the heart-shaped pond at the park's entrance. They'd sat on a bench, watching ducks and dragonflies and a picnicking family. Once the family left, he'd taken some pictures.

This painting highlighted a curve of the shallow rock wall, with gently-rippling water and a single, upturned feather. Amy's breathing settled, and she slipped back into hostess mode, her spirit lighter. She circulated around the room, greeting those who weren't in conversations, and made her way to the entrance as one of the caterers came in carrying a tray.

On her rounds, she occasionally met Michael, Aunt Bay or Emilie. If Gilles' sister seemed perpetually in the same room as Michael, at least she had fallen into a charming support role and dropped the coquette routine. All four knew how to process a sale, and by early evening about a third of the originals bore "sold" signs on their frames.

Amy and Michael had re-stocked the framed and un-framed prints throughout the day, as well as the note cards and pads. Amy's hip ached, and she'd retrieved her cane from the closet. She'd encountered Del several times, and she'd learned not to tense when they met. He fit the role of casual visitor — unless a person noticed his eyes.

A stout woman in a bright-flowered dress advanced toward Amy. "You're the one from that plane crash."

Amy nodded, the back of her neck prickling. Did the lady pack extra volume, or had the others in the room hushed?

Shrewd eyes flicked her up and down. "Such a little thing, too. The paper made it sound like you were crippled."

Amy smiled. "Thankfully, no. I do need my cane when I'm on my feet too long." She leaned on it now.

The woman clucked her tongue. "Nasty world we live in. People taking down planes."

Amy's grip tightened on her cane. "The investigators ruled it an accident. I'm told they were quite thorough."

"Don't believe everything you hear." The woman tapped the frame of the painting beside Amy. "He does good work."

"Yes, he does. People have said it's almost healing."

"You're in a good place here, dear. I hope you thrive." She gave Amy's hand a quick squeeze and moved to the next painting.

Amy took a few slow breaths to steady herself. She hadn't lied, but had she given the impression that she'd accepted the verdict? Not that anyone here was likely involved with the killers.

"Well played."

Del's voice in her ear kicked Amy's heart into panic mode, and she couldn't stop a gasp. She turned it into a run of light coughs. When she trusted herself, she turned to face him. "Thank you. For that, and for being here today."

He nodded, then strolled away.

Amy ducked into the office for more notepads and found Emilie at the desk, writing up a sale. Amy stopped beside her. "Enjoying yourself? I think the day's going well."

"Definitely." Emilie looked up, eyes narrowing. "Who's that guy? With the moustache. I just saw you talking to him. He's been here all day."

What to say? Amy picked up a handful of pads from the shelf. "Michael asked him to come today for security. More subtle than a uniform."

"We've never needed security before."

As if it were Amy's fault. Emilie was her mother's daughter. "I told you someone wants me to leave. We didn't think they'd disrupt the open house, but better safe than sorry." She left the room.

Michael came through the gallery entrance. He brightened when their eyes met, and he joined her outside the office door. "I was on my way for some of those pads, but you're ahead of me, as usual. How's the hip?"

"Sore, but manageable." Amy glanced around the room. "It's been a great turnout. We have more customers each year, and they're buying — even with the economy the way it is."

"That's why I like the prints and these pads and cards. They're less pricey. Struggling people need art more than the rich ones."

Amy checked to be sure Emilie was still in the office. "Emilie asked about Del. I'd told her someone wanted me to leave, so I said he was here in case they tried to cause trouble today. Naturally, she blamed me."

Michael's brow crinkled. "Is it just me, or is she getting worse?"

"Hush, or she'll fix your hair again."

He flinched. "I need to do something about this. I don't want to hurt her, though."

"I know." Reluctantly, Amy left him under Emilie's watchful eye and distributed the notepads around the displays.

As she crossed the entryway, the front door opened. Troy

stepped in, one hand wrapped in a bandage. Amy's professional smile warmed to personal. "Hey, Troy, I'm glad to see you in one piece. How are you?" So she knew him better through phone calls and texts than their one meeting at the interview. He was on her side, and he cared — about her safety and about the truth. Caring had nearly cost his life.

Troy waved his bundled hand. "Could have been worse." None of the people around them seemed to pay any attention. "Where's Michael?"

Amy pointed back into the gallery. "He'll be glad to see you. Grab a drink and snack from the caterers. They'll be around again in a few minutes."

Troy ducked his head. "Catch you later. I see you're on a mission." He started for the gallery.

The entryway displayed only paintings. Amy carried on to the living room. Only a handful of people lingered here, mostly those in need of a few minutes in a seat. Amy's hip put her in that category, except she was beyond the point of a brief respite. Tonight she'd need a long, hot soak in the tub.

Painkillers, too. Why hadn't she taken one already? Amy placed the remaining notepads and exchanged pleasantries with the visitors, noting the caterers had them well-supplied, then made her exit and trudged up the stairs.

She took the pill bottle from her dresser and manipulated the child-resistant cap, resolutely ignoring the soft bed. If she lay down, she'd never get up again. A quick glass of water from the bathroom, and Amy headed downstairs again.

Her path crossed with Michael's as she went back into the gallery. The guests wouldn't notice, but his smile was thinning, and his eyes had a weary look. Amy touched his arm. "You poor introvert. It'll be over soon. Did you see Troy?"

"You're the one in pain, and you're worried about me? I got myself into this, remember. And yes, we talked. He has pictures of his car on his phone. It's hard to believe he walked away from that." Michael moved aside to allow a guest to pass, then stepped closer. "If anything happened to you—"

"It won't. It—" Amy closed her mouth. It could. Too easily. And she wouldn't see it coming. Her head darted side to side until she saw Del. She looked back at Michael. "We have to trust your friends to do their job. And trust God to look after us."

A measure of life returned to his smile. "That, we do." He brushed his fingertips against hers and turned toward the entryway.

Amy stood a moment to watch the activity before working her way through the gallery. Passing Del, she paused. "You'll be so sick of these paintings after today."

"They're restful, but I'm not paying too much attention to the inanimate parts of the event. Except the food. I'm attending to that." He passed a hand across his stomach.

"I'm glad it's been quiet."

"Me too. Slow is better than exciting, for me." Del winked.

They carried on in opposite directions around the room. Amy spotted Emilie coming out of the office. Personal conflicts aside, Gilles' sister seemed to be out-selling them all. Not that it was a competition. Getting Michael's work out was what mattered.

Emilie looked around, probably hunting Michael. The gallery door chimed, and Amy turned to welcome the newcomers.

Newcomer. Ross Zarin pulled the door closed behind him. When he saw Amy, he smiled and threaded his way among the art and visitors. He took her hand. "You look lovely. I hope it's been a good day."

"Thanks for coming. How's your father?" Amy slid her hand free. What if Emilie saw the gesture and used it to goad Michael? Or would it diminish her perception of Amy as a threat?

His dark eyes twinkled with a charm that should have had Amy melting to a puddle at his feet. "My father is fine, and he sends his best. He is very pleased with our latest paintings, and charged me to come home with another one."

Amy swept her hand to embrace the room. "Tonight it's this area and through into the main house as well. Take your time to browse, and sample the caterers' snacks as well. They're delicious."

As if summoned, one of the black-garbed caterers approached with a tray of water and food. Ross selected a glass of water, cradling it expertly in long, brown fingers. "Thank you. The food is tempting, but I'll pass." He sipped, and turned searching eyes back to Amy. "How goes the closure?"

Amy blinked, then caught his meaning. Time to trot out her story again. "I'll never have answers to everything that happened that day, but I don't need to keep searching. I can say goodbye to Gilles and begin to live my life."

Ross nodded approvingly. "Wise words. And what will the rest of your life look like? Will you continue here at the gallery?"

Emilie spoke from beside them. "Hi, Ross. Sorry to startle you, Amy." She looked at Ross and gave her head a pitying shake. "She's jumpy. Someone's been upsetting her — wants her to go away."

Those dark eyes grew piercing, as if they could see into Amy's fears. "Who would do this to you?"

Amy glanced around the room. Nobody stood near them, but still she kept her voice down. "This isn't a good time to talk about it. I don't know what to say, anyway. It must be someone I've upset by asking about the plane crash, but I don't know who. They've been sending messages telling me to leave."

"To leave? Why would that link to your accident?"

Amy spread her hands. "I haven't done anything else lately to rock anyone's boat. Gilles and Emilie's father was upset with me for reopening the family's pain. Maybe someone else was more upset about bringing up the investigation. If I don't draw any more attention to it, I hope the harassment will stop."

"One can hope." His eyes remained serious.

A man in a designer sweater approached the three of them. "Could one of you young ladies help me? I'm interested in the spider web painting near the main door."

Amy made to excuse herself, but Emilie cut her off. "No, you were in the middle of a conversation. I'll go." She gestured toward the entryway. "Lead on." She followed the customer from the room.

Standing in the middle of the room meant they were blocking traffic, as light as it now was. Amy edged toward a row of paintings. "One of the things I love about working here is I don't have to pick a favourite. I can enjoy the originals until they're sold, and there are always copies of the prints."

Ross followed her lead, and they moved slowly along the line of paintings. "Purchasing for the hotel chain means I needn't worry if I'll tire of it or if another choice would ultimately please me more."

They'd nearly circled the room. Emilie bustled past with her customer, and with a surprisingly friendly smile for Amy. Either the girl had up-sold him to buy two paintings, or the sight of Amy with Ross gave her a false sense of security. The two disappeared into the office.

Amy glanced around. Few patrons lingered in the room, and those who did seemed content to browse. "I need to get back to work. While it's quiet is a good time to check and restock the smaller products."

As she turned, Ross nodded toward her cane. "This much time on your feet is painful?"

"I'll be sore tomorrow, but it's a small price. I enjoy these shows, and I'm so proud of Michael's work."

His gaze warmed. "I hope he realizes what a gift it is to have an employee like you." A crease appeared between his brows. "But for your own health, wouldn't it be better to find a job that didn't involve so much physical strain? Amy, come and work for my father. Your business and marketing skills—"

A pair of strong arms slid under Amy's and wrapped her ribcage. Tightly. She gasped, and they loosened a fraction.

"Hello, Ross." Michael spoke before she turned to identify her assailant, and the first note of his voice turned her fight-or-flight to unnatural stillness.

Michael didn't do private displays of affection, let alone public ones. Amy glanced toward the office. If Emilie saw this, the feathers would really fly. Was this how he planned to discourage the girl's crush? Amy relaxed against his chest. Whatever the cause, she'd be a fool to resist it.

Ross' face had gone still. He raised one eyebrow at her, and she gave a small smile.

Michael kept talking. "I'm sorry to foil your attempt to steal my best worker, but I must. Amy and I—" Warmth filled his voice. "—have a private understanding. We were waiting for the next anniversary of the accident, out of respect for Gilles' memory and his family, but I see you've forced our hand."

Ross' eyes chilled to those of a hawk. They raked Amy's face and stabbed at Michael. "A simple 'no thank you' to the offer would have sufficed."

"Perhaps, but it would have put Amy in the awkward position of turning down a valued client without being able to say why. You deserve better than that. You've been so supportive to Amy, taking her to the crash site and all. This way you can be happy for her instead of concerned." Michael's voice dropped a notch. "If you could keep it to yourself until the anniversary, we'd appreciate it."

"Me and the others in the room."

Michael's embrace shifted as if he'd shrugged. He spoke into Amy's hair. "Do you mind terribly?"

Amy snuggled deeper into his hold. His heart beat against her back, almost as fast as her own.

Ross nodded gracious defeat and raised one hand. "Allow me to be the first to offer congratulations. May you be very happy together. Now, if you'll excuse me, I have a painting to select, and time is running out."

Michael held Amy in place for a long moment after Ross walked past them to the main house. A few other visitors smiled indulgently before turning back to the artwork. Amy's racing heart and Michael's arms didn't leave room for her lungs. Her breath came in shallow gasps.

What just happened? This wasn't about Emilie at all. He couldn't mean it — could he? Amy wanted to turn and read his face. See love there.

But she wouldn't. Michael didn't love her. He'd have shown some kind of sign by now.

This moment, crazy as it was, would be her treasure to remember. She wouldn't be the one to break it.

"I'm sorry." His arms slid away and he retreated.

Amy spun. The pain in his eyes matched what she'd heard in his voice. "Michael?"

"It was the first thing I could think of. I had to get you away from him."

"Why?"

"You need to stay here for now. With me. Safe. Until Del's group ends this. I'm sorry I embarrassed you. I didn't mean—"

The words kept on, but Amy's hearing froze. Cold and

shaking inside, she walked away. Past a few patrons, seeing them only as obstacles to avoid. Toward the entryway. The stairs. Her room.

Emilie would be delighted to have her out of the picture, and Michael deserved the girl's undivided attention.

 *Chapter 26*

Amy woke the next morning hungry and with a throbbing ache in her hip. Moaning, she rolled over in bed and tried some gentle movement. Good thing she'd done her stretches last night and taken a second pill.

All she'd wanted to do was succumb to an endless sleep last night, but Michael's words — his touch — had jangled her mind and emotions. Stretching had been as good a way as any to pass the time, and maybe it helped lull her body into tiredness.

Michael and Aunt Bay had each called to her through the closed door. Amy hadn't responded. Emilie's tinkling laugh had penetrated the room, as well as the shuffles and scrapes of tear-down after the open house. Troy's voice was in the mix as well. Good thing he stayed. Amy hadn't wanted Aunt Bay picking up the extra physical effort, but facing Michael again was not an option.

Amy pushed her hair away from her eyes. She couldn't hide forever. This morning would be awkward. And of course she'd committed to attending church with them today. No lying in bed until they left.

The thought propelled her to her feet. It was still early. She'd have time to soak in the tub without interfering with their bathroom usage. Amy gathered what she'd need, wrapped herself in her robe, and headed for the door.

A square of white on the floor stopped her. She

205

recognized Michael's writing.

Dear Amy,

I'm so sorry I upset you. Honestly, I wasn't trying to take liberties — especially in public like that. I know you're embarrassed, probably offended, and I hope there's a way to make this right.

My actions were inappropriate both as a friend and as an employer. All I can say in explanation is that working for Ross and his father is not a good option. Please stay here with us until the danger is resolved, and if you want to leave after that because of my behaviour, I'll be as generous with a severance package as I can. You do the books, so you know that can't be much.

Humbly,

Michael

P.S. Please don't let this keep you from church this morning. If you want me to, I'll stay home.

Amy's heart was a dead weight. Could he make his lack of feelings for her any plainer? Still she couldn't crumple the note and toss it in the wastebasket. If she had to leave this place, she'd want every connection with him, however tiny.

Church. As hard as it would be to go with Michael, she couldn't ask him to stay away. It wasn't his fault he'd trampled all over her heart and left it on the floor among the easels. And she wasn't about to back down from this next step in her relationship with God. Belonging to Him would matter more than ever if — when — she no longer belonged here.

All quiet in the hallway. Amy sneaked from her room.

When she returned, sounds of life drifted from the other bedrooms. She was still combing out her hair when one of the other doors clicked open and footsteps passed outside. Amy tensed, but no voice called to her.

It must have been Aunt Bay on the move, because when Amy arrived in the kitchen after dithering over what to wear, Michael's aunt sat with her coffee and toast, dressed and ready to go. Her face relaxed when she saw Amy's attire. "You're still coming with us."

Amy gripped the back of the chair opposite Aunt Bay. "What did Michael tell you?"

"Very little, but Emilie was more than happy to oblige."

Given the girl's high spirits during the cleanup, Michael's act hadn't fooled her. What did Ross think? And what should Amy do about it? She owed him nothing, and she didn't want to mark Michael — or herself — as a liar. Maybe she should let it go. If she ended up needing that job, she'd deal with the deception then.

"Find yourself some breakfast and sit, child. You were asleep last night when the pizza arrived."

Or trying to sleep. Amy found some grapes and served herself a dish of yogourt. Digging in the cupboard for the granola, she asked, "So what did Emilie say?"

"Her theory is that Michael has some kind of fixation about you still belonging to Gilles, with his role being a surrogate protector. Working for the Zarins would move you out of Michael's control, so he pretended you two had a personal connection to keep you here. Why a prospective employer would care about your love life, I don't know."

A fixation that wouldn't let her move past Gilles? Amy set her food on the table, trembling hands rattling the dishes. She looked at Aunt Bay. "Michael doesn't lie. But he did."

His aunt nodded and took a drink. "Of course she told me this while he and Troy were carrying easels to the basement."

"You still don't think he has some form of... illness?"

"I do not." Aunt Bay spread blueberry jam on the last triangle of toast.

Amy went back to the counter and concentrated on pouring a mug of coffee without spilling. Michael didn't care for her romantically. That much was clear. It made sense that his jealous response was on Gilles' behalf. All his protectiveness, his holding her back from moving on — how could Amy not have seen what he was up to? No wonder these threats had him so on edge.

Her heart bled out through her soles. It wasn't a matter of how long it would take for him to develop feelings for her. Michael was loyal to a fault. He'd never allow himself to love his best friend's girl.

How could she venture into church this morning, a big step on its own, with this new knowledge crushing her? Amy's lips quivered. "I think I should stay here today after all."

"Please, Amy. It's not safe for you to be alone, and you wouldn't want to be with me. Don't make Aunt Bay miss church." Michael's voice from the doorway came out husky.

Amy whirled. How much had he heard? "Are you guilting me?"

"I didn't mean it that way. I—" He flung his arms wide, his face twisting. "I've caused enough trouble. I don't want to spread it to Aunt Bay, too."

Dark-rimmed eyes, a red spot where he must have nicked himself shaving... he looked terrible. Amy took half a step toward him before she caught herself. The lost look in his eyes went beyond grief, as if he'd wrestled all night with Gilles' ghost and been found wanting. Amy's heart twisted. *I love you, Michael. No matter what's wrong in your mind.*

She crossed the room and stood looking up at him, aching to wrap him in her arms and offer comfort. He'd done that for her before, standing in for Gilles, but being on the receiving end might be a breach of his unnatural loyalty. "Michael? It's okay. I'm not offended. And I'll go with Aunt Bay. Shouldn't you go back to bed?"

His eyes widened, and his face lost its rigid cast. "Can you forgive me?"

"It's done. Now, get some sleep. We'll set the alarm when we leave."

Michael shook his head and turned to the coffee pot. "I'll nap later. Days like this are when I most need to be in church."

Aunt Bay lifted an eyebrow. "I think I'll drive."

When they arrived in the parking lot and Amy saw the open doors of the church, the reality of her choice hit her. Yes, she'd meant her prayer on Wednesday night. And Aunt Bay had showed her verses in the Bible that said God would accept anyone who came to Him with a sincere, longing heart.

Amy licked dry lips. Would there be anyone here like the church ladies of her childhood? Whispering, pitying, judging? She tried to calm her breathing. Nobody would know her past. Michael and his aunt didn't see it as a problem, and they wouldn't bring it up.

Walking into the building still felt like being sent to the principal's office in school.

A smiling woman handed them each a program. "Good morning!" She hugged Aunt Bay and Michael in turn and half-reached for Amy, a question in her eyes. Amy smiled and extended her hand to shake.

Aunt Bay made introductions and led the way into the seating area. She stopped midway to the front and gestured to a side row. "You might not want to be in the thick of things your first Sunday here."

Amy glanced at the chairs. "Could I sit between you?"

She'd asked for her own security — and to sit beside Michael, truth told — but the flicker of his eyebrows and the sad smile he sent her way said the gesture reinforced her earlier words of forgiveness.

As he stepped past her into the row, Amy whispered, "Don't beat yourself up. You're making this bigger than it really was."

He didn't look like he believed her.

Settled safely between the two of them, Amy looked around. She thought she recognized one or two faces from the other night. Possibly from the open house, too. A few people noticed her and smiled a welcome. Most people looked friendly, and there was a good spectrum of ages. "Will Troy be here?"

"No," Michael said. "He goes to another church. They're the ones with the Tuesday group I'm in."

"It would have been nice to see someone else I knew."

One of the women she'd seen with Aunt Bay on Wednesday approached from the front of the room. She sidled into the row ahead of them and beamed at Amy, holding out her hand. "It's so good to see you this morning. I'm Fiona Moring, a friend of Beatrice." The woman's hand was warm, her grip sincere.

"I'm Amy. I work with Michael, and he and Aunt Bay have been like family to me." Heat flooded her face. "But you'd know that already."

Fiona arched a brow. "Beatrice does talk, yes. But she has only good to say about you. I've been praying for a long time that you'd feel comfortable to join them on a Sunday."

"You were praying for me? You didn't even know me." What had Aunt Bay said?

"Beatrice loves you. I knew about your tragic loss. That was enough." Fiona's smile reached the depths of her eyes. "God bless the three of you. I'll catch you later, Bay." She moved back to the aisle and walked back to her seat.

A small band took position on the stage. Gentle music filled the room, but the people chatting at the back made no moves toward their seats. By the time the minister stepped behind the podium, three more women had stopped to welcome Amy. Although they cast worried glances at Michael, all they asked was how his open house had gone. Would they be gossiping about his health later? Or praying for him? Amy felt certain Fiona would be praying.

She would, herself, although she didn't know what to say. Was there something God could do about Michael's strange overprotection? Something that could give them a future?

The music stopped, and the minister said, "Good morning, everyone. Thank you for coming today, whether you're a regular part of our congregation or a visitor. May the Lord suit a blessing to each one of us today."

Did his eyes linger on Amy? Or was that her insecurity talking? *Shameful. Mistake.* Amy frowned and formed her own thoughts against the accusations from the past. *Accepted. Child of God. Jesus loves me.* She took Aunt Bay's hand.

After a few announcements, the band kicked up the tempo. Amy tried to sing along with the words on the screen, but she'd never heard these melodies before. Except for one that sounded vaguely familiar. Maybe she'd heard it in Michael's studio.

When the ushers started passing offering plates, Aunt Bay whispered, "You're a guest. Don't feel obligated to give."

Amy found a two-dollar coin in her wallet, and slid it into the plate as it passed. Her heart wanted to give back something, no matter how small. Nothing she could give would be big enough to say a proper thank you.

She'd expected the sermon to be dry, but the minister — Pastor Verrall — told a story about one of Jesus' disciples trying to walk on water, and how Jesus rescued him when he started sinking. At least he'd had the courage to try — and to ask for help.

After the service, Michael and Aunt Bay introduced Amy

to more of their friends. Amy's head was crammed full of names by the time they reached the door. Pastor Verrall squeezed her hand. "You are welcome here, Amy."

"Thank you."

Aunt Bay stepped closer to her. "Amy gave her heart to the Lord this week, Pastor. Wednesday night, when the Warners were here to speak."

"Then welcome not only to our meeting today, but to the family." His voice radiated with the same excitement that lit his face. "I'd love to meet with you and hear your story. When you're ready, of course."

The way he backed off... had she flinched? Amy's stomach tightened. She believed God accepted her. Would she ever be able to trust church people in general?

Aunt Bay jumped into the gap. "Amy lives with us. When she's ready, you can come for tea."

"And homemade brown bread?" He rubbed his stomach.

Aunt Bay's smile had a distinct air of satisfaction. "Of course."

Pastor Verrall reached for Michael's hand. "You don't look so well, my friend. Just tired from yesterday, or do we need to talk?"

"I'll be okay, thanks."

"I'll pray to that end. Take it easy today. You've earned it."

The wind had a definite bite as they walked to the SUV. Aunt Bay put her arm around Amy. "I'm glad you came with us. Now let's get this tired man home."

Home... what would they find there? After the phone call, the letter, and the mutilated doll, Amy's enemies had done nothing on Saturday. They wouldn't just stop. What would come next?

Chapter 27

Michael insisted on being the first to approach the house, the first to enter. Amy didn't argue. If there was anything terrible to be found, she'd see it anyway, but she was not in a hurry.

The alarm beeped when he opened the door. Good — no one had been inside to set it off or somehow disarm it. Amy glanced into the shrubbery on each side of the doorstep as she passed. No dolls or other warning signs.

They did a full walk-through of the house and found nothing out of place. Amy dropped her purse in her room but kept her phone, just in case. She kept Del's security device, too.

How long would it take his team to wrap this up? They knew their targets. The need for a valid chain of evidence made perfect sense from a legal standpoint, but as a potential victim, Amy wished they could arrest first and worry about proof later.

She met Michael coming up the stairs eating a banana. He saluted with it. "Lunch. Then back to bed as ordered." He didn't meet her eyes.

"Sleep well. Yesterday was a long day."

He mumbled something about the night being longer.

Amy took the remaining stairs slowly. Could he really mean to preserve her as a living memorial to his best friend? Was there help for something like that, or would she have to leave here — leave him — to find a full life? Which would hurt more in the long run?

In the kitchen, the message light flashed on the phone. Amy picked up the handset. Michael must have checked it and left it for her or Aunt Bay. Caller ID settled that question. Neal Williamson.

He'd phoned an hour ago, inviting her to lunch. Amy hit the call-back button. When he answered, she said, "Neal? It's Amy. I'm sorry I missed you this morning. We were at church." Would that be an issue for him? They hadn't talked about faith.

"How was yesterday?"

"The open house went well. Each year it attracts more buyers, and it's a great launch for the Christmas sales season."

"Good... listen, do you have some free time today? I could pick you up. We could do some sightseeing. Have dinner together?"

Would this flip Michael out? Especially since Neal already wanted to take her back to Saskatchewan? Amy stood taller. It didn't matter. Neal was her father, and she wanted to see him. Maybe she needed to take a few more of these intentional steps outside Michael's boundaries. For her own sake, and also for his. Could it help him see her as no longer tied to Gilles?

She walked to the window and looked out over the lawn. The day was overcast, but not cold. Fine for traipsing around tourist sites. "I'd like that. What time works for you?"

They made their plans and ended the call.

Amy started putting together a salad. She and Aunt Bay had time for lunch and a quick rest before Neal arrived.

She was waiting by the door with her purse, camera and cane when his car turned into the driveway. Amy slipped out with a quiet goodbye to Aunt Bay while Michael slept.

Neal greeted her with a smile. "I haven't seen Peggy's

Cove yet and they say it's a must. Shall we start there and then head back to the city?"

"Sure. I feel bad about you having to drive all this way later to bring me home."

"For the chance to spend time with my daughter? Don't be silly."

The road curved nearer to, then away from St. Margaret's Bay. Neal had a light rock station playing on the satellite radio, and he kept up an easy conversation as he drove. He turned onto the narrow road leading to their destination. "Barren, isn't it? The rocks are something else."

Huge, rounded boulders of granite dotted the landscape. Amy nodded. "Can you imagine the glaciers moving them around like pebbles?"

Neal parked, and they wandered toward the lighthouse. Amy pointed out the profiles of fishermen carved into the rock wall. "Isn't that amazing? They say it took ten years to sculpt. The artist was a painter, too. Michael loves his work."

Neal bought them each a cone of artisan ice cream. "Not much here but rocks, is there? And the lighthouse."

"And the restaurant and gift shops. People like to climb on the rocks and watch the waves. I can't go very far — the different elevations mess with my hip, but I'm happy to sit and watch you explore."

"Another time. Today I don't want to miss a minute with you." Neal led the way to an empty bench facing the ocean. "So tell me about Amy. We've talked about your mom, and a bit about your childhood, but who are you now?"

Amy's camera lay in her lap. She wound the strap around her index finger. "I'm pretty boring. I worked my way through university to save as much as I could of Mom's life insurance as a safety net, then started a career at a bank in Ottawa." Her fingers stilled, and she stared at the waves' hypnotic motion. "My one, wildly spontaneous act was to chuck it all and move here to marry Gilles. He died, and here

I am."

She turned to Neal. "I don't mean that to sound like self-pity. I stayed because Michael and his aunt supported me when I needed it, and I kind of — grew into their family and into a job at the gallery."

Neal's eyes probed hers. "And you're happy?"

Amy looked at her hands. "I've been happy, until this craziness started with the sabotage rumours and threats. An accident's easier to accept than attempted murder. But I love working at the gallery."

"And you love Michael."

She nodded, still looking down.

Neal's arm slid around her shoulders. Amy nestled into his embrace and absorbed the wonder of having a dad after all these years — one who cared about her.

Adopted by God... accepted by her birth father... pining for a man she couldn't have. But held, in the middle of the pain. She tried to keep her voice steady. "I guess you've learned more about me than you wanted to know."

"I wish I could have been there for you." Neal released her, but stayed near enough to touch.

Amy fidgeted with the camera in her lap. "I was so hurt by what you said after the accident, but I'm glad you didn't offer me a place to stay then. This time at the gallery has been precious. Even if I do end up leaving."

"You're welcome to live with me as long as you like. I, um, gather you don't think Michael returns your feelings. He's very protective. Too much like an older brother?"

"Something like that."

A seagull dove and snatched something from the rocks, then wheeled away with its prize.

"You said if you do end up leaving... you still think you're safer here for now?"

The hypnotic motion of the waves lulled Amy back to a place of calm. "I don't know. That's what the investigator says. And I'm not ready to give up on Michael yet. Plus, his aunt... I'm a brand new Christian, and she's kind of a mentor to me."

"Absence might make the heart grow fonder."

Or tip Michael clear over the edge. What if he started stalking her? "Knowing I have a safe place to hide is a big help. And I do want to visit you. For now, I think I should stay put."

"I'm not happy about it, but I have no right to push." Neal stood. "Shall we walk? Maybe ice cream wasn't a good idea with this breeze."

"But it was tasty."

They meandered through a few gift shops, and made the trek to the lighthouse. Amy watched a group of teens clambering up the granite slopes, leaping across crevices. She and Gilles had done the same, before the accident that changed everything.

When they returned to the car, Amy eased herself into the passenger seat, trying not to wince.

Neal must have noticed the hitch in her breathing. "Too much?"

"I shouldn't have left my cane in here. Yesterday was a long day on my feet."

"Unfortunately, this rental didn't come with heated seats."

"Right now that would be an amazing luxury."

The car nosed down the narrow lane to the main road. Neal glanced at Amy. "Give me directions back to the city? Or should I use the GPS?"

"Turn right, and we'll go a different way than we came. Not that the scenery's much different. Can you imagine being out here when the fog rolls in? It's like another planet."

"It's beautiful today."

"In good weather, sunrises and sunsets are spectacular.

We've come a few times to take pictures."

The drive gave Amy's hip time to settle down. Directing Neal into the city outskirts, she said, "I'm okay for more walking. I'll be smart and use the cane. Is there anything special you'd like to see?"

"I explored Point Pleasant yesterday afternoon, and the Maritime Museum."

"How about the Citadel? We can park on the grounds and not have to climb the hill." As they wove their way toward the downtown core, she pointed out her favourite cheesecake spot. "For next time."

Neal chuckled. "Works for me. And there will be a next time, whether it's business or a holiday. We have a lot of catching up to do."

Half way through touring the Citadel, Amy ducked into the washroom and used tap water cupped in one hand to wash down some pain medicine. The site wasn't large, but by the time they finished, she was limping.

The lines around Neal's mouth deepened. "Note to self. My daughter is not a quitter. Admirable, but for now let's stop. Where's a good spot to eat? I'd like to take you somewhere nice. Somewhere we won't be rushed and where it's quiet enough to talk."

Amy climbed into the car, gritting her teeth until her hip muscles relaxed. "There's a spot near the water where Gilles and I went a few times. It shouldn't be too crowded on a Sunday night."

Her phone buzzed. Michael, saying she'd been out long enough? Amy checked the message anyway.

Troy. *Call me?*

She told Neal which direction to take and tapped a quick reply. *Later tonight?*

Troy acknowledged, and Amy put her phone away.

Conversation stayed light over their meal, touching on memories, hopes and what they liked or disliked. When prodded, Neal talked about his time in professional hockey and about building a new career in his thirties. Would that be Amy, too, leaving the gallery work she loved and starting over in her mid-twenties? Going back to banking felt like a sentence instead of a career, now that she'd experienced the art world. Yet if Michael really was ill — or misguided — and couldn't or wouldn't be helped, how long before she gave up? Showed her father she was a quitter after all?

Amy declined dessert, and Neal did the same. "I need to take you home before your house mates think I've abducted you."

"This has been such a good day." Amy picked up her purse and retrieved her cane. "To think I almost refused to meet you."

Neal's smile held a touch of sadness. "Only after I threatened legal action." He paid for their meal and escorted Amy from the restaurant, one hand resting gently against her back.

Tension crept into Amy's muscles on the drive home. In anticipation of a jealous response from Michael, or regrouping to face the nameless, escalating threats?

Neal didn't speed, and Amy didn't mind. Maybe neither of them wanted this day to end.

When they arrived at the gallery, the sight of Emilie's car added to Amy's growing sense of heaviness. Or maybe it was a good thing. In host mode, Michael was less likely to complain about Amy being out.

She turned to Neal. "Come in for coffee?"

He squeezed her hand. "You're tired, and they may be, too, after yesterday. I'll walk you to the door and say hello."

"Thank you for everything. Including the listening ear."

"I think that's part of the standard job description for fathers. So I count it a privilege. We'll keep talking once I'm home, I hope."

"Me, too. But I'll try to stay upbeat."

Neal stopped, one hand opening the door, and held her gaze. "If he makes you cry, I'll have to come back and straighten him out."

Amy bit back a giggle that could too easily turn to tears. "I may take you up on that."

Opening the door, Amy braced herself against a wave of high-pitched laughter. "Gilles' younger sister," she whispered to Neal. "She has a thing for Michael."

His brows lowered. "Competition?"

"Hardly." Amy grinned. "He didn't realize until I told him, and now he doesn't know how to discourage her."

Michael came into the entryway, looking more rested than he had before but still ragged around the edges. "How was your day?"

Behind him, Emilie's laugh cut off, as if she'd just noticed he left the room. "Michael?" She followed him into the open area, her eyes narrowing when they met Amy's.

Amy smiled. "Emilie Renaud, Neal Williamson. Emilie, Neal's my father."

"You have a father?" The girl's voice came out in a squeak.

Michael lifted an eyebrow. "Is it that unusual?"

"No, but—"

Aunt Bay came down the stairs, and Michael turned. "I wondered where you'd gone." From his accusing undertone, a private visit with Emilie had not been his choice for the evening.

Amy shared a look with the older woman and tried not to smirk.

"Did you two have a good visit? And Neal, do you have time for a drink?" Aunt Bay crossed the open space toward them.

"No, thank you, for the drink. But it's been a fantastic day. Everything fine here?"

Amy interpreted his question to mean "no more threats?"

Aunt Bay's lips tightened, and she glanced at Michael.

Before either of them could speak, Emilie jumped in. "If you're Amy's father, did you know someone's threatening her? Michael didn't want to tell her about the note we found last night." Emilie put a hand to her mouth, eyes round, as if she'd accidentally said too much.

Neal stepped nearer to Amy and slid a protective arm around her shoulders. "Show me."

Frowning, Michael shook his head. "The police took it. Amy, I wasn't trying to hide this from you. I wanted to wait until morning, not ruin another night's sleep."

Emilie seemed oblivious to his glare. "It was in a little envelope, like you get at the florist's. 'Leave now, while you still can.'" She delivered the line in a spooky tone, like something from a bad horror movie.

Her childish delight sent a shiver through Amy. Neal pulled her closer. "Are you sure you won't come home with me?"

Why stay? Amy had no future with Michael. It would tear her heart out to leave him and Aunt Bay, but hearts healed. She'd have her father, and God. She could start over. Go back into banking if she had to, or maybe find another gallery to work in. Del wanted to keep them all together for protection, but how would Amy's nameless enemies even find her with Neal?

Amy opened her mouth to agree. A glint in Emilie's eyes stopped her. If a jealous university student took this much satisfaction in twisting these threats to scare off a perceived rival, how much more would the person who'd sent them feel? Amy locked eyes with Emilie. "I appreciate the offer, but I'm staying."

Emilie pouted and clutched Michael's arm. "If you really cared about Amy's safety, you'd make her go."

Aunt Bay snorted. "Clearly you've never tried to make Amy do anything."

Michael disengaged his arm. "It's better if she stays. Neal, I'll keep you in the loop."

Neal nodded. "I leave on Tuesday. If we don't talk before then, thank you both for your hospitality. Michael, do you have a minute now?"

Caution flitted across Michael's face, but he stepped away from Emilie with the speed of a child at the recess bell. Behind him, she frowned.

Neal turned to the door. "Let's step outside."

Michael shot a glance at Amy. She made an "I don't know" face and said goodbye to Neal. "Phone me before you go?"

He touched her hand. "Of course. Take care of yourself."

"You, too." Amy watched the two men step outside and close the door.

She turned to find Emilie watching her. The girl tipped her head toward the door. "What's that about?"

"I'm not sure."

"He wants to know you'll be safe." Aunt Bay pulled Amy into a hug. "I'm glad you had a good day. It looks like it nearly killed you."

"I'm definitely sore. Say goodnight to Michael? There's a hot bath calling me."

Emilie's face brightened. "You wouldn't have liked the show we're watching, anyway." She bounced back to the living room.

Aunt Bay rolled her eyes. "I don't know what Michael's going to do with that one, but I hope he does it soon."

"So you're helping by staying out of his way?"

"Something like that. My patience isn't what it should be, tonight."

Leaning on her cane, Amy trudged up the stairs. Was Neal talking strategy with Michael for her protection? Trying to convince him to send her away until the danger passed?

She barely knew her father. What if he did the old-fashioned   what-are-your-intentions-toward-my-daughter thing and Michael learned how she felt?

Chapter 28

The next morning, Amy made her way into the kitchen with a zombie-worthy shuffle.

Aunt Bay looked up from her newspaper and huffed. "No work for you today. If Michael has other ideas, I'll—"

"I agree completely." His voice came from right behind Amy.

She smothered a yelp and stepped sideways to let him pass. How had she not heard his approach?

Michael stopped beside her, his face serious. "We're closed today. Period. If someone rings the gallery bell, I'll deal with them." He pulled a bouquet of red roses from behind his back and held them out. "I didn't have the chance to give you these yesterday, but I've kept them in water."

A dozen silky crimson blooms, partially-opened to release their sweet scent. Amy clenched her hands by her sides. "From you? Or from Gilles?" Was this some new quirk in Michael's ploy to tie her to his dead friend?

He paled. "From me. To say thank you — and I'm sorry — for Saturday."

Amy narrowed her eyes at the flowers. "Red roses are for love. You made it perfectly clear how you feel, Saturday night." She fled from the room.

"Amy—"

"Let her go." Aunt Bay's sharp tone carried to the stairs.

Michael's voice rumbled low, defeated. Still in the

kitchen.

Moving as fast as her hip allowed, Amy escaped to her bedroom and shut herself in.

A while later, fingernails tapped at her door. "Michael's gone out for a bit, child. Come and have some breakfast."

Amy wanted to stay in the rocking chair and keep staring out the window at the clouds over the water.

Aunt Bay tapped again. "Don't make me bring you a tray. I'm not getting any younger."

The woman could still run laps around her. Amy was maimed, like Troy's article had said. Damaged in body and in heart, loving a man who wanted to bind her to her dead fiancé.

Hopelessness pressed like a physical weight until she could barely breathe. Amy gave in to it for a slow count of one hundred, then pushed up from the chair. One thing she'd learned from her mom's illness — a few minutes' surrender was sometimes necessary, but indulging in a full-length pity party only made things harder.

Amy turned the doorknob and called downstairs. "I'll be there in a minute."

When she entered the room, Aunt Bay turned from the counter. "Sit. Tea, toast, and eggs coming up."

"You don't have to wait on me."

"I choose to bless you with a little extra care. If we're lucky, it'll keep me from saying something I'll regret later."

Amy reached for the pepper grinder and slid it from hand to hand. "I was out of line. Poor Michael. But I can't live like this much longer."

Aunt Bay brought tea in a china cup and saucer.

Amy looked up. "Why so fancy?"

"I want you to stop and think. A bit of elegance can do that."

It was a pretty cup, robin's-egg blue with a delicate lace pattern. Amy slid her finger around the rim until the heat forced her away. Think. Not about her own pain. Nor about Michael's. Something had to give, and soon, but not by way of an Emilie-style outburst. If it meant her leaving, that needed to be a rational choice carried out in a civilized manner to minimize the hurt on both sides.

Steam swirled across the surface of the tea. "Aunt Bay? Does God care about the details of our lives? Does He have an opinion about our choices, as long as we're not disobeying Him?"

"He tells us to trust Him and not tackle life based on our own understanding. The Good Shepherd goes with his flock to the pasture. He doesn't just turn them loose and hope they'll stay out of trouble." Aunt Bay scraped butter across fresh toast.

"So how do I know what He wants me to do? To stay or to go, and how to be safe while Del takes his own sweet time collecting evidence?"

Michael's aunt set a plate of toast and scrambled eggs at Amy's spot and took the chair across from her. "First of all, God's in this for the long term. He wants a relationship with you more than He wants to answer your questions. You — and I — need to learn to listen. And to trust Him."

"But how?"

"His Word shows us right and wrong, but it also reveals His character. The more we know about Him, the easier it is to believe His promises and His presence. You're used to handling everything on your own, and He wants to teach you to work with Him."

Amy picked up a toast triangle and pushed the eggs into a pile in the middle of the plate. "How do I work with Him about these threats? And about Michael?"

"Prayer is a good place to start. Ask God to involve Himself, and commit to doing what He says — even if you don't like how He works things out."

The first mouthful of eggs wedged in Amy's throat. Aunt

Bay was preparing her to let Michael go. But wasn't that what she'd already known had to happen? Amy swallowed the lump of food. "You think Michael's okay. I think he's making me into some kind of living shrine to Gilles. How do we find out what God thinks?"

Aunt Bay huffed. "I suspect God wishes He could knock the pair of you upside the head and shake some sense loose. But He saves the dramatics for key points in history."

"If Michael is healthy, why is he so... possessive? It's like he feels this obligation to care for me, but he can't let me leave Gilles in the past and move on." Amy shifted her tea to the side, sloshing some into the saucer. "Did you see his face when I asked if the roses were from Gilles? He doesn't want me to know what he's doing, but he's deliberately tying me to a dead man."

"So that's what the question meant. Child, if I couldn't figure it out, how do you know he did? Perhaps he thought you expected Gilles to communicate from the grave."

Amy ate without enjoyment. Was it possible her overreaction this morning had confused Michael more than accusing him? He was clueless about Emilie's and her feelings toward him. What other nuances might he miss? Should she flat-out tell him she loved him? Explain how pushing her back to Gilles came across as rejection? But if Amy was right about his obsession, this might be the ultimate betrayal of his friend. Could a fragile mind survive it?

She gulped her now-cool tea and carried her dishes to the sink. Aunt Bay had the frying pan soaking. Amy put her things in the dishwasher, and plunged her hands into the soapy water to wash the pan. "Thank you for breakfast. And for still loving me."

"Child, the problem is we love you too much."

Amy's phone buzzed in her pocket. She grabbed a towel to dry her hands, and checked the caller ID. Troy — she hadn't called him last night. She answered before it could go to voice mail. "Troy, I'm so sorry. I forgot."

"No worries. Are you alone?"

"No, why?"

"I want you to sound like what I say is a great idea. Even if you think I'm nuts."

"Sure." She added a smile for good measure. "What's up?"

"It's about Saturday. I saw your face after Michael's stunt. He has no idea how you feel about him."

"Tell me something I don't know." Sarcasm. Not good. "Sorry."

"Come on a date with me. To shake him up."

"That's a great idea." Not. Had she managed an eager tone like he asked? Amy walked to the window so Aunt Bay couldn't see her expression. Leaving the room would look suspicious.

"It'll break his rules and he'll be upset, but do you want him to see you're over Gilles, or not? Nothing else is working."

What could she say to that? Nothing positive. Amy's breakfast turned over. Troy's scheme could destroy everything. "When?"

"Tonight, if you're free. Or tomorrow. I'm working days this week, for a change."

"I'll let you know, okay?"

Troy chuckled. "Think about it. Pray, too — Michael told me about that, and I'm pumped to hear more. Honestly, this isn't a weird pick-up. Michael's a great guy and a good friend, and I love him too much to let him stay miserable."

"Is he?"

"Trust me, Amy. He is. I need to get back to work. Text me your answer? We can do any time six or later. Dinner and maybe a movie. And talking."

"Thanks. I'll text you." She hung up and turned back to the sink. Aunt Bay had left the room. Amy finished washing the egg pan, as slowly as she could. *God, what do You think of this?* Troy's plan would shatter the unnatural peace she'd already weakened. She didn't dare agree.

Chapter 29

The day dragged, without anything to keep Amy's mind off the need to apologize to Michael when he returned. She sat in the living room with Aunt Bay, working on his sweater while keeping an eye out the window for his van. When he finally pulled into the driveway, she stuffed her knitting back into the bag.

Her hip protested when she stood. "Pray I can say this right and not make things worse?"

Michael's aunt nodded. Amy hurried to the entrance. When she heard his footsteps on the concrete, she opened the door.

He stopped, as if assessing the threat level. "Hi."

Amy stepped back to let him in. "I'm sorry, Michael. I shouldn't have blown up like that. You were being kind, and I overreacted." She tried to laugh. "Roses aren't cheap."

The pain didn't leave his eyes. Was he still blaming himself for Saturday? He shrugged. "I put them in the gallery. Can we talk? Maybe walk down to the water?"

"Sure. Aunt Bay's in the living room."

Michael poked his head into the room to say hello and tell his aunt where they were going. Amy walked with him through the house.

He stopped in the kitchen and set his shopping bag on the table. "I stopped at the Christian bookstore. They don't have any copies of the magazine with the Harry Silver interview yet, but what I went for was this." He pulled a flat box from the bag. "I'm not trying to buy my way back into your good graces, but I wanted to give you something that shows I care. With no hidden meaning to tie you to something you don't want. Will you take this?"

Amy reached for the box as he held it out. The label said it was a Bible. She opened the cover and found a pale green book.

"Green, for growth. That's all the symbolism, I promise. I chose a translation I like, but I didn't write an inscription in case you wanted to change it." His grin was hesitant. "Aunt Bay will be mad. She wanted to buy you one."

The leatherette cover felt soft against Amy's fingertips. She took the slim volume from the box. "Thank you, Michael. I'll treasure this." Especially if she had to leave here.

His forehead smoothed. "You're welcome. There's a reading guide inside to take you through the entire book in a year, but Aunt Bay has some better ideas on how to introduce you to the highlights first."

Amy set the Bible back in the box but left the cover open. She placed it on the table. "You really didn't need to buy me a gift. But I do appreciate it. Would a hug be appropriate?"

He opened his arms. His embrace was light, brotherly. Brief. The jealous ghost of Gilles would approve.

Stop that. The man was being kind — again — and again Amy was letting it push her buttons. Now she was blaming her dead fiancé, too. Which one of them was coming unhinged? Amy rolled her eyes at herself and followed Michael to the back door.

They strolled down the grassy slope toward the water, under trees that would soon turn from green to oranges and yellows. Amy had already spotted a few early splashes of colour from her bedroom window. Ordinarily she loved the fall, but it was a time of death and decay. Of endings. Was

God trying to tell her something? How could she know for sure? Del had told her to stay. Not that he outranked the Lord.

Michael cleared his throat. "I owe you an explanation. For Saturday."

"You wanted me to stay here until whoever's threatening me is arrested. Del said the same thing. It would be harder to keep us all safe if we're scattered." Amy stared straight ahead. "Ross was just making an offer."

"Emilie thinks you're... romantically interested in Ross. She said that's what upset you on Saturday."

"And you believed her?" Amy whirled. "Michael, she's crazy about you. She'll say whatever she can to keep me off your radar. I used to think she was my friend, but since you and I did the road trip to Toronto, she's been playing mind games — with us both, it seems. What else has she told you?"

Michael looked away. "Once she met Neal, she said you'd planned from the start to stay here instead of letting him look after you — that you wanted to trap me in a relationship, as a surrogate for Gilles." He snorted. "Before that, she was always playing up your grief, how there'd never be another man for you and you'd stay single to honour his memory."

He met Amy's eyes. "I believed her, for the longest time. Until she switched stories faster than she changes her hair colour."

Amy moistened her lips. "Gilles will always be a part of me, but please don't tie me to him. I'd like the chance at another relationship... with the right person." Her cheeks heated.

"Ross."

"Ross is a friend. That's all."

Some of the tension left Michael's face, but his eyebrows pulled together. "There's more to Ross than you see. I need you to promise to stay away from him."

Amy shook her head. "He's always been a perfect gentleman. And you can't worry about him stealing me from Gilles — his dad's going to arrange a marriage with a suitable Muslim girl. Which I am not."

"Stealing you from Gilles?"

Holding her ground, Amy searched his eyes. "Isn't that what you're really afraid of? That I'll find someone else? Be unfaithful to Gilles' memory?"

"Um... Gilles would want you to heal, and to love again." Michael's mouth turned down. "He would not want you spending time with Ross."

"They didn't know each other."

"He knew enough. Please. Promise me."

Amy walked along the edge of the grass and perched on a flat rock facing the water. "Emilie says you're trying to keep me bound to Gilles, like a living exhibit. She's lied to us both, but every time I try to rejoin the human race, you find a reason to hold me back. Now you're not even telling me about new threats, in case I might try to leave. What am I supposed to think?"

A gentle wind stirred the trees and lifted strands of Amy's hair. She brushed them away from her face. "It's time to open the sanctuary gates. Unless you mean to turn them into a cage."

Finally Michael spoke. "I've overprotected you, but I couldn't bear to see you hurt again." He climbed down the short set of stairs where the land fell away to a stony shore and stood looking up at her, hands spread wide. "I was wrong."

"So you won't mind if I go out tonight. With Troy." The words tumbled over one another.

Michael's hands dropped to his sides. He seemed to shrink. "Troy."

"He asked me this morning. I like his dedication to truth.

And he's kind of hot."

Michael walked to the water's edge and scooped up a handful of stones. One by one, he hurled them into the bay. Then he stood, feet braced wide. Staring at... what?

Amy smoothed her hair and let it fall behind her back. If he'd been bluffing, she'd called him on it. If he was mentally ill, what had she done? "Michael?" Amy pushed to her feet and made her way carefully down the stairs and across the stones.

She stopped a pace behind him. "Michael. Talk to me." After a minute, she touched his shoulder. "I'm still here."

He turned and looked down into her face. "Healing from Gilles doesn't mean you need to rush into a new relationship. Being single is okay."

"I know that. Aunt Bay is a prime example of a fulfilled single life. But what if I want to fall in love again... and have a family?" Heat rose in Amy's cheeks. He couldn't miss the longing in her voice.

The wind lifted her hair again. Michael caught a lock that grazed his cheek. He let the hair slide through his grasp, and twined the ends around his fingers. "What about me?"

Amy was a statue. Watching him play with a ribbon of her hair. Trying to read his face. "What about you?"

"Would you... be willing... to try dating me?" He spoke to the strands of her hair.

Amy's heart banged in her ears. She moistened her lips. "I—" Was this what Troy intended? Or did they have to go through the charade of a date? Amy ached to melt into Michael's arms. Accept his hesitant invitation and scrap Troy's plan.

Cold swept her. Why had Michael asked? He'd expressed his lack of feelings for her pretty clearly on Saturday night. Why this reversal? Amy's stomach dropped and she gasped. "It's not you — it's still about Gilles. You want to take his place so no one else can have me."

She spun, but her tethered hair yanked her back. "Let me go!"

"I'm trying! Hold still. But, Amy, that's not what I meant. I—"

Her hair came free and she bolted for the house, heart pounding. At her fastest, on level ground, Michael could have caught her without losing his breath. Amy scrambled up the stairs and across the grass. When she looked back, panting, from the doorway, he knelt huddled by the water, only the top of his back visible.

Amy threw herself into a deck chair. She couldn't face Aunt Bay this way. Once her breathing slowed, she pulled out her cell and shot Troy a text. *Yes. Tonight.* Not that he'd be able to help.

~~~

Neal phoned while Amy was getting ready to meet Troy. Good thing she'd started early. It gave her time now to talk. His tone spoke concern. "You're not worn out from yesterday, are you? You looked pale when I dropped you off."

"It's been a busy few days. But I'm so glad we've been able to spend some time together." Amy turned her back to the mirror and used a hand mirror to check the back of her hair, carefully woven into a French braid. She'd taken more care with her appearance for this one night than she did in an average week.

A silk blouse of antique gold — a gift from Gilles — brought out the highlights in her hair. Slim-fitting chocolate pants kept her from feeling over-dressed. Amy checked her makeup in the tiny mirror. Subtle, but effective. "I left Michael to enjoy Emilie's company last night and had a good soak in the tub. He's been trying so hard to be kind to me today... you didn't scare him when you left, did you?"

"Maybe. I gave him my best face-off glare, and told him he was responsible for not only your safety but your happiness as well. He turned a little white around the eyes." Neal's chuckle carried a satisfied ring. "Good to know I haven't lost my touch. Seriously, I hate leaving you like this. Empty threats are bad enough, but these sound serious. I know you have a security system, but still... If you need to get away, you'll let me know, right?"

"I will." Amy slid a gold bangle onto her wrist and held it up to the light. "I have a date tonight. A friend thinks it might wake Michael up."

Michael had confined himself to his studio, from what she heard music-wise, until Aunt Bay called him to supper a few minutes ago. Would he come out of the kitchen to say goodbye? Or to confront Troy? Amy put the bangle back into her jewellery box. If he didn't surface, she'd wasted all this for nothing. Not that she had anything better to do.

"That's my girl. Take the fight to him. Listen, my flight's not until tomorrow afternoon. I know it's a work day, but could we do brunch? Michael and his aunt too, if they'd like? We could meet halfway, and I'd drive to the airport from there."

"Michael may not be speaking to me, and Aunt Bay usually has plans on Tuesdays, but I'll ask them. I'll come if I can. My knight in shining armour doesn't want me going out alone since the threats started."

"Worst case, I'll pick you up. We'll just have to eat earlier and closer to the gallery. Text me when you know. And good luck tonight. I need to go now. We have a closing dinner tonight and I'm about to be fashionably late."

"Enjoy." Amy ended the call and took another look at her earrings. She still liked the effect. Good. Troy would be here any minute. His responding text had asked her to keep him waiting. She hoped they weren't taking this too far. And that it would work.

The doorbell pealed. Amy jumped. She made herself count fifty slow-ish breaths before collecting her purse and a light jacket and opening the door.

Troy's light tones drifted up the stairs. Michael responded, stiff and low. Amy grinned. Good for Aunt Bay, leaving him to answer the bell. The older woman was visibly unhappy with the tense atmosphere, but so far she'd resisted speaking her mind — at least to Amy.

At the top of the stairs, Amy caught Troy's next words. "It was only a matter of time before guys started asking her out. You're not showing any interest. Why should I hold back?"

She stepped lighter. Slower, so they wouldn't notice she was there. Michael muttered something indistinct and Amy scooted a couple of stairs lower to make him out. "You, of all people. You know how I—"

Troy spoke over his words. "Amy, you look great."

So much for eavesdropping. Hiding her annoyance, Amy took the remaining stairs at a normal pace. "Thanks. You clean up pretty nice, yourself." She forced herself to focus on Troy and not glance at Michael. "Sorry to keep you waiting."

Troy reached for the doorknob. "You're worth the wait. After you." He opened the door and made a sweeping gesture with his free arm.

Amy turned to Michael. "Don't worry. I'll be safe with Troy."

"As long as nobody tries to run him off the road again." His voice said angry, but the lines in his face cried hurt. Deep hurt.

Hurt because she'd stepped outside of his control? Against every instinct of her heart, Amy offered a light "Don't wait up," and walked out the door.

Troy pulled it shut behind them. His bandaged hand barely touching Amy's back, he escorted her to his car. "Walk happy. He's watching."

Amy tipped her head to look up at Troy as if he'd said something amusing. "This is killing me."

"Me, too. Hop in."

He drove as far as the first parking lot and pulled in. Leaving the car idling, he leaned against the headrest and blew out a long sigh. "I feel like the worst kind of sleaze. But he needs a kick-start, or neither of you'll be happy."

Amy watched the passing traffic. "You don't really have to take me to dinner. We can get fast food somewhere. I'll pay for my own."

"You know he'll ask where we went." Troy put the car in gear and started moving.

"He wanted me to cancel and go out with him instead."

Troy shot her a look. "Why didn't you? That's what this is all about."

"Troy, he keeps throwing Gilles in my face — Gilles wouldn't like this, would want me to do that—" Amy took a deep breath. "What if everything he's done, even asking me out to keep me from going with you, is to tie me to Gilles' memory? Is he trying to be a surrogate? A stand-in for his dead friend?"

The words stuck in her throat, but she pushed them out. "How could I risk a relationship with him, never knowing if he was just playing some kind of sick role?"

Troy made a strange, gulping sound. "That's not the case."

Amy loosened the seatbelt strap against her shoulder. "He said there's something he struggles with. Something you know about and pray for. Tell me the truth. Is Michael mentally ill?"

"No! He's under a lot of stress right now, the same as you, with those threats. For the rest, you can trust what he says, but you'll have to ask him yourself."

Chapter 30

It was after eleven when Troy parked in front of the house. They'd chatted over Thai food and caught the latest comedy at the cinema. Troy still looked as guilty as Amy felt for upsetting Michael, but he'd insisted on finishing what they started. No going home early.

Before getting out of the car, he said, "Tell Michael I won't be at our meeting tomorrow night. I don't want him to stay away on my account."

"You two will be okay, won't you?"

"Once you're comfortable to tell him why we did it. Talk to him, Amy. And don't listen to those crazy fears. They're lies."

Amy searched his face. "You're sure."

"If I wasn't, would I risk upsetting him like this?"

They walked to the house and paused on the step outside. Amy turned to Troy. "You don't have to come in and face him. Thank you so much. Pray for us both?"

"I'm already on it." He gave her a gentle hug, then stepped back.

Amy unlocked the door and stepped inside to the security system's beeping. Michael wasn't waiting at the door, but a light shone in the living room. She poked her head back out. "Good night, Troy. Thanks again."

She reset the system before it triggered an alarm, then approached the lit room. Had tonight helped Michael see she was over Gilles? She'd have to apologize again. Ask if his offer was still open. *God, this is worse than high school.* Amy had been wrapped up in care-giving for her mother. There'd been no time for the typical teenage angst.

Aunt Bay unfolded from her chair as Amy entered the room. No sign of Michael. The older woman moved slowly, blinking, as if she'd fallen asleep in front of the television. She fumbled with the remote and turned off whatever show had been playing.

"Aunt Bay, why are you still up?" The van was outside, but even if Michael had gone out, Aunt Bay wouldn't wait up for him.

"We had a break-in. The police left about half an hour ago."

No wonder she looked pale. Amy's heart dropped. "What happened?"

Aunt Bay's lips twisted. "Thank God we were both out, although Del thinks they waited for the house to be empty."

"Why didn't you call me?"

"The damage wasn't going anywhere, and the house and grounds were full of policemen. Michael said he didn't want to ruin your date, but I think he needed time to process this alone." Aunt Bay's voice broke. "They vandalized his studio. You need to see it, and you need to not freak out."

"Why would I—"

"Wait and see." Aunt Bay took Amy's arm. "He's in his room. I'll go up with you, but I'm going to bed. These old bones aren't as young as they used to be."

They climbed the stairs together. Amy hugged Michael's aunt and whispered "Good night." She threw her purse and jacket on her bed before tapping on his door. "Michael? It's me."

Furniture creaked, and footsteps approached the door. His expression froze Amy in place. She'd seen Michael hurt, angry, even afraid for her. She'd never seen him like this.

His complexion had a grey cast, like when Nathin first called, but on top of the shock was a hardness to his jaw and around his eyes. The eyes themselves were red-rimmed and haunted. He looked more like a man wrestling demons than one whose art had been attacked.

Amy couldn't stop a gasp. "Aunt Bay said it was bad. Michael, I'm so sorry. This has to be about me. I'll go. Tomorrow. With Neal."

"No." A muscle twitched on the side of his neck. "You need to stay. Del set a watch on the house, and we're to keep those security devices with us at all times."

Michael's face, his voice, made Amy want to cry for him. She reached out a hand. "Show me."

Panic flickered in his eyes, and he seemed to brace himself. "This began as an attack on me. A personal threat. Remember, Del said this group would be after us all now? But they found something to send you a message as well."

Amy wiped clammy palms against her pants and started along the hall to Michael's studio. She waited for him to open the door and flick on the light.

What she saw inside stole her breath. Easels upended, paint splattered everywhere, and the paintings — Michael's art, the beauty he saw and shared — slashed, smashed, smeared with paint. Her eyes filled. "Oh, Michael!"

"It gets worse." He led her on a winding route through the debris and stepped aside. "This is what they left for you."

A portrait — her own face — and glaring red words. Blood red. *Leave and you die.*

What was the mark on the portrait's neck? Amy leaned closer and her flesh chilled. They'd slashed the canvas across her throat.

Amy recoiled and hid her face against Michael's chest. His arms folded around her, warm and strong, but helpless to erase what had been done in this room. What she'd seen.

As her trembling eased, Amy's mind started to work. Her

portrait, the one Luc had commissioned Michael to paint for Gilles. Why hadn't he painted over it and reused the canvas? Why complete it and keep it here? Secretly? She'd been in this room many times and hadn't seen it. A chill stabbed to her core.

Amy pulled away from Michael, but he stood between her and the exit. She retreated as far as the mess allowed. Not far enough. "The other threats told me to leave. You're the only one who wants me to stay."

He flinched. "Would I destroy my own work?"

"I don't know. Would you? For the greater goal of controlling me? Keeping me here as a memorial to Gilles, or for some other purpose?"

Michael's laugh sounded forced. "You're a good worker, and a good friend, but that's a little extreme."

"Why do you still have that portrait? Why lie about finishing it?"

The attempted smile dropped from his face. "I couldn't destroy it. Or leave it incomplete. It's been in the back of the closet."

"You could have told me." Amy tried to spot another path to the door. "I asked Troy tonight about your secret. He wouldn't tell me, but he's convinced you're sane. That you're not trying to make me into a memorial for Gilles."

"I'm not. I promise."

"You don't want me for yourself, but you won't let me leave." The words left a bitter taste. "This—" She spread her hands over the destruction. "—comes while I'm out on a date, after I said I wanted to move on with my life."

Michael hadn't moved. He watched her like a person might watch the first tumbling stones of a landslide.

Another piece clicked into the puzzle. "You've been single since the crash. Not one date. Why?"

Faint colour seeped back into his face. "At first we were caring for you, driving you to appointments. Keeping you company."

"Try harder, Michael. That's not the real reason."

He tugged at the neck of his shirt. "My heart belonged to someone I couldn't have."

"Not the girl with you the time we double-dated?"

"No."

Amy's mouth was dry, but she had to get the words out. Had to know. Why hadn't she seen this before? "Gilles. You waited while he played the field, but marriage looked final. That's why you ran away. But you couldn't let him go, so you — or Nathin or even Del — rigged his plane to crash."

Michael's jaw dropped. He flushed, then went pale. "I think you just accused me of killing my best friend."

Amy nodded. "You kept me here as some kind of trophy. Something that mattered to Gilles and became a prize you didn't know what to do with."

"Oh, Amy..." A half-giggle, half-sob burst from his lips. He stepped toward her.

Amy backed away. Her heel caught on an obstruction, and she hit the floor hard. Something sharp poked her side. As fast as she could manage, she was on her feet, rubbing the sore spot.

"I wasn't going to hurt you." Michael held out his palms. "Don't you know me by now? Do you honestly think I could harm you?"

"The real Michael wouldn't, but you're not well."

"Amy. I did not do this. I did not have anything to do with Gilles' death. I didn't know it was anything more than an accident until Troy stirred up this mess."

"Where were you tonight?"

He sighed. "I was... upset about you and Troy, so I went out. Alone. Roamed an empty stretch of shoreline. Like I did after I met Nathin."

"Then Aunt Bay went out separately, and for all she knows you could have come back and done this. Or done it

243

before you went out."

"You've been listening to Emilie's poison too long."

"Or she's right."

Michael cleared a spot with his foot and sat on the floor. He stared up at Amy. "Emilie's stories are contradictory. And if she thought I was dangerous, why would she be trying so hard to catch me? Even I can see she's doing that, now. Look, you said Troy vouches for me. Aunt Bay will, too. If you can't trust me, trust them."

"You've fooled us all. Maybe you've fooled yourself and don't even remember doing this. But this message doesn't match the others." Amy pointed at the portrait. "It's time to face the truth. I'll stay. We'll get you help."

He'd walked her through her own pain. She wouldn't dream of abandoning him in his own.

Michael's brow wrinkled. "What will it take to convince you? Other than the arrest of the real perpetrators?"

Amy picked up a broken piece of easel and twisted it in her hands. "I don't dare believe you anymore."

His eyes narrowed. He made as if to rise, then stopped. "I'm going to stand up, and I'm going to take my cell from my pocket. I won't move toward you. There's one person you'll believe."

Once he was on his feet, he made the call. "You have to talk to Amy. Yes, you do. Right now. Del told you what happened at my studio? She thinks I did it — and that I'm behind the sabotage."

A sharp exclamation carried through the phone.

Michael grimaced. "Because I wanted Gilles for myself."

Silence. Then a string of words that Michael muffled by mashing the phone tighter against his ear. He met Amy's eyes and moved the device away from his mouth. "Do you want me to set down the phone and back away, or can I hand it to you?"

Hope fluttered in Amy's heart. Could he really prove his

innocence? Set these wild doubts to rest for good? She stretched out her hand.

Michael stepped close enough to pass over the phone, then retreated.

"Hello? Who is this?"

"Bonjour, Aimée. Whose is the last voice you expected to hear again?"

Amy squealed and dropped the phone. She glanced at Michael, then dove to retrieve it from beneath a mutilated painting of lily pads. "Who is this, really? This is not a joke."

"No, it's not. Although I wish I could see your face right now, chérie. These days I use the name Nathin Ayon. Perhaps you'll understand Michael's reaction when I called him."

"But it can't be — I have to see you. To be sure."

"You weren't intended to know about me. I had no right to turn your life upside-down like this, but you must trust Michael. For the record, he's as heterosexual as I am. He's just more... restrained about it."

"But—"

"It would be too dangerous for us to meet right now. Ask me anything. Something only we two could know."

"Your final words that day."

"Toujours Aimée. Go to Michael. Also about the medical tag."

"I may have told him that. What did we do on our first night together in your condo? Give me details."

Michael grimaced. His throat worked, as if he were having trouble swallowing.

The beloved, gently-accented voice in her ear chuckled. "We made pasta. Linguine with tomatoes and clams. We watched... *The Princess Bride*. I actually enjoyed it. We argued over who got the bed and who slept on the couch. Finis."

The band of disbelief binding Amy's chest broke, and she

filled her lungs with air. With hope. "Michael had no part in what happened? Even if he doesn't remember?"

"None at all. I trust him with my life. I trust him with you. Stay with him and be happy."

"Then you don't... Gilles, it's been two years. Part of me will always love you, but I'm over — us. It wouldn't work now." How could she be breaking up with Gilles over the phone? While staring at the man she now loved?

Michael's gaze hadn't left her face. Did he hear her meaning?

Gilles' chuckle trailed into a sigh. "I know, chérie. It's the same for me. Keep close to Michael. If he gives you any trouble, kiss him. With feeling."

The connection ended. Amy looked at the phone, then at Michael. Beautifully sensitive but clueless about women. Wounded, not murderous or unbalanced, not-gay Michael. Endorsed by her miraculously-alive former fiancé. "I didn't ask him what happened. How he—" Heat rose in her chest. "Why he let me suffer all this time."

Michael's lips twisted. "He had no choice. You know he'd never abandon you voluntarily. This is bigger than all of us. We can't say a word about Gilles to anyone. Even Aunt Bay, and especially not Emilie. Not until this is over."

He gestured at the destruction around them. "I phoned Neal, and the brunch plans are off. You being seen in the company of someone heading for the airport is a bad idea."

Michael raised his hand as if to ward off Amy's protest, but she had nothing left. He nodded, and continued. "Neal will come here. You and I will stand at the door when he leaves, so anyone watching will know you're not hiding in his car. Amy... it'll be all right. Somehow."

Heat crowded Amy's face. "I'm sorry for suspecting you. Emilie... my own fears... things that didn't add up. But there's no excuse for what I thought."

His smile lit his eyes. "You said you'd stay and help me,

when you thought the worst. Please, let me take you out somewhere. Soon. I have so much to say, but not here. Not in this — ugliness."

"I'm sorry about this, too. I can't begin to imagine how much it hurts." How could she have forgotten? "And, yes. Let's talk. Gilles gave me a tip on how to manage you." Amy grinned. Would she dare use it?

Chapter 31

Amy was first to reach the kitchen in the morning. She started coffee on auto-pilot and stared into the fridge. Neal was coming here, but was that for brunch or simply for a goodbye visit? Either way, she'd make a batch of muffins.

Thoughts of last night still jostled in her mind. The destruction. The death threat. Gilles... alive. In the midst of it all, hope. Michael was innocent of all her fears. She'd seen a deeper warmth in his face.

A floorboard creaked overhead. Someone else was on the prowl. Michael? She'd love a few quiet moments alone with him, even if there wasn't time to explore what might lie between them. Excitement zinged through her.

Aunt Bay appeared as Amy was chopping an apple for the batter. Amy's heart rate settled down. She shouldn't be surprised. Michael's aunt had the most sleep last night, or had at least been in bed the longest. Amy rubbed her forehead. Had any of them really slept?

The older woman stopped in the doorway. "Couldn't sleep?"

"Not well."

One thin eyebrow raised. "You don't sound unhappy about it. I was afraid you'd have nightmares from that painting."

She would have, in other circumstances. "Michael and I had an... interesting conversation. I know he's not doing any of those controlling things I was afraid of."

"That should clear the air a little around here. Anything else?" Was that a twinkle in Aunt Bay's eye?

Amy focused on chopping the rest of the apple, ignoring the heat in her face. "No." Not yet. "Is Neal eating with us when he comes?"

"I believe not. I may be gone before he arrives, so give him my best."

"You'll be able to stay awake at your prayer group?"

"Child, with the threats and the vandalism, I need to be there. The others would pray if I phoned, but I need to hear it." She filled the kettle for tea. "There's definitely a nap on my schedule this afternoon."

"Will God keep us safe?"

"I don't know. But He'll be with us. Del says this group is almost perfect at covering its tracks. He'd hoped to have the evidence he needed by now."

Amy stirred apple pieces into the batter and began spooning it into the muffin pan. "It makes me angry that the authorities know who they are, but can't arrest them."

"That's the price of a free country."

"I'd feel better about that if our safety wasn't part of the cost." Amy finished filling the pan and slid it into the oven.

She'd just set the timer when the front door opened. The security alert sounded, followed by the sequence of touch pad beeps to reset it. Michael called a quick "Hello" before jogging up the stairs.

Aunt Bay glanced at Amy. "Did you know he'd gone out?"

"I thought he was still sleeping."

"Or brooding."

They heard him on the stairs again. This time, he joined them in the kitchen. The smile he flashed at Amy seemed to hold a secret.

She couldn't help grinning back. "Where have you been?"

"Couldn't sleep, so I went to watch the sunrise."

Aunt Bay shook her head. "Was it wise to be out alone? That attack was personal."

"I told the guard where I'd be and how long I'd be gone. Actually, I gave him an hour more than I needed, in case I zoned out or something." Michael's face went solemn. "Nathin said these people are using Luc's dealership, and my paintings, to launder money. The vandalism was clear intimidation. There should be no danger if I cooperate."

"Which you will do." Aunt Bay's tone left no room to argue. "Del may be able to gather more evidence through you."

Amy gripped the counter behind her. "Cooperate how?"

A corner of his mouth turned down. "I'm sure I'll be informed." He poured a cup of coffee and carried it to the table. "What's cooking?"

Amy nodded. "Apple muffins." Her mind picked up on his earlier words. "We have a guard?"

"A gift from Del. They'll intercept anyone they don't recognize. Last night I showed the guy pictures of you and Troy, and described Troy's car, so he wouldn't stop you."

"Have you told Troy?"

"No." The single syllable brimmed with dark emotion.

Amy sighed, and turned to check her baking. "Troy said to tell you he won't be at your meeting tonight."

"Good."

Surprisingly, Aunt Bay didn't call Michael on his attitude. Maybe she felt he'd taken enough grief in the past twenty-four hours.

Aunt Bay left around nine. "I'll tell the guard we're expecting Neal." She sifted through the key fobs on the hooks. "The alarm remote is in someone's coat pocket again. You'll hear me beeping when I come in." She pressed the quick exit code and ducked out.

Amy turned to Michael, heart fluttering and her mouth

suddenly dry.

He smiled. "So."

"What time is Neal coming?"

"Too soon for what I want to say, and the insurance adjuster's coming, too. Del's forensics team swept the place last night."

The air between them sizzled. Amy traced a circle on the floor with her toe. "It'll be good to start the clean-up." She looked into his eyes, bracing against the pull. "Michael, what's this doing to you? You pour so much into your paintings, and to have them butchered—"

"I'll be okay. When I can forgive him, it'll be easier. I'm not there yet."

"You know who did this?"

"Ross Zarin. At his father's direction, I'm sure."

Amy gasped. "No, it has to be someone else. Whoever did this is brutal. Ross and his father are so... cultured."

Michael's face hardened. "It's an Islamic extremist culture, Amy. Radical violence. Nothing like what Safia and her family believe. The Zarins are recruiting — and funding — terrorists. That's why the evidence trail has to be solid. This is high-stakes."

"So Del isn't a detective. He's CSIS." Canadian Security Intelligence Service.

"Gilles approached them in Ottawa before he brought you back. He planned to collect evidence, but the Zarins must have suspected something. That medical tag you wondered about alerted CSIS, and they set Gilles up in witness protection. He's given a recorded testimony, but if the Zarins' group finds him, it'll weaken the prosecution."

Amy swallowed hard. By find he meant kill. "It would be my fault."

"You didn't know. But that's why he didn't want to reveal himself to you."

Her stomach twisted. "What have I done?"

An engine sounded outside. Michael hurried to the door and pressed his eye to the peephole. "That must be the adjuster. Unless you want to hear what she has to say, you could wait here for your father."

"Maybe I will."

He interrupted the security system and opened the door. The insurance adjuster was almost as petite as Amy, but the plain-clothes guard flanking her looked like he could stop a bear in its tracks.

The woman held out her card. "Mr. Stratton? I'm Chrissie Cordero. If I could have a look around, I'll get this claim processed as quickly as I can."

"Thank you." Michael nodded at the guard, who withdrew. "This is Amy Silver, my assistant. Everyone was out last night when the break-in occurred."

Chrissie stepped into the entrance and shook Amy's hand. "Damage was confined to the one room?"

Michael closed the door behind her. "Yes. The upstairs windows aren't alarmed, and the intruder smashed the glass to get in. I have more paintings on this floor, in my gallery, but it's equipped with motion sensors."

"Your alarm was set?"

"Yes. We've had threats recently."

Michael led the adjuster upstairs, and Amy retreated to the living room to wait for Neal. Her father wouldn't want to leave her here, but after the painted warning — and Gilles' exoneration of Michael — how could she leave?

She must have drifted off in her chair. A firm knock at the front door woke her, and she scrambled to her feet. Pain speared her hip at the fast movement.

Michael's voice rumbled from the upper floor. Amy called back, "I'll get it!" She hobble-hurried from the room, remembering to bypass the alarm before opening the door.

Neal's concerned gaze swept her, then he stepped across the threshold and wrapped her in a massive hug. "They have to stop these guys."

Behind him, the guard spoke. "That's the plan, sir." He closed the door.

When Neal released Amy, he looked down into her eyes. "Thank God you were out when this happened."

"Michael thinks they wanted the house empty." Amy shivered. Could it really have been Ross? Not quietly controlled and elegant, but venting fury and hate? Her knees wobbled.

Neal's hand shot out to steady her. "Let's sit. Living room?"

"Sure." Amy leaned on him until she could collapse in a chair. "I'm sorry. We didn't sleep much last night."

"I'll bet. Where's Michael?"

"Upstairs with the insurance adjuster. Aunt Bay's out for her meeting. She asked me to say goodbye."

"A formidable lady." Neal leaned forward in his chair and kept his voice low. "How did your date go?"

Amy blinked. She'd almost forgotten the evening out. "Michael was upset. I feel bad, with everything else that's happened."

"Destroying his art must be quite a blow."

"You should see it." She remembered the death-threat portrait. "Or maybe you shouldn't."

Neal's jaw set. "He told me about your painting."

Footsteps rapped on the stairs. Amy beckoned Neal nearer and whispered, "But I know now that Michael's not acting out some weird obsession over me. He's fully sane, and he wants us to spend some time together."

Neal grinned. "Go for it."

Michael's voice grew fainter. They must be checking the gallery. Did the adjuster need to see some finished products? It made sense that a half-completed painting wouldn't be valued as high as one ready to sell.

Amy stared at her hands. "We're about to hit his peak

sales season. We have what's in the gallery, because it closes for the winter, but Michael wanted to release a few new paintings."

"But no one was hurt."

She nodded. "That's what we have to keep remembering." No one was hurt yet. Had Michael told Neal this was connected with the previous threats? "Let's talk about something else. How did your meetings go?"

"Well enough. It was great to finally see this part of the country — not to mention finding my daughter."

"I'm glad you came."

They chatted until the insurance lady left and Michael joined them.

Neal rose. "I'm sorry about what happened."

Michael nodded. "Thank you."

"You can't repair any of the paintings?"

Michael kneaded the back of his neck. "No, but it doesn't matter."

Amy looked up at him. "Why not?"

His eyes held a fierce glint. He tapped his temple. "I still have the images. In here. Plus my photos. The next paintings won't be the same, but if this was a practice run, they may be better." Michael rocked back on his heels, lips curved in a bring-it-on smile.

Amy stared at him. "You're amazing."

His expression softened, and he dropped onto the couch. "It's not me. I had a lot of time to think, and pray, overnight. I'm still angry, but a bit of perspective seeped in."

Neal settled back into his chair. "I know Amy's portrait was to be for her fiancé, but if you decide to paint her again, I'd be interested."

Amy repositioned her leg on the footrest. Gilles might want a photo of her now, to remember their time together, but he'd hardly want a full-sized portrait. Especially if there was a new woman in his life.

It was a disturbing thought, but Amy couldn't expect him to stay single and mope over her. They'd shared a love-in-a-million, at least on her side. Her feelings now for Michael were less of a whirlwind, but no less strong.

Gilles had let her go. She had to do the same for him, now that she knew he had a future. She let her hands fall open in her lap, and looked up to find both men watching her. "Sorry, did I miss something?"

"Everything okay?" Michael offered a reassuring smile.

"I'm fine. Or I will be, when certain people are behind bars."

Neal stood. "Until then, stay safe. I have to go, but I'll be checking in." Did his tone take an extra significance as he glanced at Michael? He reached for Amy's hand to help her up. "Think about coming for Christmas?"

"I will... Dad."

He froze, then pulled her into a hug. "My girl."

Amy and Michael waved goodbye from the front step. Once Neal's car vanished down the road, Amy walked out onto the driveway and back toward the house, stopping to inspect the flower beds. "There. I'm clearly visible as still here."

Michael held the door for her, then locked it behind them. The light in his eyes warmed her. "Walk with me down to the water?"

The phone rang, and he grimaced. "I'll get it." He strode into the kitchen. "Hello?"

Amy didn't bother going upstairs for her cane. Holding onto Michael on uneven ground would be a bonus.

As she entered the kitchen, Michael kept talking. "It was personal, Safia. They clearly targeted Amy and me. Your family isn't at risk. I'm sure if you phone the police, they'll confirm that."

He listened some more. "I appreciate that, and I'll let Amy and Aunt Bay know. We have a guard on-site in case our vandal comes back, but tell your pint-sized warrior to stay away from any strangers he sees — and to keep his eyes open." He laughed. "Okay. Thanks for calling."

Replacing the phone in its cradle, Michael frowned. "Safia said she asked Aunt Bay to babysit on such short notice last night because they had an urgent call from another Muslim family in the city who had a crisis. She said the family was pretty upset, but seemed calmer when they left, and when she phoned them today everything's okay."

"You think Ross or his father applied some pressure, once they knew Aunt Bay was the only one still at home?"

"I'll phone that in to Del. And I need to get something from upstairs. It'll just take a minute, and we can go for our walk." He pulled his cell from his pocket as he left the room.

Amy stared out the kitchen window at the green lawn. How could one guard keep tabs on the whole house, front and back? Movement to the right resolved into the man walking from the side of the house. He stopped to scan the trees, then circled around the back and headed around the other side.

Michael's soft footfalls pulled her attention away from the view. He held out a pink rosebud. "I hope this is a safe place to start."

She took it by the stem, avoiding the thorns, and brushed the tightly-furled pink petals against her lips. The faint fragrance teased her nostrils. "I—" Her pounding pulse said it was time to take a risk. Amy cleared her throat and forced herself to keep eye contact. "I'd accept a double dozen red roses from you, Michael... if I knew you meant it. Last time... I didn't know what kind of message you wanted to send. Or from whom."

His eyes widened. When he didn't answer right away, she blurted, "But there are better things to spend your money on. I didn't mean — if you ever did want to say—" She looked down. The rosebud trembled in her hand, tickling her chin.

"Amy..." Michael stepped nearer.

She looked up, afraid of what she'd see on his face. How could she dump her feelings out like that, over a tentative peace offering?

The elusive gold flecks glowed in his eyes. "As it happens, I do have a better idea for the money. But if that's what you needed to believe me, I'd count every dollar well spent."

"I—"

Someone knocked on the front door. They jumped apart, and Michael let out a low growl. "Good timing." He grinned at Amy. "You put that in water, and I'll see what's so important out there."

Shaking, trying to process what had almost happened — had he really been about to kiss her? — Amy dragged the step-stool over to the cupboard and climbed up to reach a bud vase on the top shelf.

The guard's voice reached her, and Michael's. Then the door slammed.

Michael stuck his head back into the kitchen as her feet hit the floor. His face looked set in stone. Angry stone. "Zarin. Ross. Wants to pick up the painting he bought at the open house."

Amy couldn't stop a little squeal.

He held up his hand. "The guard's sending him to the gallery door. I'll handle this alone."

"But what if—" The words burned her suddenly-parched throat.

"Del said the attack means they know I know about them. Not from Gilles — they'd think Luc told me when he was trying to stop us asking questions."

Us... Amy bit her lip. She'd latched onto Troy's suspicions alone, against Michael's advice.

"Don't worry — and don't come near him. Ross wants to

see how I'll react about last night. This is intimidation. Not another attack." Michael's chin came up. "Although if he does try anything, Del brought cameras and microphones last night. I don't know where he found everything so fast. He can collect evidence and send the cavalry." Michael took off through the house.

Amy stared after him. How long would the mythical cavalry take to arrive?

She didn't dare let Ross see her. What if she gave something away about Gilles? But she couldn't stay here at the mercy of her imagination.

One hand gripping Del's security device, Amy hurried from the room and sneaked toward the connecting doors to the gallery.

Chapter 32

Amy peeked around the edge of the stairs. Michael had closed the French doors to the gallery. She saw him let Ross in and lead him toward the office, but she couldn't hear a word.

She raced back to the kitchen and down the workshop stairs. How sensitive was the baby monitor they used to let them hear the gallery's door chime?

Since the time Aunt Bay had been startled by voices from the basement, they'd left the receiver turned off unless Amy or Michael was working down here and on call for customers. Amy scanned the shelf for it now and her heart sank. If Michael had taken it to his studio since the last time she'd used it here, it was buried and probably in pieces.

A nearby plastic crate functioned as a step. With the extra height, Amy could reach behind the cans of wood stain. She clenched her teeth. If her fingertips met anything small and furry, or crawly, Ross would hear her scream. Instead they slid off smooth plastic. She tipped one of the cans forward until she could reach the monitor lying on its side at the back of the shelf.

Her hip protested as she dropped her foot to the floor. Should have led with the good leg. Right now, it didn't matter. Amy spun the dial from *off* to *max* and pressed the speaker to her ear. Voices, indistinct but getting clearer. They must be carrying the painting from the office into the gallery proper.

"...with the amount of your work we've been acquiring for our hotels."

Amy dialled back the volume.

"I'm sure we can work something out. Although after last night's vandalism, I won't have as much to offer." Michael's tone was brittle.

"I sympathize. And I hope nothing like this happens in the future."

There was a pause. If only she could see their faces, read their body language.

Ross continued. "Amy's questions seemed to have stirred things better left alone. How is she?"

"She'll be okay."

"I understand she received threats before your work was destroyed. It would be tragic if anything were to happen to her." Ross' voice barely changed, but his menace came through loud and clear.

Amy shuddered. This was not the man she'd thought she knew. Her fingers ached from her death-grip on the monitor. She flexed them, one at a time.

"Tragic indeed. And unlike Luc Renaud, I would have nothing left to lose."

Serious undercurrent in Michael's words, too. Amy could picture the look on his face. Stern, unflinching. A shade darker than usual.

Silence dragged. Then Ross laughed, light and controlled. "Your aunt might not appreciate being overlooked. In any case, such grim events are to be avoided."

"At all costs. Let me bypass the alarm for your exit. We don't need to set the thing off for nothing."

Amy sank onto the plastic crate. She dropped the monitor in her lap and cradled her face in her palms. "God, won't You help us? Keep us safe?"

The speaker carried the sound of the door closing, then

Michael's footsteps receding. Amy went upstairs to meet him, but he didn't come into the kitchen right away. Watching to see if Ross really left? Debriefing with the guard?

When he finally appeared, he came straight to her and took her hands. "I know it was him, and he knows I know. I think that's all he wanted to establish."

Amy gripped his hands. "I heard you on the workshop monitor. Michael, I'm scared."

"Me, too." A smile softened his face. "For now, we're safe. Walk with me? We'll leave a note for Aunt Bay, and I mentioned it to the guard. I'll just go hit the alarm bypass button again."

Amy tore a sheet from the memo pad on the fridge and scrawled *Walking with Michael. Back soon.* She left it beside the rosebud.

He opened the door. "I meant to tell you, there are wireless alarms on all the windows now, including yours. Bedrooms and bathroom are camera-free, but they put microphones everywhere."

Michael put out a hand to help Amy down the steps from the deck. He didn't let go when they reached the grass.

They strolled in silence for a few minutes, until he stopped and leaned his back against a tall pine tree, its needles whispering high above them. "I need to ask you a question."

Amy looked down at their linked hands. "Okay."

"What you said about the red roses today... now that I know what they mean... is this new? Since you started suspecting me of ulterior motives?"

"But I believe — the person who spoke for you last night." No saying Gilles was alive, not even out here with only the squirrels listening.

"I'm glad." He moved her hand in a little bouncing motion. "Amy, this matters. Which came first?"

"I was... fond of you before I started paying any attention to Emilie. Why?"

The lines around his mouth relaxed. "Otherwise, it wouldn't be healthy. Like a type of Stockholm Syndrome or something. Where the captive bonds with the — in this case perceived — captor."

"So last night I was afraid you were unstable, and today you're worried about my mental health? Aunt Bay would call us both nuts."

"Hey, there's a big difference in degree. I needed to be sure before I told you—" Michael lifted her hand and placed a gentle kiss on the back.

The current nearly lifted Amy off the ground.

His eyes shone brown with gold. "I've loved you for so long. I finished your portrait so I'd have a reminder when you went back to the world you had before Gilles. When you stayed, I hoped you'd come to love me once you healed... all those times you thought I was throwing Gilles back at you, I was reaching. Hoping you'd say you were over him. By the time you did, I'd lost your trust."

A crooked grin split his face. "That's my deep, dark secret that you worried about."

Amy remembered to breathe. "I can't believe I'm hearing this."

His grin died. "I misunderstood."

"No, you goof! I've wished so hard, so long, and I thought you'd never notice me. You hide your feelings very well."

"I didn't want to frighten you."

"Well that worked well." Amy raised her free hand to his cheek. "I love you, Michael. And I'm so glad you're not a murderer or an obsessive creepy guy. Or longing for my former fiancé."

Michael rolled his eyes. "You've got a wild imagination."

"But I'm not imagining this, right?"

"No. And my heart's still on the table."

Amy arched an eyebrow at him. "Even though you're giving me trouble from the start. Luckily, my phone adviser last night told me how to handle you."

"I may regret this."

"You'd better not." Amy stood on tiptoes and pulled his head down for their first kiss.

~~~

Strolling toward the house, hand in hand with Michael, felt... complete. As if Amy's heart were a puzzle and all the pieces had settled into the places for which they'd been cut.

She looked up at the broken window to Michael's studio, now sealed with plastic. Too bad the larger puzzle of her life still had such rough-edged holes.

The alarm beeped its warning when they opened the back door. Michael called, "It's us, Aunt Bay." He jogged to the security panel and cleared the alert.

Amy hesitated in the kitchen. *Fatherless. Conceived in sin.* The old shame rushed back. What if Aunt Bay judged her unworthy of Michael's love?

"Stop it," she whispered to herself. "I belong in God's family. Adopted. Loved. Accepted. She believes that. I do, too."

Amy stroked the pink rosebud for comfort, then marched after Michael. She found him in the doorway to the living room, talking with his aunt. As Amy approached, he held out his hand. A smile warmed his face.

Aunt Bay huffed. "It took you two long enough."

"It was only a short walk." Amy resisted the guilt that rose at the sharp words. She grabbed Michael's hand. "Has something else happened?"

The older woman shook her head, eyes glinting. She pointed at their joined hands. "I meant that. Seeing what was right in front of you. If you get married soon enough, I can go on that spring cruise."

Amy laughed. For this, she'd had to fight off the old voices? She threw her arms around Aunt Bay and received a fierce hug in return.

"Welcome to the family, child."

Michael hadn't said a word. Surely he knew Aunt Bay was joking. He would propose, though, once they'd been together long enough to sort out their relationship... wouldn't he?

Amy pulled free of Aunt Bay and turned to face him.

He stood leaning against the door frame, shaking his head gently. "Incorrigible. Just like you said." At least he didn't seem offended. Or opposed to the idea.

Michael held Amy's gaze for a long moment. Warmth flickered inside her.

Then he shrugged. Stepped forward and dropped to one knee in front of her.

Amy's heart stopped.

"I hope we both knew this was coming, so why not now?" Adoration glowed in his eyes, his smile. "Amy Silver, will you marry me?" He held the pose a little longer, then stood and took her hands, still holding her gaze. "You don't have to answer today. Take as long as you need... to say yes."

She could get seriously lost in those eyes. "Yes."

Michael winked and reached for her. "Close your eyes, Aunt Bay." His kiss held a promise to love, honour, and cherish — and to delight.

When it ended, Aunt Bay had left the room. Amy nestled into Michael's shoulder. "Even Gilles waited until we'd had our first date before he proposed."

"Yes, but we've lived together for two years."

Together, but apart. "Michael? Now's not the time to set a date, but let's not wait too long."

"How do you feel about a Christmas wedding? Neal could

come here instead of you going there."

"This Christmas?" Less than three months away.

"If you need more time, we'll take it. I want this to live up to your dreams."

Amy trailed her fingers along his spine. "You are my dream. The ceremony is a bonus. Besides, I don't do frilly and fussy. Especially when we're paying for it ourselves."

"Miss Silver, you are indeed a woman after my own heart."

Amy giggled. "I have to tell my dad. And Troy." She tried to frown at Michael but couldn't pull it off. "You need to talk to Troy. The whole 'date' thing was his way of shaking you up to ask me out, yourself. He saw how I felt Saturday night, and took pity on me."

"I wish I'd seen it. I was too afraid I'd scared you and ruined my chances. But I had to get you away from Ross."

"I hope we can both keep away from him."

"Amen." Michael dropped a kiss into her hair. "Let's go find Aunt Bay."

His aunt was in the kitchen. The table held a plate of sandwiches and a green salad. Three matching china mugs waited on the counter beside the stove. "Amy, tea or coffee?"

"Tea, please."

Aunt Bay raised the teapot to pour, while Michael reached for the coffee pot. As soon as they'd settled at the table, Aunt Bay said the shortest blessing Amy had ever heard, and then fixed them with alternating stares. "Well?"

Michael shrugged. "She changed her mind."

"You did not."

"Of course I didn't." Amy swatted at his arm and turned her attention to Aunt Bay. "Incorrigible must run in the family."

Aunt Bay insisted on hearing their story over lunch. Michael told her what she wanted first, and finished with an update about the insurance adjuster's visit. "We should hear from the company soon, but I can start cleanup this afternoon."

His aunt clucked her tongue. "Such a shame."

Michael pressed his knee against Amy's. "I don't know. It was a cruel, personal attack, but that's what broke through the misunderstandings and brought us together. Honestly? When this guy's safely behind bars, I ought to thank him."

"Just pray it'll be soon." Aunt Bay's grim tone lifted the hair on Amy's arms.

Once the table was cleared, Michael excused himself to make some calls. He snapped Amy a salute. "Troy is on my list. I owe that man a steak."

"Is that all I'm worth to you? A single steak?"

"It'll be a thick one. Marinated."

Amy snatched a tea towel and flicked it at him, but he ducked out of the room.

Aunt Bay chuckled. "Well, that's half the trouble lifted from this house. He's been a walking rain cloud for a long time, and you haven't been much lighter."

Amy hugged her again. "Thanks for putting up with us. Why didn't you tell us what the other felt?"

"Child, I may be outspoken, but I don't meddle."

Amy's cell vibrated a text alert. The Alberta number again. Gilles — Nathin. She skimmed the words. *M said to text you. What's up?* "I need to reply to this. I'll just be a minute."

"Take your time. I want to have a lie down before you two start pulling trash out of the studio."

Squinting at the screen, Amy typed, *Your advice worked. He proposed. Thank you. For everything. Stay safe.*

The phone buzzed again. A winking emoticon with a grin that was practically a leer.

Amy stuffed the device back in her pocket and walked to the window. Looking out over the water usually lulled her, but today she had too many emotions and reactions jumping hoops inside. Michael loved her. In three months, they'd be married. Unless Ross carried out his death threats.

She pressed her forehead against the glass. He had no reason to harm either of them. Michael was cooperating. But what if Ross found out about the investigation — or about Gilles?

Was it weird that she wanted to invite "Nathin" to the wedding?

An incoming phone call made a welcome distraction until Amy checked the call display. Emilie. Tension crept between her shoulders. "Hi Emilie. No classes today?"

"Next one starts in twenty minutes. Dad texted that someone broke in and trashed a bunch of paintings. Is Michael okay?"

"He's handling it better than I would have."

"That's Michael. Amazing. Dad said one was a portrait of you. Slashed. Amy, you need to get out of there."

"The message said to stay."

"Don't you see? That's Michael. Trying to control you. Listen, if you don't have the money, I'll buy your ticket. You have to go."

"Emilie. Stop. Michael is perfectly fine, and you know it. You're not going to scare me away."

Was Emilie behind the threats? But then the only painting damaged would be the one of Amy, and how would the girl have known it existed?

Plus, the beheaded doll had a strong Islamic-extremist feel.

Amy braced a hand against the back of a kitchen chair. "Listen, Em... you're not going to like this, but you need to know. Michael and I are getting married."

Emilie's breath hissed. "Don't trust him. It's just another way to manipulate you."

"I'm sorry. You need to let him go. Find someone your own age, who likes to party."

"I'm coming out there. As soon as my classes end."

"Fine, but he won't be here. He has plans on Tuesdays."

"Then I'll come tomorrow afternoon. I have a test in the morning. Which I will fail now, because of you." Emilie let out a theatrical sob, and the connection cut.

Amy groaned. Something to look forward to. Not.

Chapter 33

Amy tied the last bundle of splintered easel wood. On the other side of the room, Michael filled another garbage bag. They hadn't accomplished much yesterday afternoon before his meeting, and she hadn't wanted to be in here alone.

She kept finding herself staring at Michael. It was still a little surreal. She'd wished he could love her, hoped for it, and even prayed. Why did it feel so unbelievable?

He met her eyes and his expression cleared. "Getting tired?"

"A little. But I can sit here and watch you."

"Slave driver."

His tone said he understood her true meaning. They'd shared many moonstruck gazes over the past twenty-four hours.

Being together made this overwhelming chore more bearable. With paint flung all over the walls and floor, gouges in the walls, and the broken window, the insurance adjuster had suggested bringing in a contractor to redo the entire room. The crew couldn't come until Monday, but clearing away the debris was a step toward healing.

Better still, they'd pushed everything to the sides and Michael had set up one of the display easels from the gallery. This morning he'd bought a mid-sized canvas and some basic brushes and paints. The white rectangle shone like an invitation.

Amy loved what the persistent, unbreakable act said about him.

Aunt Bay tapped at the door frame. "I'm going over to Safia's. I'll be back when Emilie's car leaves."

"Chicken."

Michael's aunt shot him a mock glare. "Cluck, cluck. I suspect the drama level will be high today. This way, I won't say something I'd regret."

He lifted an eyebrow. "You're known to speak your mind, but I've never heard you regret it."

"Let's not put that to the test."

Amy pushed to her feet and stretched her legs. "She's not here yet, is she?"

Aunt Bay shook her head. "I'll see you later."

"You're not taking those fresh cookies, are you?" Michael added one last scrap of canvas to his bag and tied it shut.

"Only some."

Michael made a show of checking his watch. "Break time. Come on, Amy. The cookies are calling."

They followed Aunt Bay down the stairs. Michael's arm around Amy's waist pulled her close. "Coffee and cookies on the couch. Might lead to kissing."

This was real. The love in his tone, the current between them. The belonging. Suddenly December seemed too far away.

Amy leaned into his hold. "Kisses you can have. But that's all until our wedding."

Michael stopped on the bottom stair and turned to face her. "Amy, I take the Bible seriously. I'll never let things go too far before we're married. Even if it means a lot of cold showers."

She kissed the tip of his nose. "My mother taught me the consequences by example. Gilles was horrified. But he loved me enough to wait."

"But you lived together."

"So do we."

"In a one-bedroom apartment."

"With a couch. You can ask — um — Nathin. He and Gilles were very close." Amy winked. "That's why we had such a short engagement. Now, where are those cookies?" She headed for the kitchen.

She hadn't finished her coffee when Emilie arrived. Nestled in the circle of Michael's arm, Amy watched the car approach. "She must be beyond mad. I've never seen her drive slowly like that."

Michael sighed. "She took Gilles' death hard. I've tried to be a surrogate brother, but I think I created a monster. I never meant to hurt her."

Today's guard intercepted the girl before she reached the house. Amy and Michael shared a look. Neither moved until the doorbell rang.

Michael bypassed the code and took Amy's hand before opening the door. "Let's be gently clear about this from the beginning."

He exchanged a few words with the guard and stepped back to let Emilie in.

The girl hadn't just changed her hair colour this time. She'd done a complete makeover. Amy blinked a few times and tried not to stare. Light brown hair in a subdued style, enough like Gilles' that it might be her natural shade. Minimal makeup, understated clothing and jewellery... was that a cross on her necklace?

As soon as the door closed behind her, Emilie's eyes welled. And targeted Michael. "I can change. Be whatever you want. You like plain women? I can be plain. Dull. At least until we're alone." Her voice dropped to a throaty purr on the final word. She held out pleading hands. "I can give you way more than she can."

Practice makes perfect. Amy barely caught the words before they burst out. Her cheeks warmed.

Pity washed Michael's face. He shook his head gently. "Emilie... never sell yourself out — not for anyone. You're worth so much more than that. I'm sorry it hurts you, but Amy and I belong together. I never meant to give you any other impression."

Emilie wilted against the door, hands behind her back, head drooping. Her shoulders shook, and she indulged in a few loud, gulping sobs.

Amy twisted to look at Michael, and she mouthed *what do we do?*

He shook his head.

With a lung-shuddering sigh, Emilie seemed to pull herself together. She dabbed at her eyes with her sleeve. Sniffing, she faced them. "It's because of your poor paintings, Michael. You're not thinking clearly. Let me see what that awful person did to you."

Michael led the way upstairs. Emilie tugged Amy's arm and pulled her back a step. Eyes glittering, she hissed, "This isn't over. You're gone. Today. Michael is mine."

And Amy'd been worried about Michael's stability? "Em, it was only a dream. He's not even your type." She freed herself from Emilie's grip and sped after Michael. Surely the girl wouldn't try to get rid of her by staging a fall on the stairs?

Breathing hard, Amy reached Michael's side and took his hand.

He turned, a gentle frown wrinkling his forehead. "You okay?"

"She's not. As soon as she's gone, we need to call Luc. I'd do it now, but who knows what she'd do if I left you alone?"

His eyes widened. "Spare me."

Together, they stepped into the wreckage of the studio. The blank canvas spoke hope to Amy. Out of destruction would come fresh beauty.

Emilie followed them in. The room looked much better

after their efforts, but to someone who hadn't seen the worst, it was clearly a shock. Hands to her mouth, Emilie stared around at the piles and garbage bags. She mumbled something that sounded like a French curse.

She picked her way to the window and peered through the plastic. "Someone's out there!"

Amy kept her eyes on Emilie while Michael hurried to look. "Nobody's there."

"He was moving fast. Under the trees. From the water." Whimpering, Emilie clutched at Michael's arm. "What if it's him — the one who did this? Coming back to finish the job?"

"Emilie, calm down. I didn't see anything."

"He's there! Your guard has a gun, right? Please, make him check!" Her voice shook. She let go of Michael and sank to the floor, resting her head against the wall.

Amy caught Michael's puzzled look and shrugged.

He pulled out the security device Del had given them, and pushed some buttons. "Hi, it's Michael. Our guest thinks she saw someone running in the back. From the water toward the house. Could you check it? Thanks."

He ended the call and punched another code before slipping the device back into his pocket and crouching beside Emilie. "He's going to look, okay? And he'll phone me back. Take some deep breaths. Do you want me to get you some water?"

"No! Stay — both of you. And call Aunt Bay to come in here with us. It's safer if we're together. What if he gets into the house?"

"Aunt Bay's at the neighbours'. But we're safe here. You'll see."

Michael came back to Amy's side. He leaned close, his breath warm on her ear. "Something's definitely wrong with her."

Emilie thumbs moved over her phone, then she rested it on her leg. Amy muttered to Michael, "That better not be a social media update saying she's in danger."

"More likely a panic text to a friend, who'll spend the next ten minutes worried sick."

The way Emilie stared at her phone made Amy think Michael's guess was right. "I hope she didn't text Luc. He might believe her."

Michael went back to the window. "This is blurry, but I can see the guard. There's nobody else moving around."

Emilie's phone blared a heavy metal ring tone. She reached for it in slow motion and held it while the song played.

Walking back to Amy, Michael made a gagging face.

She grinned. "Emile? Are you going to answer?"

The girl looked up. Suddenly pale, she touched the screen. "Hello? No, I'm not all right. I'm still scared. They don't believe I saw anything, and that guard's wandering around but he's not really looking, and what if the guy's really there and he comes into the house?"

Michael's pocket buzzed. He answered the security device. "Nothing? Thanks for checking it out."

Emilie was still prattling on the phone.

Michael spoke over her words. "Emilie."

She flinched. And paused, mouth open.

"The guard says there's nobody out there."

Instead of responding, she spoke into the phone. "I only came out here to help Michael, but he doesn't see, and I don't know what else to say, and where are you—"

"Enough." The voice, harsh and clipped, came from behind them.

Amy was already in motion when Michael pulled her to the side. Away from the doorway.

The intruder was dressed in black, with a black stocking over his head. Black gloves. Black gun, targeting Amy and Michael. His free hand flicked at Emilie. "Put that away now. You played your part well. Where is the old woman?"

"At a neighbour's house."

"We'll move quickly, then. Collect their phones for me."

White-faced, Emilie climbed to her feet. Approaching Michael first, she held out her hand. "I'm sorry. It has to be this way. You'll thank me, later."

"Emilie—"

"Silence." The command was more frightening for its low tone.

Michael passed over his cell. "Or what, Ross?"

Emilie started at the mention of his name. Then her chin firmed. "The other one, too. The one you used for the guard."

Michael took his time complying. When the device left his hand, he seemed to deflate.

Too-bright eyes drilled Amy. "Now you. This is all your fault."

"You know I don't always have my phone on me. Remember the time it took two days for me to see your text?"

"You got it right away. You were just playing with me."

Ross spoke. "It's in her back pocket. I saw it when I arrived."

Sighing, Amy surrendered her cell. Would they notice the less bulky outline of her security device in her front pocket? If not, how could she send an alert? *God, help?*

Ross held out a plastic bag for the phones. When Emilie dropped them in, he said, "Yours, too."

"What? Why?"

"You don't know what kind of spy-ware Amy may have planted on your phone. Get a new one."

Amy squealed a protest, but Emilie tossed her phone into the bag without another word. The girl stalked back to Amy. "You should have obeyed the warnings I sent."

Michael's arms came around Amy and held her tight, as if he feared Emilie would take her by force. "You sent the warnings?"

Ross snorted. "Surely you didn't think anything so clumsy came from me?"

Emilie stiffened. "It was your idea!"

"To frighten her. Not to scare her out of reach. Luckily for us both, she's too besotted with her painter to leave."

"You're taking her away now. You promised."

"I will." His voice took on a pensive tone. "The beheaded doll. I wish I could make that prophetic, but they'd never believe it of you."

"Believe what?"

"You, my feisty little infidel, are going to kill them both. Beheading is military. Instead, you will shoot them, overcome by grief at their engagement. Then, in remorse, you will shoot yourself."

Emilie threw herself at Michael. His arms holding Amy didn't move. "Michael, let him take Amy away. He won't really shoot her. He'll make her Muslim and find her a good home. Away from here."

Amy's throat closed. She knew what happened to women abducted by Muslim extremists.

Michael held her tighter. "Why hide behind a woman, Ross? It's not the military way. Have you gone soft, living here?"

Ross spat a string of foreign sound. "I surrender my personal satisfaction for the greater good. My work brings others into the fight."

Amy twisted her neck to stare at Michael. "What are you doing?"

"What would Del want us to do?" Meaning layered his tone.

She forced her mind to concentrate on the puzzle. Del... wanted evidence. Had installed cameras and microphones in the house. Amy gulped. "Be careful."

Michael lifted his chin at Ross. "Have you even seen

battle? You can trash paintings, manipulate young women. Sabotage airplanes—"

Emilie gasped. "You didn't—"

Michael pushed on. "You're always in the shadows, Ross. Aren't you good enough to fight with the big boys?"

Another snarled curse. "Do you think I like polluting myself in the cesspool of North America?"

"It beats being shot at. Dying. Plus I'm sure you enjoy the amenities."

A barrage of foreign words seared the air. "Infidel dog! You should take days to die. But I am a good son. A good servant of Allah. I will obey my father."

"You serve out of fear. You'll never be enough to satisfy either of them."

Emilie whimpered. "Michael, did he really kill Gilles? I thought she was lying about the crash being sabotage."

"I'm sorry." Michael's voice held infinite regret. "If I'd known you'd been talking to him—"

"Enough." Again the military tone. "Emilie. You will shoot them."

She was crying now, shaking so badly while she clung to Michael that Amy could feel it on his other side. "I — I don't have a gun."

"I do." He produced a second one, small, compact, efficient-looking.

Emilie fell to the floor, sobbing. "No! I didn't—"

"Stand!"

She bounced to her feet. Positioned herself between Michael and the gun. "It won't work if you shoot us this way."

"True. Perhaps Amy found the two of you together, and fired the shot in jealous rage. Then, of course, killing herself."

Amy slid from Michael's arms and ducked behind him. With his torso blocking Ross' view, she wrenched the security device from her pocket and engaged the emergency call signal. How could help arrive in time?

"Step out from behind them. Now."

Amy locked her arms around Michael's waist and rested her forehead against his back. She'd rather be between him and the gun, but not when it meant being in front of Emilie. What might the girl do?

Michael spoke again. "So you kill us. My paintings don't move that much money for you, and losing a second child will destroy Luc. Don't you need his dealerships either?"

"Renaud has another daughter. Grandchildren. And a wife."

"Have you not seen him lately? The man is crumbling. One push and he topples. How many laundry schemes do you have in place?"

"More than you know. Emilie. You will step aside. Now."

"You promised I'd be with Michael!"

"You will be. In death. Move."

Emilie screamed at him.

Michael lunged as if to catch her. "Emilie, you don't have to be in front. But we have to stay together." Had she tried to rush at Ross?

Amy squeezed Michael's ribs. "We can move together."

He stepped forward, guiding Emilie.

Amy followed, still holding onto him.

"Stop!"

"Shoot us like this and you've lost your cover story." Michael kept them moving. Faster.

Something crashed through the plastic over the window. Crackles, bangs and the sound of shots filled the room.

Michael shook free of Amy's grip before the object thudded into the debris. He dodged Emilie and charged at Ross. "Amy. Emilie. Down!"

Forget down. Amy ran after him.

Ross hit the floor, cursing. Amy fell on Michael, and felt

Emilie land on top of her.

A new voice shouted, "Put that fire out. Then get these civilians out of here."

Amy lifted her head. The room swarmed with men. Two smothered flames with their jackets. Another helped Emilie stand, then reached for Amy. She took his hand and let him pull her to her feet. Her legs wobbled, but she stayed upright. Seconds later, Michael pulled her into his arms and she was drowning in his kiss.

He drew back and stared at her. "Are you okay?" One hand stroked from her temple to her jaw.

Amy nodded. If she spoke, she'd be crying. Instead, she held him as tightly as she could. The trembling started anyway.

Michael spoke against her hair. "I knew something wasn't right, so I pinged Del when I spoke to the guard. Took them long enough to act."

The guard was there, too. With a grim hold on a manacled Ross. Someone had pulled off the stocking mask, and their attacker's face burned with hatred.

Del stood in the doorway, surveying the room. "Michael, Amy, Emilie, come with me. Woody, keep a leash on our warrior."

"You got it, boss. A very short one." He sounded like he hoped there'd be a reason to use force.

One arm around Amy, Michael urged her toward the door. He stopped and turned back. "Emilie? It's over. Come on."

She burst into tears and ran to him. "I didn't mean any of this to happen! He said he'd help me — not do this!"

Michael nodded. "We'll go downstairs, and we'll talk about it, okay?"

Emilie spun and marched straight to Ross. "You're an embarrassment to true Muslims. You, you... terrorist." She spat in his face and stalked away.

His face twisted in hate, and a torrent of invective flowed from his lips. The spittle slid down his cheek into his beard. The guard made no move to wipe it off.

Amy followed Emilie, quickly before she gave in to her own desire to retaliate. Kicking a restrained man where it hurt would put her on his level. Where she did not want to be.

Michael's hand holding hers made a warm spot. The rest of her body felt like ice.

Chapter 34

Del stuck his head out the front door. "All right. You can come in."

Aunt Bay rushed past him. She hugged Michael, Amy, and then Emilie. "Thank God you're safe! Dafiq saw someone climb out of Emilie's car and sneak to the house. I contacted Del."

Amy wilted against Michael. Help had been on the way long before she called. If she'd known, would she have been less afraid?

Another man stood at the threshold, watching. A stranger. Or — Amy gasped. Hissed at Michael. "Is that—?" But she didn't need his answer. She slipped from his side and walked toward the door. Slowly, her eyes never leaving those bright, brown ones she'd last seen dazed with pain.

He held out a hand.

She took it. Smiled. Dove into his arms and held on as if she were the only thing keeping him anchored to this world.

"Women still run to me."

His chuckle was the same, but his touch... definitely didn't spark the same reaction. Amy stepped back and grinned at him like an old friend. "Nathin. Thank you. For everything."

He winked at her. "Send me an invitation to the wedding. I hope to bring a guest."

"I want to hear your whole story — but you need to talk

to Emilie."

Gilles frowned. "I can't believe she did this."

"She needs help." Amy turned back to the group. "Emilie?"

Del ushered the others into the living room. Michael stopped just outside, waiting.

Gilles closed the front door and walked with Amy to meet his sister.

Emilie stared dully at him. Sudden light flashed in her eyes. Her lips quivered. "Gil—"

"It's Nathin for now. But it's me." He pulled her into his arms and let her sob on his shoulder.

Amy met his gaze. "Join us when you can."

She crossed the floor to Michael and looked up into his face. "Were you worried I'd change my mind? About us?"

"Not really." But his gaze flickered away from hers.

"Michael. Your best friend is now my very good friend. Nothing more. You are my one and only, lifetime love." She traced the collar of his shirt with a finger. "That means you're stuck with me."

"Mission accepted." He squeezed her hand. "Let's join the debrief."

Del stood with his back to the window, tapping the fingers of one hand against his leg. Likely impatient to get on with his job. Amy and Michael sank onto the couch.

Amy looked over at Aunt Bay in the recliner. "I wonder how Safia's managing to keep Dafiq away."

The older woman smiled. "She took him for ice cream. And told me we were all welcome to go to her place if we had to."

"There was a little fire upstairs, but they put it out quickly."

Michael shifted nearer. "The insurance adjuster will not be pleased. But it made the distraction we needed to jump Ross. I'll take that any day."

Amy shivered. "I don't ever want to be that scared again."

"You're likely in shock, child. I'll make you a hot drink as soon as I'm allowed into the kitchen."

Del shifted his feet. "As soon as the prisoner is removed. Which will happen as soon as our friends in the entryway decide to join us."

Amy tucked her feet under her and concentrated on the warmth emanating from Michael. "Del, thank you. That's not enough, but... thank you."

"You're welcome. Thanks to Michael for challenging Zarin verbally. Every bit of evidence helps. We want this pair put away for a long time."

"Pair." Amy blinked. How could she have forgotten the scope of this? "Reza Zarin. Did you get him?"

"A strategic response team apprehended him not long ago."

Gilles led Emilie into the room. The girl didn't make eye contact with anyone.

Amy jumped up. "You two sit here together. Emilie needs someone near."

For a second, the girl glanced at her, surprise on her face. Then she looked down again. She subsided into a corner of the couch. Gilles sat close enough that there was room for another person between him and Michael.

Mindful of Michael's doubts, Amy opted for the other chair.

Emilie spoke to the floor, her voice barely audible. "I'm sorry."

Del cleared his throat in a way that said "time for business". His shoulders squared. "Miss Renaud, your actions will require an investigation. Beginning with a psychiatric evaluation. You'll be taken from here to hospital, where we'll arrange for your family to meet you. Nathin will leave you before they arrive. Please understand his former identity is not to be revealed until this case comes to trial.

We need to get him back into hiding. He shouldn't even be here."

"Couldn't keep me away."

"But can I keep you alive?" Del walked to the door. "You can transport the prisoner now." He glanced over his shoulder at Gilles. "You, keep out of sight."

Del occupied the doorway until the men escorted a still-cursing Ross from the house. Then he resumed his position at the window. He inclined his head toward Aunt Bay. "Thank you for your cooperation. The kitchen is yours. But I'm about to ask these folks to tell their stories."

Conflicting emotions chased across her face. As Aunt Bay started to rise, Amy said, "I'm warmer now. Or we could all move into the kitchen."

Aunt Bay settled back in her chair. "You deserve to be comfortable."

Del fixed Emilie with a stare. "We know what happened here in the house. Tell us the background. How you got involved with the Zarins and what you thought would happen here today."

Emilie paled even further. "I met Ross here. At the gallery. He seemed interested in Amy, so I tried to encourage him."

"To what end?"

"She wanted Michael. But I've loved him forever. I wanted Ross to take her away."

Del tapped his pen against his chin. "Literally?"

Red filled her cheeks. Her hands twisted on her knees. "Not at first. He's gorgeous. Why couldn't she fall for him? When she didn't, I sent some warnings. To scare her away. To make her think she wasn't in a safe place. But she wouldn't go."

"Did Ross know about these warnings?"

"He did. He was mad, though, when he found out I was telling her to leave."

"Why?"

"He didn't love her, but he didn't want her to go away, either." Emilie's fingers picked at her skirt. "Men! Why do they all go for her? What's wrong with me?"

Amy's heart echoed that need to be loved — to belong. She ached for the girl. Couldn't Emilie see herself? How bright, popular, energizing she was? Had it become all about the disappointment of not attracting Michael?

Del glanced at Amy as if gauging her reaction, then continued his questions. "And how did today's plan come about?"

Emilie sniffled. "When Amy told me she and Michael were engaged, I was devastated. I texted Ross. He promised he'd think of something. Then he asked me to meet him today before I came out here. I needed to talk to Michael face-to-face, to make him see."

She let out a hiccuping sob. "Ross was so kind. He said, what if he could take Amy away and I could be with Michael? I drove to his condo. He hid in the trunk. My job was to get everybody up to the studio, pretend to see someone in the back. When Michael sent the guard to check, Ross slipped in through the front door."

Del held up a hand. "How did he bypass the alarm?"

"He borrowed the remote key fob the night of the open house."

"Were you aware that he later broke in and vandalized Michael's studio?"

"He was clever about that, using a window, so the remote would be a surprise for later."

"And so, knowing he had already committed criminal activity, you willingly aided him in a kidnapping attempt?"

"It wasn't like that! He had to take her away so I could have Michael." Emilie's face darkened. "Except he lied to me. He wanted to kill us — all of us. How could Michael love me if we were dead?"

"How indeed?" Aunt Bay's tone was dry.

Gilles draped an arm around his sister's shoulder and pulled her close. "We'll get you help, Emilie. Don't be afraid."

She started from the couch.

Del positioned himself between the girl and Amy. Gilles tugged her back to her seat.

Emilie dissolved in sobs. "Not afraid? I've ruined my life. I'll go to jail! Because of her. And Ross. Michael will never love me now. Our parents will disown me. My life is over!"

Del paced back to the window. "You'll be remanded for a psychiatric assessment and you will go to trial. But you have family and friends who will stand by you."

Emilie turned her face to Gilles' chest and sobbed.

Gilles' arms circled her. "This is as much the terrorists' fault as my supposed death. She wasn't like this before. They've destroyed my entire family."

He'd built a new life at least. But Luc, Emilie, and Honore had paid a higher price. Only his married sister and her family seemed untouched. Or was that simply because Amy hadn't interacted with them since the crash, to know?

Emilie's shoulders heaved. Her sobs spoke despair, not her usual drama. What would become of her? She'd nearly caused their deaths. Now she had to live with the fallout.

Amy's heart twisted. "Em? For what it's worth, I forgive you. If you want, I'll still be your friend."

Emilie's sobs might have slowed, but she didn't respond. Gilles' smile carried gratitude.

Del tucked his notepad into a pocket. "Time to take you to the hospital." He shook hands with Michael, Amy and Aunt Bay. "I'll be in touch. Take some time to talk this through among yourselves. We have the recorded evidence, but we'll have some questions as well."

He held out a hand to Gilles. Between them, they guided Emilie to her feet and led her from the room.

BONUS SCENE

Chapter 20.5

[Would you like to have seen Michael's and Gilles' reunion? I couldn't include it in the novel, for spoiler reasons and because everything else is in Amy's point of view, but I really wanted to eavesdrop on this scene, so I wrote it. ~Janet]

The van's turn indicator clicked as Michael drove into the parking lot of a three-star, drive-up motel. He backed into a spot against the shrubbery to hide his license plate. The plain, brown van had no distinguishing marks to identify it as his.

He sat a few minutes, watching. Light traffic continued normally on the road. Michael turned off the engine. He slipped from the van and crossed the parking lot to the unit marked 117. Feeling like a spy in a bad movie, he rapped softly on the door and stepped back to be visible through the peephole.

Before he was ready, the door swung inward. A shadowy figure hissed, "Inside. Quickly."

As soon as Michael obeyed, the door shut behind him. The deadbolt clicked home, and the security chain rattled.

All senses alert, Michael waited for his eyes to adjust to the dim room.

A shadowed figure closed a crack in the curtains and flipped the light switch. He turned. "Michael."

Michael choked. "Gilles."

Gilles' eyes narrowed. "Nathin. I told you, that name will get me killed."

They clasped each other's upper arms and shared a long look. Lines etched Gilles' — Nathin's — face. His pupils carried the faint dilation of a prescription painkiller. Everything about the man seemed faded.

But he was alive. "What's going on? How — why — did you fake your death? And why come back now?"

Gilles dropped into one of the wooden armchairs beside the room's tiny desk and waved Michael toward the other. "My father's company is being used by terrorists to mask the movement of funds. When he found out, he gave in to their threats and let it go on." Pain twisted Gilles' face. He stopped and massaged the back of his neck. "Sorry. This is life, since the crash. The long flight here aggravated the injury."

He pulled a few slow breaths before going on. "I didn't know until I started at the Halifax dealership. I blew up at Dad, and took off to cool down." He smirked. "I was young. Indestructible. I could fight them and win."

Michael nodded. "You always won."

"Exactly. I came back, pretended to be on board. But I'd contacted the Canadian Security Intelligence Service and was working with them to gather evidence." Gilles held out his hand. "I swear I had no idea I was bringing Amy into danger. I'd have chucked it all and stayed in Ottawa with her."

Michael's mind flashed an image of Gilles and Amy, carefree, laughing, swinging a little girl by the hands. The toddler looked just like her mother. The scene twisted a bitter-edged knife in his heart. It could still happen. He swallowed hard. "They'd have still known you knew."

Gilles shrugged. "Maybe."

"What happened at the hospital?"

"CSIS had given me a medical alert tag. When the first responders phoned it in, my contacts descended on the emergency room and arranged for me to 'die' on the table."

"But your family — Amy—"

"They lost me. CSIS said it was best. I've been in witness protection since then, and my handler is not happy about me being here. Essentially I've left the program."

"What does that mean for you?"

"I don't know." Gilles slid a takeout menu from the desk and rotated it in his hands. "They have my recorded statement. If I'm killed, it won't harm their case. When Amy wouldn't take my warnings, I had to talk to you in person."

"But not to her."

"Amy shows her feelings too clearly. Her happiness that I was alive, her sudden fear of the terrorists... she'd be an instant target."

"Who would see?"

Gilles rolled the menu into a tube and tapped it against his leg. "My friend, they're using your products, too, in the money laundering. In lower dollar amounts. The Zarins. Reza and Ross." He cursed. "Ross is short for Rostam, a legendary hero warrior. He's done a stint fighting over there, and now he's here radicalizing young, disenfranchised Canadians for the cause."

Michael's entire body surface poised on the edge of a shiver. "Ross. He's been taking an interest in Amy."

"How?" The word came out like a bullet.

"Chatting in the gallery. He took her to visit the crash site. Invited her to lunch today."

Gilles stared. He didn't seem to notice he'd crushed the paper in his fist. "Keep him away from her."

The knife twisted again. "Now that you're back—"

"Michael, I am not back." Gilles leaned forward, eyes

revealing his pain, and whispered his next words. "Gilles Renaud died that day. Nathin Ayon has a new life. His concussion, the damaged neck muscles, are healing, but he's — I'm — a different man. Believe it or not, I sell life insurance. I'm doing well with it, too."

He swept his arm around the room. "I could afford better than this, although not as much as my predecessor. This is close to your gallery and not somewhere they'd look for me." He stood. "If they ever start looking for me, I'm dead. Amy's in danger, but I can't take her back with me. They'd look for her and find us both."

Gilles stood. "Coffee?" He took the mini carafe and filled it from the bathroom faucet.

Michael watched him dump the grounds into the filter. "Please."

Once the water started to hiss and burble, Gilles circled the cramped room. He stopped in front of Michael. "How is Amy? And the indomitable Beatrice?"

"Fine. Amy's healing. She still has pain in her hip if she stands too long. I don't know what this will do to her emotionally."

"If all goes well, she'll never know."

"You'd do that to her?"

"Wouldn't it be best? She's over me by now. I'm over her." Gilles passed a hand over his face. "Don't look at me like that. Death ends relationships. I think I'm falling for my physiotherapist. If she can see beyond the rehabilitation project, we may have a chance."

The room seemed to tilt. Michael gripped the arms of his chair. "You're not here to reclaim your fiancée."

"Michael, she's not a package I forgot in a taxi." He poured coffee into two thick, porcelain mugs and fanned out packets of sugar and powdered whitener on the table.

Michael grimaced and opted for black. "No, she's not. Amy is a person who lost her love. Her future. Your family cut her off. So did her own father. If Aunt Bay and I hadn't taken her in—"

The plastic stick made a faint tick-tick as Gilles stirred sugar and whitener into his drink. "I didn't script any of this. We had no warning. But come on, *ami*, you're the winner here."

"I've had to watch this beautiful soul suffer through abandonment and physical therapy while she grieved, knowing my best help couldn't touch her deepest hurts. You know how I feel about her. How is this winning?" Michael's hand jerked, and coffee splashed the table. He grabbed the stack of napkins and blotted the mess.

"I don't understand." Gilles dropped back into the opposite chair. Ignoring his coffee, he picked up the crumpled menu and began twisting it. He raised his eyes to Michael's. "My friend... my very best friend... the minute I saw you and Amy in the same room, I knew you were perfect for each other. In my selfishness, I kept you apart. Cut my truest friend out of my life to keep a treasure who shouldn't have been mine. When you acted honourably and withdrew, I was relieved. Can you forgive me?"

"I would have done the same thing. There's nothing to forgive." Michael risked a sip of coffee. The bitterness curled his tongue. "Plenty of girls dropped me for you, but you're wrong to think Amy would be like that. I'm hardly a better prize."

A flash of the old arrogance crossed Gilles' face. "Not better. A perfect match." He laughed. "Amy's loyalty is also a match for yours. I saw how it would play out. She'd fight it each step of the way. You'd both deny it and live in misery to give me a hollow victory. When my own love faded, you'd feel too guilty to get together. It would make a terrible novel. But now—"

Gilles saluted Michael with his mug. "She's working with you every day. How are you not a couple yet?"

Michael's world was still off-kilter. "You really believe this."

"I do."

"I had hoped... not that I took her in for this... but I'd hoped she could love me." He sighed. "Every time I move in that direction, she shuts me down."

A grin played on Gilles' lips. "Perhaps you're making the wrong moves. If we live through this, I'll give you some pointers."

"If we live. You must have a plan, or you wouldn't have contacted me."

"I wanted to warn you. My CSIS contacts would have let you be collateral damage to catch the bigger prize. Now I can tell them you're definitely in the Zarins' sights. They can work with local law enforcement, and hopefully give you protection. Tell me everything suspicious that's happened."

Half-way through Michael's recap, a door banged in the next room. He nearly jumped out of his chair. "Sorry. You were always the adventurous one. I just read about things like this."

Gilles took notes, and at the end asked for Michael's cell number. "If you hadn't changed it, this would have been much easier. I received a very startled reply when I tried to text you. Give me Aunt Bay's, too, if she has one."

"Why?" Michael gave him the numbers.

"I might need a second opinion about Amy's feelings. Once the dust settles. Or I may just ask her myself. By text, of course. A dead lover showing up to ask about her next one might not go over too well."

Michael snorted. "I'm glad you're still crazy."

"Like a coyote. You want to get Chinese takeout, for old times' sake, or do you need to get back?"

"I can't go home until I get my head around this."

A NOTE FROM JANET SKETCHLEY

Thanks for reading *Without Proof.* If you liked it, **please consider posting a brief review** at your favourite online bookstore or with Goodreads or one of the other social book sites. And tell your friends about it. Word of mouth is still the best way for readers to find new books.

This completes the Redemption's Edge series, and I hope you've enjoyed spending time with the characters in these novels as much as I have.

I hope you'll check out my **Green Dory Inn Mystery series**, set on Nova Scotia's picturesque South Shore. Meet Landon Smith, a young woman making a fresh start after a traumatic past; warm-hearted innkeeper Anna Young; and some quirky neighbouring characters.

Book 1, **Unknown Enemy**, is a novella. The remaining books are full-length novels. This is a continuing series, so you're encouraged to start at the beginning.

If you want to keep in touch with what's coming next, you're invited to **sign up for my author newsletter** at janetsketchley.ca/subscribe.

It's worth mentioning the difference between Islamic extremists and other followers of Islam. As a Christian, I believe Jesus' words that He is the only way to relationship with God. His invitation is open to all who choose to accept it (see the Gospel of John). I do not believe that ordinary Muslims like Safia and her son are evil. They simply haven't yet met the God of grace and mercy. The Christian's job is to be Jesus' ambassador to those who don't know Him, whatever their faith or lack thereof.

If you haven't read the other Redemption's Edge novels, you may have questions:

What exactly did Amy's cousin Harry do? Could he have truly found redemption, despite his crimes? *Heaven's Prey*, Redemption's Edge 1, tells his story — and the story of Ruth Warner, the prayer warrior whose faith could have cost her life.

What would it be like to live with the public shame of having a family member who's a dangerous offender? What if Harry's enemies, who can't touch him in prison, decide to target his sister Carol and her son? Redemption's Edge 2, *Secrets and Lies*, is Carol's story.

Again, thank you for reading. I hope it was fun, and that God blessed or encouraged you somewhere in the story.

~Janet

~~~

Janet Sketchley is an Atlantic Canadian writer who likes her fiction with a splash of mystery or adventure and a dash of Christianity. Why leave faith out of our stories if it's part of our lives?

Janet's other books include the Redemption's Edge Christian suspense series and the devotional books, *A Year of Tenacity* and *Tenacity at Christmas*. She has also produced a fill-in reader's journal, *Reads to Remember: A book lover's journal to track your next 100 reads* (available in print only, with two different cover design options). You can find her online at janetsketchley.ca.

Subscribe to Janet's newsletter at janetsketchley.ca/subscribe or follow her on BookBub at bit.ly/JanetSketchleyBookBub.

DISCUSSION QUESTIONS

1.   Amy's petite stature and the need to be independent since her mother's death have taught her to stand up for herself and rely on her own judgement. Do you think that made it harder for her to believe Aunt Bay's and Troy's reassurances of Michael's sanity?

2.   Aunt Bay is outspoken, yet she's careful not to say things she might regret. Is it harder for you to speak your mind or to restrain your words?

3.   As the point of view character, Amy's perceptions make her an unreliable narrator at times. Did you feel like Aunt Bay, that you'd like to make her see clearly, or were you content to watch her learn for herself?

4.   Why do you think Aunt Bay and Troy wouldn't tell Michael or Amy how the other felt? Would this be wise in real life?

5.   As a child, Amy internalized and accepted the judgements about her. This left her overly sensitive to her birth circumstances, even when those around her saw that it wasn't a barrier. How easy is it for us to believe the lies that diminish our worth or exclude us from relationships where we could blossom? What difference could it make to ask Jesus how He sees us?

6.   Once Amy discovers that God loves her, she starts fighting the "voices" of childhood with what she's learning about herself as His child. Have you ever used this sort of strategy to fight the battle in your mind?

7.   Aunt Bay, Michael and Troy are all people of prayer. What part does prayer play in your life?

8.   Aunt Bay tells Amy, "I suspect God wishes He could knock the pair of you upside the head and shake some sense loose. But He saves the dramatics for key points in history." What are some of the more subtle ways God opens our eyes to what He wants us to see or to do?

9.   Nathin may be farther from God now than ever, due to his life experiences. How do you think God might yet draw him to His heart?

10.   Can you relate to Amy's childhood fantasies about her father? What do you think about her struggle to forgive him for rejecting her as an adult? And what do you think about her forgiving Emilie at the end?

11.   One type of fear keeps Amy silent about her birth. Fear of another kind keeps her and Michael from revealing their hearts to each other. It's easy to see this in other people, but what whispers of fear might be keeping us from living transparently with those around us?

12.   What do you think about Aunt Bay's words that "We should never blame God for what happens. But when you know He could have prevented something, it can be a struggle to accept that He didn't."

13.   Aunt Bay has built a relationship with Safia's family. As she shows practical love to her neighbours and prays for them, she'll see opportunities to share her faith. What questions do you think the events in this novel might raise for Safia? Do you think this young mom and her family may yet discover the truth about Jesus?

14.   If you've read the first two Redemption's Edge books, how did you feel about seeing Ruth, Tony, Carol, Joey and Chance again? What do you think of Harry's decision to go public with his conversion story?

OTHER BOOKS IN THE
REDEMPTION'S EDGE SERIES:

Heaven's Prey (book 1 expanded anniversary edition)

High octane Christian suspense meets women's fiction in this battle of wits between the prayer warrior and the fallen hero.

Ruth Warner is broken. Her adult niece's violent death at the hands of a serial rapist-murderer leaves her bitter. Tempted to reject her faith, Ruth instead finds healing through praying for the victims' families. But pray for the predator himself? Never. Until she does—and then a botched kidnapping pegs her as his next victim.

Ruth has invested too many prayers and tears to give up now. Not when his coming to faith is the only way to save her life.

Secrets and Lies (book 2 expanded anniversary edition)

A widow in hiding. A vengeful drug lord. And a teenage boy ready to come of age.

Carol Daniels is afraid to be found. Starting over in a new city to escape an anonymous threat, the single mother is desperate to protect her sixteen-year-old son. But a chilling phone call from a local crime boss reveals a menace she can't outrun.

Terrified and out of options, she agrees to find her convict brother's hidden fortune. Facing this crisis alone is overwhelming, but the one man she wants to trust has a past she can't accept. With the clock ticking, will Carol break under pressure or survive to forge a stronger life with her son?